THE FARMINGTON COMMUNITY LIBRARY
FARMINGTON HILLS BRANCH
32737 WEST TWELVE MILE ROAD
FARMINGTON HILLS, MI 48334-3302
(248) 553-0300

D0284637

FEB 15 2011

FEB 15 2011

BANISHED

30036010708558

BANISHED

sophie Littlefield

delacorte press

This is a work of fiction. Names, characters, places, and incidents either are the product of the author's imagination or are used fictitiously. Any resemblance to actual persons, living or dead, events, or locales is entirely coincidental.

Copyright © 2010 by Sophie Littlefield

All rights reserved. Published in the United States by Delacorte Press, an imprint of Random House Children's Books, a division of Random House, Inc., New York.

Delacorte Press is a registered trademark and the colophon is a trademark of Random House, Inc.

Visit us on the Web! www.randomhouse.com/teens

Educators and librarians, for a variety of teaching tools, visit us at www.randomhouse.com/teachers

Library of Congress Cataloging-in-Publication Data
Littlefield, Sophie.
Banished / Sophie Littlefield. — 1st ed.
p. cm.
Summary: Sixteen-year-old Hailey Tarbell, raised by a mean, secretive grandmother, does not know that she comes from a long line of healers until her Aunt Prairie arrives with answers about her past that could quickly threaten her future.
ISBN 978-0-385-73852-1 (alk. paper) — ISBN 978-0-385-90735-4 (lib. bdg.) — ISBN 978-0-375-89495-4 (e-book)
[1. Healers—Fiction. 2. Identity—Fiction. 3. Grandmothers—Fiction. 4. Aunts—Fiction. 5. Supernatural—Fiction.] I. Title.
PZ7.L7359Ban 2010
[Fic]—dc22   2009032711

The text of this book is set in 12.5-point Adobe Garamond.

Book design by Stephanie Moss

Printed in the United States of America

10 9 8 7 6 5 4 3 2 1

First Edition

Random House Children's Books supports the First Amendment and celebrates the right to read.

For Sal.
Growing up is hard, but you are doing a beautiful job.

ACKNOWLEDGMENTS

This book was touched by many hands along the way, and I am grateful to you all.

Barbara Poelle, my agent who employed the roadside-assistance-phone-call and cocktail-napkin methods to develop my idea,

Claudia Gabel, who took a chance on me,

And Stephanie Elliott, my editor, who worked tirelessly to help me shape the story.

Writing this book reminded me of a time when I was doing my best to grow up, and I would like to thank the friends who were there. Bob—first and foremost. Mary. Julia, Sonja, Anne, and MaryAnn. Joellen and Margaret, and Ellen and John. And of course Kristen and Mike, who are always there.

PART ONE: GYPSUM

PROLOGUE

JUNE 1995

WAKING UP HURT. Her head pounded and there was something in her eyes, something sticky and warm that made it hard to see.

She blinked hard and her eyes cleared, and she realized she was in a car.

Not just any car—her boyfriend's car. It was a pretty white Celica, and she brushed her hand against her lap, feeling smooth, silky fabric, and remembered—it was prom night, and they were driving out to Boone Lake and he'd brought champagne, a bottle on ice in a cooler. She had slipped into the girls' bathroom to fix her lip gloss and dab on a little extra perfume before they said goodbye to all their friends, to the school gym decorated with streamers and helium balloons, to the teachers, who smiled and nodded at them because they were nice kids, kids who got good grades and didn't make trouble.

Except that her boyfriend had been drinking since they got to the prom, and he wasn't drunk, no, not drunk exactly, but they'd been laughing as he took the turns on State Road 9 just a little too fast, his hand slipping along the folds of her emerald green skirt.

And she hadn't stopped him. Because she liked having his hand there. And she couldn't wait to kiss him some more. And she liked going fast and reckless around the turns because it felt like the future, felt like the day when they would drive away from Gypsum and never come back.

But something had happened.

There were no lights in the car now, not even the glow of the dashboard. But the headlights were still on, one shining straight into the woods, to the right of the tree they'd hit.

The other beam twisted at a crazy angle. It lit up his body, lying on the ground ten feet from the car, bent in a way that didn't look the least bit natural.

She started screaming, yanked at the buckle of her seat belt and pushed against her door—it wouldn't open, it was stuck or jammed, and she crawled to the driver's seat, her knees grinding on something sharp—oh, it was the windshield, the windshield had shattered, and she realized with horror that it was her boyfriend's body that had broken it. He never wore his seat belt—he'd gone flying through the windshield, across the hood of the ruined Celica, and landed on the hard ground, broken and bleeding.

The driver's-side door opened easily and she stumbled out of the car, tripping on the hem of her dress, her beautiful strapless dress that no one knew had come from the St. Benedict's thrift shop in Tipton, that fit her like it had been made for her alone.

She bunched the skirt in her fists and ran to her boyfriend, stumbling in her high heels before collapsing on her knees next to him. His hand, thrown out palm-open as though he'd been reaching for something, twitched and his lips moved. His eyes were glassy and unfocused and she bent close to hear what he was trying to say.

"Hurts . . . ," he managed, licking his dry, cracked lips.

"No, no, please don't . . . ," she murmured as she tugged his tuxedo jacket open as gently as she could.

What she saw made her throat close with fear. It was too much. There was too much damage. The wound was open and black and glistening in the moonlight, so much blood draining into the cold, dry earth.

Her hands flew to the wound, her fingers working quickly to find the edges of the gash, the words coming to her lips even before she realized she'd made a decision.

But he spoke first. "I . . . I love . . ."

His voice was so weak she almost missed it, but comprehension flickered in his beautiful brown eyes, and he looked at her the way he did when he picked her up for school, the way he had the first time she'd passed in front of his locker last year, the way he did when he searched the crowd for her face after every play at football games.

It was a look that saw her, knew her, really knew her, the way her mother never would and her father, whoever he was, never chose to. It was the look she'd hung every dream, every foolish hope on, and as he blinked twice, his eyes rolling up and going opaque, she said the words.

She said the words the way her grandmother had taught her, the syllables slipping like gossamer ribbons past her lips, words she'd chanted a hundred times on a hundred long-ago nights lit by sputtering candles and her grandmother's eyes bright with purpose. A hundred times, a hundred nights, but tonight was the first time she prayed with all her soul that the words would work.

A twitch, a sigh—she broke off in the middle of a word whose sound was burned into her memory, but whose meaning she didn't really know, not the way her grandmother did. Her boyfriend twitched again and blinked, and she stilled her fingers on his face.

"Don't leave me," she whispered. "Oh, please don't leave—" Her heart thudded hard in her chest because he wasn't gone; he'd almost died but she'd brought him back, she'd said the words.

He was back.

She was bending to kiss him, to throw her arms around him, when his eyes blinked again and stayed open—

And there was nothing there.

"Vincent," she breathed, her heart going cold. "Vincent, please, please, Vincent, please—"

But he said nothing. His eyes were empty and his lips were still, and the forest around them was dark and silent as a stone.

CHAPTER 1

NOW

WHEN I WAS EIGHT, the social workers finally made Gram send me to school. Until then, she told the authorities she was homeschooling me, but after years of her never turning in her paperwork or showing up for the mandatory meetings, they finally got fed up and told her I had to go to regular school. Gram gave in; she knew when she was beat.

The first thing I noticed about the other kids was that they all looked like they could be on TV. I called them Cleans. Their clothes were new and ironed smooth. Their hair was shiny and combed. Their nails were trimmed and free of the black grime that I'd had under mine as long as I could remember. No one had to tell me that, compared with these other kids, I was dirty.

That didn't stop the kids on the bus from reminding me. By the end of my first humiliating ride to school, I'd been called a bunch of names and accused of having cooties and lice and a witch for a grandmother. It was the same thing on the ride home, even though Mr. Francheski pulled the bus over, stood up and hollered, *"Was all you kids raised in barns? Where's your manners? Be nice to this new girl."*

When I got home that first day I was crying. This was long before Chub came to live with us, and even though I knew better than to hope for anything from Gram, I dropped my book bag on the floor and ran to her favorite chair, in front of the television, where she was smoking and watching *Montel.* I blubbered out what had happened, how the kids had said I was dirty and called me trash. Gram barely shrugged, craning her neck to see over me to the television.

"I guess you know where the soap is at," she snapped. "And you can drag a brush through that hair, you want. Now git."

Now, eight years later, I had washed my hair the night before and blown it out with a hair dryer I'd saved up for. I was wearing mascara and lip gloss that I'd bought with the money I'd made working for Gram.

But everything else I had was secondhand, a fact I was always conscious of as I walked the halls at Gypsum High. My clothes were never right. My backpack was never right. My shoes, my notebooks, my haircut, wrong, wrong, wrong—and everyone knew it. Gypsum might be a two-stoplight town in the middle of nowhere, Missouri, but there was a structure like anywhere else: popular kids and in-between kids and losers. And people like me, so far down there wasn't any point in bothering to classify us.

I had gym second period. My locker was next to Claire Hewitt's. Claire always smelled faintly of baby powder and motor oil, and her hair frizzed in a cloud around her shoulders. But as I spun my lock, even she flinched away from me.

When you're near the bottom of the school social ladder, like Claire, the only thing that can really hurt you is to be associated with someone even lower. And there was no one lower than me. Not Claire. Not Emily Engstrom, with her limp and her lazy eye. Not even the Morries. No one at all.

I started changing into my gym clothes, not bothering to say anything to her. What would be the point?

"Hey, Hailey," Shawna Rosen said, appearing at my side without warning. "Are those *nurses'* shoes you're wearing?"

The girls trailing her pressed in closer to me and stared down at my feet as Claire slammed her locker door shut and slipped hastily away. I could practically feel their excitement. They were never happier than when they could remind some poor girl of the enormous distance between her pathetic existence and life at the top of the heap.

Sometimes, when Shawna and her crew came after me, I stood my ground. I stared into their overly made-up eyes and telegraphed disdain. But this wasn't one of those days. I shuffled backward, away from Shawna and into the wide aisle between locker rows, bumping into someone behind me, tripping and nearly falling. My hand shot out to steady myself against the wall of lockers, and I was dismayed to see I'd run into a group of Morries.

"Sorry," I mumbled, but they were gone before I finished speaking, melting down another aisle without a word.

You almost never saw one of the Morries alone. They stuck together at the edge of the halls and the back of the classrooms and the cafeteria tables farthest from the food line in silent clumps of three or four. Like me, they didn't participate in any sports or clubs or extracurricular activities. The girls wore their hair long, hanging in their faces. The boys were so skinny their dirty, frayed jeans hung off their hips.

They never volunteered in class. If they were called on, the girls would mumble so quietly that teachers soon gave up on them. The boys were bolder, surly and argumentative and sullen. They didn't care at all about their grades.

They were called Morries after Morrin Street, the main road that ran through Trashtown, which is what everyone called the run-down neighborhood outside of Gypsum half a mile past our house. I don't know who started calling them that, but if there had ever been a time when the Trashtown kids mixed with the Cleans at school, that time was long gone.

Shawna and her friends got bored with me and wandered off, but I still had to hustle to finish getting dressed, and I was late to gym class. Ms. Turnbull and Mr. Coughlin didn't notice, since they were busy dragging the vaulting horses and balance beam and parallel bars out of the closet. We counted off and lined up behind the equipment. No one looked very happy about it, but my reasons were probably different from everyone else's. It wasn't that I was bad at this stuff. The problem was that I was good—*too* good.

I used to wonder if God had compensated for making me such a freak, for my lack of friends and horrible home life, with natural athletic ability. If so, I'd love to give it back. I was fast and I was strong, I could balance and throw and catch with amazing accuracy, but instead of helping me fit in with the other kids, it brought me—what else?—more trouble.

In sixth grade my PE teacher noticed I had the third-highest mile time in the school. He had me run sprints and then another mile, eight times around the track, clocking me with his stopwatch. Each time I passed him I could see his expression growing tighter and more excited. When I finished he jogged over to where I was stretching out—they were constantly harping on us about stretching after exercise—and told me he wanted me to start training with the middle-school track team.

I was so surprised I couldn't come up with a response quick enough. It had never occurred to me that anyone would ask me to join a club or a sport. But of course I couldn't do it. Gram would never have allowed it. She didn't even want me attending school. If the social workers hadn't forced her to send me, she never would have let me out of the house except to do errands.

Once, in grade school, I received an invitation to a birthday party. I ran home, my heart pounding with excitement. I knew that the girl didn't really want me there, that her mother had made her invite every girl in the class, but I didn't care. I had never been to a birthday party—Gram didn't believe in celebrating birthdays, so mine passed every year with no cake, no presents, no singing—and I desperately wanted to go.

Gram read the invitation, her cracked lips moving as she sounded out the words, and then she frowned and tore it into pieces. "No need for you to mix with them kids," she said.

Years later, when my gym teacher insisted on sending home a permission slip for track, Gram wrote in big block letters across the section of the form where she was supposed to fill in my medical information: HAILEY DOES NOT HAVE MY PERMISHION TO DO ANY SPORT.

Ever since then I'd been careful not to let anyone see me excel at anything.

But today would be tough. I was in the vault line. I stared at the old leather-covered thing, wondering how I could feign clumsiness. It would be hard; if I just hit it head-on, it would hurt plenty. But I wasn't sure I could stop myself from hurtling over it neatly. How was it possible to act clumsy when you were sailing through the air, your instincts taking over?

I managed, but it took all my concentration. I also forced myself to stumble off the balance beam and pretended to be too weak to support myself on the parallel bars. When Mr. C glared at me and shook his head with disgust, I felt a flash of pride.

If he only knew.

I was at the back of the vault line, congratulating myself on escaping attention again, when Milla Swanson reached the front.

Milla was a Morrie, a thin girl with hair the color of mustard crusted to the lid of a jar. She approached the vault with uncertain little steps, head down as though she hoped the floor would swallow her before she got there. I was only half watching as she got to the old wooden springboard, but I saw her hesitate—instead of the step-bounce-leap they drilled into us, she wobbled and then almost tripped as she jumped toward the vault, her hands scrambling on the leather padding. That happened sometimes; kids hit the vault wrong and sort of slid or fell off the other side, usually in embarrassment with a bruise or friction mark. It had happened to me once or twice when I'd purposely messed up.

But when Milla struck the vault, momentum carried her into the side, and the impact sent her flying backward. She fell on her back, and I winced at the sound her shoulders made as they struck the springboard—that had to hurt—but then there was another thud and a reverberation I could feel through my feet on the hardwood gym floor, as her head bounced off the edge of the springboard.

The two girls at the front of the line jumped back with little shrieks, and then there was a second when no one moved as Milla rolled gently to a stop at the base of the springboard, her arms flopped out at her sides.

Someone screamed.

Ms. Turnbull and Mr. C came running, but I got to Milla

first. I didn't even know I was moving until I was crouched by her side, reaching for her hand, but Ms. Turnbull slapped my hand out of the way.

"Don't touch!" she screamed, even though Mr. C bent down and picked up the same hand I'd been reaching for.

I backed away, but I didn't want to. There was something inside me, some roiling force, that was making my fingers itch to touch Milla, that was sending the blood in my veins surging through my body with hot insistence. I wanted—no, I *needed*—to help, to put my hands on Milla. Even as I realized how bizarre my impulse was, I had to fight not to act on it.

I stepped back into the silent crowd of kids making a circle around the vault. Ms. Turnbull and Mr. C talked in hushed voices, feeling for a pulse and waving their hands in front of Milla's eyes, which were open but unblinking. Ms. Turnbull put her face close to Milla's as though she was going to kiss her on the lips, but then she turned away.

"She's breathing," we all heard her say.

"She's unconscious," Mr. C said in a panicked voice. I saw the flyaway ends of the hair he combed over his freckled scalp trembling as he crab-walked away from Milla's body like she was on fire, and I realized he had no idea what to do, despite all the years he'd taught us basic CPR.

"I'm going to go call." Ms. Turnbull scrambled to her feet and sprinted toward the gym teachers' office.

In the seconds it took for me to break away from the crowd of kids and rush to Milla, there was not a single sound in the gym. No one spoke, or coughed, or called my name. No one tried to stop me. But when I picked up Milla's cool, limp hand with its ragged fingernails and rough calluses, I stopped hearing anything else anyway.

At least, I heard nothing in the gym. Inside my head a strange whispered chorus started up, a murmured chant that made no sense.

A second later, my vision went. I don't think I closed my eyes, but everything else disappeared and it was as though I was looking into time going forward and backward at once, like I'd jumped off a cliff and hovered somewhere in black empty space.

"Milla," I whispered. I felt my lips move, so I was pretty sure I'd actually spoken, and then I had that same blood-rushing feeling again, like every bit of energy inside me was being pushed to my fingertips, where it dissipated into Milla's body.

I let go of her hand and my fingers moved over her neck and face until they found her scalp, which was hot and damp, the hair plastered across a long bump that swelled under my touch. The rushing sensation intensified, and my own heart seemed to slow and falter, and I started to sway, but somehow I couldn't let go, couldn't stop touching Milla's injured body. Just when I felt like I had exhausted the last of my will, something shoved me hard and I fell onto my shoulder. My vision and hearing returned instantly.

"What the hell do you think you're doing?" Ms. Turnbull screamed, her face purple and her hand raised high as though she was about to hit me. Maybe she would have, except that Milla, lying at her feet, rolled over and threw up.

It turned out to be a good thing because Ms. Turnbull forgot all about me. Milla sat up, wiping her mouth against her sleeve, hiccuped a couple of times and looked like she was going to cry, but as Ms. Turnbull shouted questions at her she answered them, in a voice too low and mumbly for the rest of us to hear.

I retreated back into the crowd of kids. A couple of them started to ask me what had happened, but then the door to the gym burst open and Mr. Macklin, the vice principal, came in and started yelling at all of us to go to the locker rooms and get dressed for next period, that everything was under control and none of our concern.

I went with the rest of them, but I couldn't help glancing back over my shoulder at Milla, who was trying to stand up even while Ms. Turnbull pushed her back down to the floor.

Milla was watching me. The look she gave me was hard to understand: fear battling contempt, with barely a trace of gratitude.

The only emotion completely absent from her face was surprise.

CHAPTER 2

THAT AFTERNOON I walked to the grocery store rather than riding the bus. I needed to walk; my mind was unsettled because of what had happened in gym. I couldn't stop playing it over and over in my head: the sound Milla's head made hitting the floor; the way her skin felt under my fingers; the blinding, swirling feeling when I touched her.

When I got home, carrying grocery bags the last mile, Rascal bounded across the yard to meet me. He was part blue tick, part beagle, part something else. Gram got him from one of her customers after some stray got through a fence and impregnated a prize hound. The customer was going to drown the whole litter, but Gram took a shine to Rascal. For a while, anyway—she got tired of him when he wasn't a puppy anymore.

He nuzzled my hand, then slipped in the door and went

straight to Chub, who was sitting in front of an open kitchen cabinet, playing with the pots and pans while the lids rolled around on the floor.

"Russo!" Chub exclaimed, clapping his hands and throwing his arms around Rascal.

"Russo" was one of Chub's better words. He called me Hayee, and he could say "wah" for "water," and "chah" for "chair." Other things he had his own special names for, sounds that had nothing to do with the actual word, like "shoshah" for "flower" and "bobbo" for "truck." Most of the time, he didn't make words at all, just hummed, sounds rising and falling like a song only he could hear.

I knew that there was something wrong with Chub. I tried to figure it out by doing research on the Internet, but there were so many causes of developmental delays, I didn't even know where to start. I knew that eventually the social workers were going to demand he be tested, but I wasn't anxious for that day to arrive because I was afraid they'd put him in some group home for kids like him. And I didn't want Chub to go. Ever. Besides Rascal, he was all I had to love.

When Chub first came to live with us, Gram changed. She spent time with him every day, murmuring softly to him while I did the chores, holding up toys and flash cards and trying to get him to talk. Those were good days. If Chub did something new, if he crawled toward Gram or reached for the shiny blocks she held up, she felt like celebrating; she turned off the TV and didn't drink as much and even complimented me on whatever I made for dinner.

But when he had a bad day, when he wouldn't repeat the sounds she made, or ate dirt from the yard, Gram seemed to sink a little lower in her chair. As I got more and more attached to Chub, I realized that Gram saw him as a project, an experiment. And when she couldn't fix what was wrong with him, she lost interest.

Within a couple of months, she was back to spending her days in the chair, watching TV and smoking. She began drinking earlier in the day and barely paid any attention to Chub, but she kept cashing the checks the state sent for his care, and he became mine to look after just like Rascal had.

"You git my cigarettes?" Gram wheezed from her chair. She asked me that every time I came home from the grocery, as though I'd ever forget. She went through a pack and a half a day. I handed her the four packs of Marlboro 100's along with the receipt and a few coins. The cigarettes cost almost half what I'd spent at the grocery, but I knew better than to suggest Gram cut back. The one and only time I'd tried, she'd slapped my face so fast and hard it took my breath away.

Gram was mean, but she was also weak and sick most of the time, so I could stay out of her way if I tried. She woke in the morning coughing up nasty stuff and spitting into the sink, and she fell asleep drunk in her chair most nights. She ordered me around like a servant. I didn't mind the housework so much—I had kind of a thing about keeping the house clean, and I would have done it even if she didn't tell me to. And she paid me, even if it was a fraction of minimum wage.

I unpacked the rest of the groceries and got to work making sloppy joes. Sautéing the frozen peppers and onions, the ground beef, stirring in the tomato sauce—I'd done it a hundred times before, but it still brought me a sense of calm, especially with Chub playing at my feet and Rascal dozing in the corner of the kitchen where I kept a stack of old blankets for him to sleep on.

Gram, laughing at something Tyra Banks said on her show, farted loudly, and I thought for the thousandth time how glad I would be when Chub and I left this house for good. I knew you weren't supposed to feel that way about your grandmother. Grandparents were supposed to be overprotective and hopelessly out of touch, but you were still supposed to love them. They were supposed to listen to your troubles and offer you advice from all their years of experience.

"Something weird happened at school today," I said as I stirred the ketchup and onion soup mix into the skillet. Gram had never given me a single piece of advice worth remembering, and as I started to speak I already knew it was a mistake, but I had to talk to someone about Milla. "Milla Swanson got hurt in gym."

"Uh-huh," Gram said without taking her eyes off the television.

"I mean, like hurt pretty bad. I think she was unconscious for a while. A head injury."

"Mmm."

"But I . . . well, I think I might have . . . um. The thing is, I just wanted to help, you know? Because Ms. Turnbull went to call and—"

"What did you say?"

Gram's voice, sharp and shrill, startled me. I set the spatula into the pan and looked at her. To my surprise she was struggling to push herself out of her chair, grunting with the effort.

"Just that Milla fell off the vault and hit her head." I went to help Gram. She seized my hands and pulled herself up, her back cracking.

"Was there blood? Skin cut? Bone showing? What did you do?"

Gram's questions had an edge to them, an urgency I had never heard from her, and I wondered what she knew that I didn't.

"It wasn't really any big deal. Just a bump."

"You said she was unconscious." There was excitement and accusation in her voice, and her eyes were bright and intent.

"Well, maybe for a minute."

"And you touched her?"

"Um . . . yeah."

"On her head?"

"Well, yes, I mean, first her hands and then, I guess, mostly on her hair."

"What did you say?"

"What did I *say*?"

"It's not a hard question, Hailey. What did you say when you were touching her?"

"I didn't—I don't know. I mean, I might have said her name, and something like, 'Don't worry,' or, 'It's going to be okay.' I really don't remember."

But as I answered Gram something stirred in my mind. There had been . . . something. A strange sound track, whispered nonsense syllables, barely audible over the rushing of my blood.

"That's all? You didn't say anything else?"

"No. Nothing else." I was a little frightened by Gram's intensity, especially when she closed one of her clawlike hands around my forearm, her long fingernails digging into my flesh.

"Have you done this before, Hailey?" she asked, leaning close enough to me that I could smell her breath, a foul combination of cigarettes and rot. I had to resist the urge to pull my arm away.

"Done *what*?"

Her burning eyes searched mine, and I felt like she was looking for signs that I was telling the truth—and for something else as well, something I couldn't understand. We stood that way for what seemed like a long time, and I felt fear unwind inside my gut, fear that fed on my confusion and the high emotions of the day.

"I think you know," Gram finally hissed, squeezing my arm with a strength that surprised me. "You know what you done. All this time I been waitin' on you, I finally gave up, and now you gone and done it."

I yanked away from her, my heart pounding hard. "Dinner's going to burn," I mumbled. I picked up the spatula and stirred the mixture in the pan, my face hot in the rising steam.

I could sense Gram standing behind me, watching. She was scariest when she was thinking. I'd rather have her hit me or yell at me any day than stare at me like that, when I didn't have a clue what she was thinking about.

"It don't change nothin'," she muttered, so softly I almost didn't hear her.

By the time I dared to turn and look, she had shuffled back to her chair, and her eyes were half closed as she watched a lawn-care commercial. I made three plates of food and got Chub set up at the table with a paper napkin and a glass of chocolate milk. I took Gram her plate and a fresh beer and set it on her TV tray. She barely grunted a response, but I kept an eye on her as Chub and I ate dinner. She ate carelessly, bits of ground beef falling to the tray or the floor, where Rascal would find them later. After a while she rubbed her napkin across her mouth and tossed it on top of her half-eaten dinner, and I breathed easier, hoping she'd forgotten the confusing conversation.

She was expecting customers that night. While I did the dishes she muttered to herself, now and then raising her voice as though she was having a conversation with someone. I was passing by her chair on my way to put Chub down, when she shot out her gnarled, yellow-nailed hand and grabbed my wrist.

"You know you're the future, Hailey," she said, lips twisted in a grin that revealed the gaps where she'd lost teeth. Gram wouldn't see a dentist, so her teeth were gray in places and several were missing. "You're the one who's gonna carry on the legacy."

I tugged my wrist back, but Gram held on tight. She'd said things like that before; it was nothing new. Years ago I'd asked what she meant, and Gram had got all coy and winked and said I'd know soon enough. It gave me the creeps, the way she stared at me with her milky eyes bright, almost hungry-looking.

"You got titties now, girl, don't you," Gram said.

Instinctively I covered my chest with my hand. It was barely even true. I was still skinny through the hips and it was clear I'd never be curvy the way Jill Kirsch and Stephanie Lee were, the way that caught the boys' attention as they walked down the school halls.

But it was horrifying to think that Gram had noticed, that she had been *looking* at me . . . that way.

"And your monthlies," she continued, wheezing and coughing into her sleeve.

I hadn't made an effort to keep it a secret. When I got my period a few years earlier, I knew what to do from eavesdropping on other girls at school, and I stored my box of tampons in the bathroom medicine cabinet. But hearing her say the words made my stomach roil, and I jerked my hand so hard that her fingers bounced off the arm of her chair as I backed away.

Gram only laughed, a croaking sound that sent spit flying, some of it landing on me. I couldn't get away from her fast enough.

"What're you so shy for, Hailey?" Gram wheezed. "Your mama was sure hot for it. Wa'n't right in the head and couldn't talk sense, but that didn't keep her from sashaying around like a cat in heat when she got grown."

That stopped me cold. Gram never talked about my mother. All I knew about her was that she had died in childbirth and that she wasn't "right in the head." I thought maybe that last part was why Gram wouldn't talk about her, some sort of grief that had got all twisted up into ugliness and silence—Gram wouldn't even tell me her name, and there were no pictures of her in the house.

"What—what—" I stammered, and Gram's lips curved up in smug satisfaction. She had me. I hated her for it, but she had me.

"Oh, so *now* you got time to talk to me," Gram said. "Yes indeed. You don't need to know anything about your mom other'n she was ripe as an August peach and lookin' to get picked. Got knocked up with you soon's the fellas come around sniffin' at her, that one did."

"Who—" I started, and then I licked my dry lips, hating myself for the question I was about to ask. I'd asked often enough before to know that she would never tell. "Who was my father?"

Gram's laughter turned into a coughing fit, but the tears she wiped from her rheumy eyes were full of mean amusement. "That—" she began, then gasped her way through another round of coughs. "That's quite the question, ain't it? Could be anyone."

I had learned a few things about Gram, living with her for sixteen years. I didn't miss the narrowing of her eyes, the way she drew her lips in. Gram was lying to me. Only, I didn't know why. What was she hiding? Sometimes it seemed like we weren't even related to each other—she was so frail, as though her body was just waiting to die, and I had never been sick a day in my life. But she also knew me better, in some ways, than I knew myself. I hated that. I couldn't help thinking of the conversation earlier, the way she'd asked all those questions about Milla, as though she had some secret knowledge about what had happened. One thing was sure, though: nothing would make Gram tell me anything she wanted to keep secret.

It was pointless to keep talking to her. I tried to walk away, but Gram stopped me.

"What's your hurry, Hailey?" she said. She stubbed out her cigarette in the ashtray I'd already emptied twice that day, and held out her arms. "We got callers. Here, git me up."

Only then did I hear the sound of a car in the yard. I did as she asked, seizing her hands and pulling harder than necessary, so Gram stumbled as she stood. I let her lean on me as she cracked her knuckles and worked her neck one way and the other.

When I was sure she wouldn't fall, I took Chub to get ready for bed. Ordinarily I'd bathe him, but Gram's callers were likely to start drinking beer and need the toilet before long.

I brushed Chub's teeth with a soft-bristled brush and the strawberry-flavored kids' toothpaste I'd splurged on. I wiped him down with a clean cloth and changed his pull-up. He was four, way too old to still be in diapers; I'd tried everything I could think of to get him to use the toilet, but nothing worked.

As I wiped down the sink, he wrapped his arms around my thighs and said, "Loo, Hayee." He said this from time to time, and I was convinced it was "I love you, Hailey," even if I didn't have any way to prove it. I knelt down on the floor and hugged him, breathing his sweet baby scent. "Me and you," I whispered. "Always."

In two more years I'd be eighteen. I'd graduate from high school and the social services people would stop coming around checking on me. And if we were lucky, we'd go so far away that they'd never be able to find Chub.

On the other side of the door I heard voices, and I recognized the loudest: Dunston Acey. Not good. I tried to slip quietly to my room, but before I reached the door his whiskey-rough voice came after me.

"Hailey, come out here so's I can see you!"

I froze, trying to decide if I could pretend I hadn't heard

him, but Gram's voice followed: "Git the boy put down quick, girl, we got company!"

I did as they said. Once I'd sung to Chub and rubbed his back, and his breathing had gone deep and even with sleep, I couldn't put it off any longer. They'd only come into the room and turn on the lights and wake Chub up. Nothing stopped Gram and her customers when they were partying.

I walked into the kitchen and said hello with as little enthusiasm as possible.

Three pairs of eyes regarded me—Gram and Dun and another man, who was standing in the shadows in the far corner. When he stepped into the light, I saw with a sinking heart that it was Rattler Sikes.

Of all the sorry and mean and no-good men who came through our house, Rattler was the worst. He was one of the only ones who didn't do drugs or, as far as I knew, drink alcohol, but once in a while he'd show up in the company of some of the others and stand in the corner of the room, watching and saying little.

Everyone knew the stories about him. Rattler was one of the few people in Trashtown who got talked about by the rest of Gypsum, probably because the sheriff had been trying to nail him for years. Only, he never managed to make any charges stick.

They said Rattler did things to women. Terrible things, things that left them messed up on the outside and the inside alike. It was only Trashtown women that he went after, and maybe that was part of why the sheriff's department couldn't bring him down. As long as trouble stayed inside the borders of Trashtown, Gypsum people didn't care much about what went on there.

They said that women would go out with Rattler—it was hard to imagine they went willingly—and then they'd be found wandering back into town in the early hours of the morning, sometimes barefoot, sometimes nearly naked, always unwilling or unable to talk about what had happened. None of them ever wanted to press charges, but those women were never the same again.

"My, you're looking fine today," Dun said, raising a bottle in my direction before taking a long drink. Gram had a policy that anything a customer drank or smoked in the house was free—for the price of a few beers and some weed, she kept them entertained and happy, and if she tacked on a premium for the harder stuff, they never complained.

"I got to git down to the basement," Gram said, sighing and fixing a look on me. I knew what she wanted—for me to go down and get whatever it was that Dun was buying tonight. But that was the one thing she couldn't make me do: I refused to get involved with her dealing. I wouldn't touch the pill bottles, wouldn't read the labels, wouldn't help her sort and bag the weed she got from a guy who drove it up from the Ozarks once a month. I wouldn't do any of it, and whenever she asked I reminded her that all I had to do was make one phone call and she was done.

Of course, I was bluffing. I would never do anything to bring the authorities in, because that would mean that Chub and I would be split up. Gram was stupid about some things, and this most of all: she should have known what Chub meant to me.

Instead, she got up, sighing and snorting, and shuffled off to the basement stairs. It would take her a while, holding on to the handrail and taking the steps one at a time, before she was back with their stuff. I saw the pile of wadded cash in the middle of the table. It would stay there until Dun checked his purchases and slid them in his pockets, and then Gram would stuff the money into her purse on the counter. That was how it was always done.

I took the only empty chair and waited. Gram expected me to make small talk, but that didn't mean I had to come up with sparkling conversation.

"Nice shirt," Dun said. "Ain't that a purty shirt, Rattler?"

I felt myself blush; my shirt was nothing special, a plain green scoop-neck top I'd bought secondhand for fifty cents, but it was old and getting a little tight across my chest.

After that, Dun asked me about school and my grades and what I was watching on TV these days. He didn't seem to mind that I gave him the shortest possible answers. Now and then he asked Rattler what he thought, but mostly he seemed content to do all the talking and drink his beer, popping the top off a fresh bottle when he finished one.

After what seemed like ages, Gram came clumping back

up the stairs. She had two brown paper bags clutched in her hands, their tops folded down. She set them on the table in front of Dun, and the mood in the room changed.

No one was looking at me anymore. Everyone's eyes were on the bags as Dun unrolled the paper and peered inside. After a second he reached in and pulled out the plastic bottles. He examined the labels, squinting. He looked like he wanted to eat them, plastic caps and all. When he was done checking the bottles, he stuffed them in a big flap pocket of his plaid shirt. He crumpled the brown bags and tossed them toward the trash can in the corner, where they bounced off the edge and landed on the floor.

I waited what I thought was a safe amount of time, and then got up and slid my chair in. "Well, good night," I said, trying to sound cheerful.

As I passed by Dun, he reached out and grabbed the waistband of my jeans.

"Off to bed already, sweetheart?" he drawled, and I caught a whiff of his tobacco-stinking breath. "You need some company?"

"Aw, Dun," Gram cackled, and slapped him playfully on the shoulder. "Don't be pestering the child."

"She ain't no child no more," Dun said, winking at Rattler. "Ain't that right."

"You know she's got to get her schooling." Gram sounded serious now, her voice scolding.

"Looks to me like she's got herself plenty of schooling.

On, on how to be smokin' hot." Dun cracked up at his own stupid joke, not even trying to hide the fact that he was staring right at my chest.

I jerked away from him, hard. Gram laughed along with him as I raced to my room and slammed the door.

CHAPTER 3

IT WAS THEIR ANNIVERSARY. *An entire year since their first official date.*

That was why she was going through his things. Other women did that, didn't they? Snooped around their boyfriends' apartments to find the velvet boxes containing bracelets and earrings, glittering tokens of love?

It was so hard to know what normal was, even though she worked at it all the time. She shopped where other women shopped, dressed as well as any of them. She got her hair cut at a salon where they brought you champagne while you waited. Why not? She had plenty of money now.

That hadn't always been the case. It took six years to put herself through college, working full-time and weekends too, six years of living in a sleep-deprived, caffeine-fueled haze before she finally graduated.

Six more years of research jobs after that, in labs all over the city, taking classes whenever she could to supplement what she learned on the job. Full-time graduate school was out of the question when she was still paying off her debts—the lab jobs didn't pay enough for her to save much money, even though she kept her expenses down by living in a tiny apartment in a bad part of town.

Those were lonely years. Even if she had time to date, the memory of her first love stayed in her mind every waking moment. Her heart did not heal. Yes, it scabbed over; the agony dulled to a low ache that was as much a part of her as breathing. But she never forgot.

She wanted to atone. Her life became an effort to make up for that early mistake. If she could just find a way to use her gift to help people—but the scientific community was not interested in the work she wanted to do.

Until the day she met him. Of course, he was only her boss for the first couple of years. He'd heard about her—heard about her reputation for hard work and reliable results, but more important, he'd heard about the research she conducted on her own after hours . . . and the thing she could do that science could not yet explain. She had told almost no one about that part, and still—somehow—he found out. And offered to pay her three times her salary to come work for him.

And now, in his laboratory, she worked the longest hours of all, but that didn't matter, did it? Because they were together, and they shared a vision, a dream. They were going to change the world.

That was what she told herself every morning as she steeled herself to go through the doors of the building where the lab was located. It was unmarked, with no sign out front, nothing to indicate the expensive equipment inside, the experts he had hired from around the world. But he was disciplined that way—he didn't flaunt it, but he insisted on the best.

And he said she *was* the best. Without her, he often reminded her, their work would be in vain. He said that studying her was a privilege. So why had it become so hard to return his affection, his touch, lately?

It was her *fault*, because relationships were so much harder for her than for other women. She tried to push the thought away as she finished looking in the drawers of his dresser and considered the sleek ebony desk in the study of his beautiful penthouse apartment with its view of Lake Michigan. Because of what had happened to her all those years ago . . . maybe it was inevitable that it would take her so long to love again.

And she *did love him*, she reminded herself as she shifted objects around on the desk, careful not to disturb the placement of the papers and pens and sticky notes and binder clips. The desk was the only messy thing in his life, this private work space in his home. The rest of it—the sterile lab, the gleaming kitchen with its stainless steel appliances, the pressed shirts and suits hanging in the closets—was so neat and orderly, it was as though no real human lived there.

She suppressed a little shiver. That was not the way she ought to be thinking about her beloved. Especially since there was a chance—he'd hinted around enough, hadn't he?—more *than a* chance, a likelihood *that he was going to propose tonight. That somewhere in this apartment was the ring he would slip on her finger, a beautiful ring, because he insisted on the best of everything, and then they would be united in marriage in addition to their passion for their work, and she would be the happiest woman in the world.*

So why was she feeling sick inside?

Nerves—that was all it was, she chastised herself, quieting the resistant voice inside. She just had to see the ring. Because seeing it would confirm what she suspected, and if she confirmed that suspicion, she could prepare for it. When he got down on one knee later tonight, she'd be ready with the proper display of delight and surprise, and he'd never know that inside her a gnawing fear was growing, a certainty that something was wrong, wrong, wrong.

She had to master that fear, to hide it away where no one would ever see it, if she ever wanted to live normally. To marry, to have children, perhaps. She would never find anyone more accomplished than her boyfriend. He was wealthy and intelligent and powerful, and he had chosen her. This was real *love, mature love, and if she found herself thinking about that other love it was only because of the terrible way it had ended. She'd fallen hard the very first time, but what had felt like love had probably just been infatuation.*

Real love was what she had now, the product of shared interests and a cautious escalation of intimacy over time. Her beloved had been patient as their working relationship slowly grew into something more.

So she would not allow the doubts in, not today. Today was special. The day every woman dreamed of, right? As she opened the file drawers next to the desk, she forced the nagging fears back to the far corners of her mind. So he had recently made a few errors that weren't like him. Everyone—even the most brilliant people—got distracted. The inconsistencies in the lab reports she'd mistakenly read, the test models and control populations that didn't look anything like what they had discussed, even the files that contained references to funding sources she'd never heard about—all of that could easily be explained. She had only a bachelor's degree, after all; everyone else in the lab—all the unfriendly staff who showed up without introduction and dove into the work without ever sharing any personal information—they were so far ahead of her that she barely understood what they were doing.

She riffled through the files in the last drawer. Suddenly, she stopped, her heart skipping as she read, and then read again, the file's label, written neatly in his handwriting.

Her name.

Her real name.

The one no one had used in years.

Behind her she heard the door open, and the click of her boyfriend's Italian shoes on the polished wood floors.

She didn't move. Couldn't move. She held the file in her hands, a file thick with papers, and stared at the name she'd thought she buried forever.

"Ah." His deep, cultured voice came from behind her. He didn't sound angry so much as amused. "Looking through my private files, are you, my darling?"

The germ of doubt inside her grew, and she began to shake. But still she held on to the file, as she slowly turned to face him. He offered his hand. Without thinking, she took it and allowed herself to be guided to the leather sofa, where they sat together, knees touching. His hands were warm, and even though the voice in her mind screamed in horror and fear, the part of herself that she had trained so carefully to be like everyone else, like normal women, did not pull away.

"We have a lot to talk about," he said. "In a way, your timing is excellent. See, I recently made some discoveries about you. Yes, you. Don't look so surprised, darling! You know I have always found you fascinating. Who could blame me for wanting to find out everything I possibly could about the woman I love? And now I can share it all with you, oh yes, because I found out something that you don't even know about yourself, something wonderful, I think. Something exciting, that will mean great things for both of us and for our work."

And then he called her by her real name, and the careful shell she'd built up through the years shattered into a million jagged shards, and she realized that she didn't really know this man at all.

CHAPTER 4

I DIDN'T SLEEP WELL that night, and it took longer than usual to get ready in the morning because someone had spilled a beer on the kitchen floor. I didn't want Chub sitting in it, so I scrubbed the floor clean. Before I left, I fixed him toast and dressed him in a cute pair of overalls, then got him set up with his stacking blocks. I fed Rascal and put him out in the yard for the day.

Maybe it was because I was so tired, but I didn't see the car across the street until the bus pulled up. It was cold for April, and I was squinting against the morning sun and blowing clouds of breath on the chilly air when I heard the bus coming and looked up. Ten yards down the road on the opposite side was a dark gray sedan with tinted windows. Our house was the only one on this stretch of road between

Gypsum and Trashtown, and anyone who came to see us just drove into the yard. No one ever parked on the road like that.

I boarded the bus, then slid in next to Coby Poindexter, leaning across him so I could look out at the sedan. The driver's-side window was cracked a few inches, but I couldn't see inside. As the bus pulled back into the street, I twisted around and tried to see the license plate, but all I could make out was a Lexus emblem.

Could it be the cops? Undercover, watching our house because of Gram's dealing? But cops wouldn't drive a Lexus, would they?

"Hey," Coby said, "how's things in white-trash land?"

I ignored him. Today, for some reason, I felt something inside me slipping. It wasn't that I was feeling any braver. Almost the opposite—like I was falling apart at the edges. The way Dun had treated me the night before, the mess in the kitchen this morning, the strange car across from our house: it was all too much. It didn't leave me enough energy to keep up the mask of indifference I worked so hard at.

"Shut up, Coby," I muttered.

It wasn't much of a comeback, but he seemed surprised. I could sense him staring at me the rest of the way to school, but I didn't pay any attention. When we pulled up in front of the school I bolted out the door before anyone else could talk to me, and went looking for Milla.

She wasn't hard to find. She was standing near the second-floor water fountain with two other Morrie girls who could have been sisters, their blond hair in greasy clumps around hollow-cheeked faces with sharp, jutting chins. I thought one was named Jean—she'd been in a few of my classes over the years.

"Excuse me," I said, louder than I intended. I was nervous. I wanted to talk to Milla about what happened, but the other girls closed ranks in front of her as though they'd practiced the move. She would have escaped down the hall except she tripped over her backpack and dropped the book she was holding. It fell to the floor, pages fluttering open.

I reached down to pick up the book just as she did and bumped my forehead against her shoulder. She yanked herself away from me with such force that I left the book on the floor.

Ever since my first week of school, when I sought them out at recess and lunch, I had found myself drawn to the Morries. Maybe it was just that we were equally pathetic, all of us badly dressed and ragged and friendless, but it felt like something more. I felt—and maybe this was no more than an orphaned child's longing for family—like we were related somehow. Like I was one of them.

I'd asked Gram about it long ago and she'd burst out in one of her breath-rattling laughs, spittle forming at the corners of her mouth.

"You ain't no Morrie," she said. "You're way better'n any Morrie girl. Don't you forget it, now."

I must have looked unconvinced, because she reached out her nicotine-stained thumb and forefinger and pinched the tender skin on the inside of my arm. She could pinch surprisingly hard, making hot tears jump to my eyes, but I didn't make a sound.

"Those Morrie *boys,* now, they're a whole nother matter," she added. "But that's for later, and don't you pay them no mind. I'll let you know when, that's what."

There were no boys around now. I looked into Milla's watery eyes and edged closer, almost enjoying the way she shrank from me.

"What happened yesterday?" I demanded.

"I don't know what you're talking about."

"You were unconscious. I saw . . . I *felt* it." I didn't say that her hands, her forehead beneath my fingers, felt worse than unconscious, they felt . . . wrong. Empty. Dangerous, broken, hurt.

"Didn't you come to my house once?" I asked in a voice that was little more than a whisper. "Last year. With that guy. You know. The one with the tattoos."

It wasn't much of a clue, since many of Gram's customers had tattoos, but the man I was thinking of had blue crosses circling his neck, disappearing into his stringy gray ponytail.

I could see in Milla's eyes I'd hit a nerve. "Wasn't me," she mumbled, lips barely moving as she spoke.

"Yes it was. Yes it *was.*"

"No. I'm, I was—"

"Why are you so scared of me?" I demanded, leaning close to her face. The bell rang loud over our heads, and I could see the kids, Cleans and Morries alike, scattering off to class, but I didn't move.

Milla shook her head, eyes open so wide I could see the pale pink veins in the white parts. "I ain't scared of you."

She tried to slip away to the side, but I put out my arm and blocked her, my hand flat against the wall. Anger traced white-hot trails along my nerves. I itched to hit Milla. I could feel my palm tingle where I imagined smacking it against her bloodless cheek.

But when she dodged in the other direction, I let her go. She backed away with little shuffling steps, her book forgotten on the floor. "I ain't scared," she said again, and I knew she was about to turn and sprint down the hall, to sit in the back of some class with the other Morries.

"I ain't scared," she said one final time, giving me a look that was part triumph and part impossibly sad. "But maybe *you* oughta be."

I couldn't pay attention the rest of the day. I had done something to Milla that had fixed her. I wasn't sure what or how, and my mind danced around the memory of yesterday, trying to make sense of it.

There had been a second, when my fingers pressed against her damp, stringy hair, when it felt as though something had shifted inside me. As though some hidden piece had broken free and now rode the currents of my bloodstream, electrified by my heartbeat and changing me from the inside out. I wasn't at all sure I liked the feeling. Being me wasn't exactly paradise, but I wasn't sure I was ready to change, either.

I thought of Gram and the brief time when she'd turned

almost human, when we first got Chub. She had changed—or at least I thought she had. For a while she was almost like a real parent, asking me about my day, about what I learned at school. She wasn't great at it—she didn't listen to my answers and I still had to do most of the chores, but when I watched her working with Chub, there was a light in her eyes, and that was more than I'd seen in her before or since.

And now she was worse than ever. Was that what was in store for me? Would I end up like her, bitter and mean? I'd tried to help Milla—I hadn't planned it, and I didn't understand it, but I had tried. And now I wanted to make a connection with her. No: the connection was already there—I just wanted her to acknowledge it. And instead, she'd made it even clearer that she wanted nothing to do with me.

I was still lost in my thoughts when I walked to the drugstore after school, and I left without the one thing I really needed, Chub's baby shampoo. I turned around after a couple of blocks and headed back.

When I had almost reached the store, I saw something that made my heart lurch: the car that had been parked outside our house that morning was pulling into a parking space. Two men got out of the car. They were medium height with short hair, wearing sunglasses and dark jackets. They moved fast and looked strong and muscular under their clothes, and they didn't smile or talk.

They could be anybody, I told myself—it was probably just a coincidence that I'd seen them twice. They could have pulled over in front of our house to check a map or to pee behind a tree or something, and as for going into the drug-store, everyone in town shopped there.

On the other hand, I had never seen them before. I knew pretty much everyone in Gypsum by sight, and these guys definitely didn't look local.

If they *were* cops, they weren't from Gypsum.

But if someone had caught on that Gram was dealing drugs, maybe the local cops had called in some other agency. Like—I racked my brain, trying to remember what we'd learned in civics. There was the Bureau of Alcohol, Tobacco, Firearms and Explosives . . . but was dealing drugs a federal crime? And who would have turned Gram in? One of her customers? Maybe they'd given up information in exchange for a better deal, if they'd been arrested for possession or something. I knew the penalties for dealing were fierce, way more serious than just getting caught with stuff.

But if they already suspected Gram, why didn't they just get a warrant and come to the house? Maybe that was what they were doing now—trying to get enough evidence to justify a warrant. Well, they wouldn't get it from talking to Mr. Hsiao—all I'd bought today was a box of trash bags, eyedrops for Gram and a three-pack of soap.

I needed to find out more. I waited until the men entered the shop, then walked quickly to the car. Trying to look casual, I peered through the windshield: there was nothing inside but a Styrofoam coffee cup in the cup holder.

I went back into the shop, slipping into the aisle farthest from the cash register. I studied the shaving cream and razors and strained to hear what the two men were saying to Mr. Hsiao.

". . . come in regularly?" A deep voice with a slightly flat accent.

"No, like I told you, she's as like to come in one day as the next. These kids, they don't stick to a schedule, you know? You mind telling me what this is about?"

"An incident at her school," a new voice said smoothly. "Can't give the details at this point. We appreciate your co-operation. And you keeping it . . . under wraps."

"And you said you were from . . ." *That's right, Mr. Hsiao, find out who they are,* I telegraphed silently.

"State services," the first voice said. "Here, my identification . . ."

There was silence for a moment; then Mr. Hsiao spoke, his voice only a little less skeptical. "Well, I've told you what I can. You could probably catch up with the girl, talk to her yourself, if you like."

A moment later they were striding back out of the store. I spotted the tops of their heads going by and ducked. I counted to two hundred before leaving the store, careful not to let Mr. Hsiao see me.

I wasn't convinced the men were from any state agency. They were too . . . anonymous, for one thing. Plus, Mr. Hsiao didn't sound like he thought much of whatever ID they showed him.

Could they be some sort of competition? Drug dealers from the next town over, maybe all the way from Kansas

City? Or had Gram got into something even worse? Did she owe money, had she stolen something valuable, cheated someone important?

The car was gone, but for all I knew it was on its way to our house. I needed to get home, but there were stretches of the road with no houses along them, no one to notice if something happened to me. But I had no idea what these men would want with *me*.

I didn't care much what happened to Gram, but I couldn't let anything happen to Chub. As I hesitated, torn between running home and trying to keep the men from seeing me, Sawyer Wesson came around a corner, walking with Milla. Sawyer was a Morrie, but he wasn't like the others. He was quiet and careful and kept himself clean. We'd never spoken, but I'd noticed him watching me a few times during lunch or in school assemblies.

Milla saw me first, and her mouth tightened into a hard line. She put a hand on Sawyer's arm, but he was in the middle of saying something to her as he tossed his cigarette to the ground and stepped on it.

"Sawyer," I called. Panic made me bold. "Sawyer, could you please walk me home?"

Only after the words were out did I realize how they sounded. I was frightened, that was all, and I just wanted some company in case anything bad happened. Sawyer was tall and broad-shouldered, with narrow eyes and black hair that reached almost to his shoulders. If you didn't know him, it would be easy to be intimidated by him.

He stopped and regarded me. He looked surprised, then wary, his eyes clouding with doubt.

"I mean—I didn't—" I started to explain, but what could I say? That I thought I was being pursued by government agents or members of the mob or, or, I had no idea who?

"That'd be okay," Sawyer said, and then I saw something I'd never seen before: his smile. It was surprising how it changed his face, making him look almost sweet.

"You were comin' to the Burger King with me, or did you forget that," Milla spat. She refused to look at me.

"I never said—"

"Whyn't you just go on with *her*, then. Seein' as you're so forgetful'n all, you prob'ly forgot who she is." If it was a bluff, it wasn't much of one, since Sawyer walked over to me without a backward glance. I had no idea what Milla meant by "who she is." Was she referring to what had happened in gym? To the fact that I was an outcast? Whatever she meant, Sawyer either didn't know or didn't care, and I felt smug satisfaction as Milla stalked off the way they'd come, defeated.

We walked half a block before I managed to think of something to say, and then at the very same moment Sawyer started to talk too.

"So how are—"

"What do you—"

And then we were both laughing and saying *you first, no you*. Sawyer kicked at a stone and it went flying across the road, hitting a tree trunk dead-on, and I thought about how it was for me in gym class.

"Did you ever want to play sports?" I asked.

Sawyer didn't answer for a moment. "Sometimes. I thought . . . I'm pretty good, you know, at throwing. I thought maybe baseball. But . . ."

He didn't need to finish. I didn't know what his home life was like, but it was safe to assume it had certain things in common with mine.

I changed the subject, and we talked about classes and teachers. I was surprised to learn that he was considering trying to get into AP American History. He'd be the first Morrie I'd ever heard of to get into an Advanced Placement class. He asked me what I liked to do after school, and I told him about Chub, and Sawyer listened and nodded and even laughed when I told him the way Chub followed Rascal around the yard, like he thought he was part dog.

"Hey," he said when my house came into view. "I just want to say I'm really sorry about, you know, Milla and what she said. She don't mean anything by it."

I doubted that was true—whatever Milla thought about me, it seemed like she felt it strongly. I tried to think of a way to ask about her, and the Morries in general, without offending Sawyer. The way he'd agreed to walk with me so readily, the way he looked at me at school when he didn't think I'd notice—I was pretty sure he had a crush on me, and it felt good. I'd never been wanted by a boy before, and I didn't want to mess it up by making him uncomfortable.

"I . . . always wondered why Milla and I were never friends," I said carefully. I was trying to figure out what to say next when a car pulled up behind us and gunned its engine. We scrambled off the shoulder into the weedy edge of the woods.

When I turned around to look, I saw that it wasn't a car at all but a battered old green Ford pickup. The driver rolled the window down and hung out an arm.

It was Rattler Sikes.

Cold fear shot through my body as Rattler leaned out the window and looked straight at me, but when he spoke, it was directed at Sawyer.

"Git on in the truck, boy," he said, and I could see that his teeth were surprisingly white and straight. His eyes were a brown so dark they were almost black, flinty and sparking some strong emotion. Maybe curiosity. Maybe rage.

"I don't—she asked me to—" Sawyer started, his gaze darting between me and Rattler.

"I didn't ask you a question, did I, boy," Rattler said. His tone stayed even, but there was a threat in it, a shadow of violence that reached into me and curled around my heart.

"No," Sawyer mumbled, his chin lowered.

"Ain't gonna tell you agin."

Sawyer glanced at me—he didn't meet my eyes, just gave me a quick view of his face, which was cast in misery and, it seemed to me, apology. He trudged around to the passenger side and got in. Inside the cab, he stared straight ahead.

Rattler continued to watch me. As uncomfortable as it was to be the focus of his attention, I didn't look away. There was something in the way he looked at me, something that kept me from running.

Rattler's voice lowered even further, a raw whisper. "You take care, hear, Hailey girl."

The truck pulled away slowly, the tires crunching gravel and spitting up loose rocks and dead leaves. Rattler's eyes tracked me, and just when it seemed like he would run off the road, he smacked the side of the cab with the flat of his hand and turned the wheel back straight on the road. He sped up and I smelled the exhaust from the hanging, corroded tailpipe.

I walked toward the house, and Rascal came bounding across the yard, ears flying, happy to see me—but Rattler's voice stayed in my head. So low, I thought again, that most people wouldn't even be able to hear it.

But *I* could hear. I could hear him just fine.

CHAPTER 5

SHE ALMOST DIDN'T STOP *outside of town, but at the last second she took the exit that led past the Show-Me Trading Post before heading out to State Road 9.*

She'd left first thing in the morning after the longest night of her life, lying in the dark and replaying that horrible scene over and over, the things she had learned about her boyfriend—and the one surprise he'd saved for last.

So much would have been different, if she had only known. It didn't help anything to think about what might have been, but deep in the night, when the silence was most profound and the dark reached all the way into her soul, it was hard to resist.

Today she would start to put things right.

The Show-Me Trading Post was even more run-down than she remembered, a ramshackle cinder-block building with gaudy displays in dirty windows, hardly the place to buy someone a gift.

But she was worried that the girl, who would never have heard about her either, might be skittish. Maybe a small token, a gesture to show that she wanted to help, could smooth things over for their first meeting.

There was nothing on the shelves that felt right, though. She considered a cardboard stand displaying fruit-flavored lip gloss, a cheap-looking bead bracelet kit, a rack of fashion magazines, before settling on a generic MP3 player with earbuds. She could buy the girl something nicer later—once they were together, once she had proved that her intentions were good.

As she slipped the player off its hook on a Peg-Board rack near the back of the store, the door jangled and two men walked in, caps pulled low.

She shrank back, slipping into the shadow of a tall refrigerator that held soft drinks and beer. She had seen those men before, at the lab. They sometimes came to meet with her boyfriend in private. They didn't look like scientists—not with their generic-looking dark jackets that did not entirely conceal the holsters underneath. Their visits were brief, and afterward her boyfriend usually grew distant for a day or two, saying little, staying in his office late and monitoring the high-res displays in his office that were tilted so that only he could see them.

One of the men talked to the cashier, showing her something small and flat. The cashier, a brassy-haired woman with glasses on a chain around her neck, answered in a voice loud enough to hear in the back of the store.

"No, don't b'lieve so," she said indifferently.

More murmuring as the man gestured insistently while his

companion glanced around. She edged back into the corner between the refrigerator and the wall and flattened her body into the small space so that she couldn't be seen from the front of the store.

"No, never," the cashier repeated. "But then again, I ain't from town. I live twenty miles down to Casey, so I wouldn't probably know her, now would I."

The man tucked the photo away—because that was what it had to be, wasn't it, a photo of the girl—and slid a bill onto the countertop glass, then flipped a card on top of the money.

"Call if you remember anything later," he said in a louder voice. Her heart pounded as she watched the two men turn and make their way out of the store.

So, he hadn't waited, then. He might have believed the story she gave him last night, her terrified attempt to convince him that finding out about the girl meant nothing more to her than good news for the research. He might have believed her lies, but it hadn't stopped him from sending the men down to Gypsum. Clearly he was determined to move forward immediately.

She had to stop him. But she couldn't just go bursting into the house and demand that the girl leave with her—not when there was no telling what the old lady had told her.

No—first she had to build trust.

She looked at the cheap trinket in her hand and slowly slid it back on the hook.

A gift wouldn't help. Bribery wouldn't help. Neither would demanding or threatening or pleading or begging.

She poured a cup of stale coffee with shaking hands. She paid *the cashier, who barely looked at her as she counted out the change, then stood in the parking lot drinking the bitter liquid before she got back into her car and drove the once-familiar streets to the house where she had grown up, a place she had hoped never to see again.*

She had a near-impossible task ahead of her. And the only weapon she had was the truth.

CHAPTER 6

AFTER RATTLER DROVE AWAY, I stood outside for a minute and waited for my heartbeat to slow down to normal before I went into the house. I said hello to Gram, and she grunted in my direction. *Judge Judy* was blaring from the television. Chub was on his stomach, scribbling with a fat crayon in a coloring book. When he saw me, he jumped up and ran over and threw his arms around my legs like he did every day, hollering, "Hayee!"

I usually loved that moment. It was the best thing in my day, getting home and making sure that Chub was safe and knowing that there was one person in my life who was always happy to see me.

Today, though, it was hard for me to return his hug without letting him see how shook up I was. I got Chub a snack and drank a glass of milk, and then I settled in with my homework, though it was almost impossible to concentrate. I kept thinking about the men in the car, and Milla and Sawyer, and Rattler. Afternoon faded into evening and I fixed dinner and gave Chub his bath. I toweled him off and dressed him in his pajamas, but it was a little early for him to go to sleep. I knew I ought to read to him, but I was still feeling upset and distracted, so I did something to help me calm down: I visited the words.

I'd found them a few years ago, carved with care into the wall of the closet in the bedroom I shared with Chub. You couldn't see them unless you actually went inside the closet, and since Gram used to keep it jammed full of junk, I didn't find them until I got old enough to organize the closet myself. I had taken everything out and was washing the walls one Saturday when I found the words, near the bottom of the wall, carved into the old wood paneling.

CLOVER PRAIRIE

Those two words sparked something inside me, almost like recognition. I wondered what they meant—I imagined a field full of clover, swaying gently in the breeze, the sun shining brightly.

But even as I pictured the scene, I knew it wasn't right. I traced the words with my finger; someone had taken care, maybe using a penknife or a sharp screwdriver, going over the blocky letters until they were grooved deeply into the wood. I wasn't the first person to trace them, I could tell. The edges were smooth, without splinters or rough edges.

I returned to the words almost every week. Something happened when I touched them, some small peace entered me, calming my anxiety and my fears.

I let my fingertips drift down the wall until they rested on the baseboard. But something wasn't right. The piece of baseboard, extending only two feet or so along the left wall of the closet, was loose. It separated slightly from the wall, wobbling under my fingers.

I tried to shove it back, feeling for the nail that had popped out, thinking I'd get a hammer and fix it.

But there was no loose nail. Instead, the bottom came away from the wall, and I realized that it wasn't nailed at all, only kept in place by the tension between the other walls.

In fact, this board wasn't mitered like the others. I tugged at it, and it came away in my hands. As I felt along the edge, I realized I'd come upon a hiding place: the paneling had been cut away in the middle, making a little hidey-hole about a foot long and a few inches deep. How had I never noticed this before?

I reached cautiously inside the hole and touched something, and the strange sensation of familiarity got stronger. I knelt down and shined the flashlight into the tiny space. With my cheek pressed to the floor I could see that there was a bundle wrapped in cloth, and papers rolled and tied with a ribbon. I took everything out and spread it on the floor in the room, where the light was better. Chub had crawled up on my bed and was turning the pages of his favorite board book, humming and running his fingers over the pictures; he could entertain himself that way for hours.

I picked up a tarnished metal frame containing a picture of a young, smiling, black-haired woman. It was one of those photos from a long time ago, when they first started printing pictures in color. The colors were all too bright: the yellow of her shirt, the red of her lips. Her hair was done in an old-fashioned style, curled close to her face, but her skin was smooth and unlined and her eyes sparkled as though she had just heard something funny.

I turned the frame over and there was handwriting on the back: *Mary 1968*. She didn't look like anyone I had ever met, but at the same time she was somehow . . . familiar. I set the frame down and unfolded a piece of fabric that had gone yellow with age.

Inside, a rectangle of white lace had been carefully rolled around a necklace. Hanging from a silver chain was a multi-faceted red stone surrounded by fancy silver scrollwork. It was beautiful and it looked very old.

The rolled pages were delicate, made of a yellowed paper that felt rough to the touch, and covered with rows of flourishy writing. The handwriting was faded, and it looked like it had been written with a brush or a fountain pen. I couldn't read all the words—there were women's names and dates on one side, and on the other side were a few lines of writing in some language that wasn't English.

I studied the names. They started with Lucy Hester Tarbell and the year 1868. I read through the names: Sarah Beatrice Tarbell, Rita Joan Tarbell, Helen Davis Tarbell. . . . When I got to the end I sucked in my breath at the final name: Alice Eugenie Tarbell, 1961.

I stared at Gram's name until I realized what was wrong: if these were birth dates, it meant that she was . . . forty-nine years old. But that was impossible. Gram was bent and arthritic and had trouble breathing and getting out of a chair. True, she'd never told me her age, but I'd always assumed she was eighty or something, as old as I could imagine.

Could the date be something else? A marriage date, maybe, or . . . I racked my brain for possibilities. Maybe something religious? Gram never went to church, never even mentioned God. But I had learned in school that families sometimes recorded names, births and deaths and marriages, things like that, in a family Bible—could I have stumbled on pages torn from *my* family Bible?

I turned the pages over and tried to read the lines of writing.

> *Tá mé mol seo draíocht*
> *Na anam an corp cara ár comhoibrí*

I had barely read the first two lines when I found that my lips moved with ease, that I was pronouncing the unfamiliar words as though I'd been speaking them all my life, line after line. It felt extraordinarily good, and right, and I didn't stop. My eyes clouded over, but I kept chanting, my voice tapering off to a whisper. When the words ran out I blinked a few times to clear my vision and saw that I had recited the entire paragraph or poem or whatever it was that had been written with such care on these pages.

I *could* have stopped—it wasn't like I'd been possessed or anything like that—but the words were there inside me, and reading just the first few brought the rest to my conscious mind. I found myself wanting—*needing*—to speak them aloud. I scanned the page a second time and marveled at the beauty of the words, and at the way I'd been able to make the strange sounds and the accent that went with them.

And then I realized I had heard the words once before.

When I had touched Milla in the gym.

When my vision had gone dark, when the sounds of the gym had faded away and left me completely focused on the rushing feeling and Milla's wounded body under my fingertips, my mind hadn't been completely silent. There had been a whisper of a voice saying these same words, or perhaps it had been my own voice, I couldn't be sure, only knew that they had unfurled like a ribbon fluttering in a breeze, there and then gone.

I ran my fingertips over the words as though touching them would answer my questions, would somehow reveal what I was supposed to do. Because I felt certain that I had been chosen for something and that Milla was part of it, and all the Morries, and Gram and Rattler Sikes and Dun and even Chub. All of it fit together in some way that I didn't yet understand, and the thought was frightening but compelling.

I picked up the necklace and held it in the lamplight. Deep red flashes danced into the corners of the room as though the stone had an energy that splintered into pieces when the light touched it.

Chub noticed the sparkling stone and dropped his book on the bed, clapping his hands.

"Preeee!" he said, laughing—it almost sounded like "pretty."

I slipped the necklace on, fastening the silver clasp with care, and then I sat next to Chub on the bed and let him look at it. He touched the stone gently and murmured and crawled into my lap, and I held him tight and rocked him.

I loved to sing to Chub, everything from songs from cartoons to my favorites from the radio. Today, I just hummed, a sad, wandering melody that came into my head. Chub sighed and leaned into me, and the humming turned to words, the words from the verse. If Chub found them strange, he didn't let on. I sang, and we rocked, and when the need to replay the verses over and over finally faded, he had fallen asleep in my arms.

I carried him to his crib and tucked him under his blanket. I slipped the pendant under my shirt so Gram wouldn't see it, and rolled the scrap of lace carefully and put it in the back of my T-shirt drawer along with the frame and the pages. When I left the room, Chub had a fistful of soft cotton blanket pressed to his chin, smiling in his sleep.

CHAPTER 7

I WAS SLIDING into my usual seat at an empty lunch table the next day when I saw him. Sawyer was sitting with Milla and a few other Morries, poking at something in a Tupperware container with a plastic fork.

Only, there was something wrong. I could see it from twenty feet away. His eye was swollen and there was a purple bruise shading his cheek.

I suddenly wasn't hungry. I threw my lunch—a sandwich and apple from home—into the trash and then walked, as casually as I could, past his table.

Up close it was worse. He had a black eye, and the other eye had an ugly red cut along the brow. In addition to the bruise on his cheek, there was something wrong with his nose; it was swollen and tilted to the right. As I passed, I couldn't help gasping. Everyone looked up except Sawyer, who dropped his chin even lower and stared at the table.

"Whatcha lookin' at him like that for, Hailey?" Gomez Jones demanded. "You're whose fault that is. *You* done that to him."

I couldn't let him say that, not in front of Sawyer. "I— I—"

Milla slammed her hand down on the table angrily, making the trays and silverware jump. "Why can't you just leave us alone?"

"Yeah, bitch—stay away," another girl muttered.

I was getting tired of the way they treated me, especially considering what I had done for Milla. "You'd be dead if it wasn't for me. Maybe you should try being a little grateful."

"Oh, right. 'Cause you *saved* me and all, right?" Milla's face twisted up in fury. "So I'm supposed to kiss your ass?"

"I don't—I never said—"

"I don't *need* you, none of us need you. You think you're above the rest of us, but you're not. You're *not*. You and your grandmother, you're broken. You're *freaks*." To my horror, Milla's eyes filled with furious tears and she bolted from the table. After a second of silence, Sawyer pushed back his chair and went after her, not looking at me.

"Happy now?" the girl said as Gomez and the others started gathering their things. "How many of us do you want to get hurt? None of this would happen if you would just *stay away*."

I stood frozen to the spot after they'd all left. I didn't

understand. I had never—*never*—heard a Morrie girl stand up to anyone outside their group, not in my whole life. I backed slowly away from the table, her words ringing in my ears. When I bumped into a chair, I turned and walked out of the cafeteria as quickly as I could.

Stay away. I'd broken some rule when I talked to Sawyer yesterday, and he'd paid for it. I didn't bother asking myself who had done that to him—it had to be Rattler, though I couldn't imagine why. I didn't blame the Morries for being afraid of him—I was plenty afraid of him myself.

When I got home, Chub was curled up on the couch, asleep.

"How long's he been down?" I asked Gram.

"Not long," she said, stabbing out a cigarette in the ashtray and reaching for her pack, then crumpling it when she saw that it was empty. "I think. Or maybe a while, I don't know."

She had no idea, I could tell. All she cared about, unless she had visitors, was her programs. I reached for the full ashtray, carried it to the trash and wiped it clean before setting it back on the arm of her chair. I went to her room to get a fresh pack of cigarettes from where she kept them on top of her dresser. But when I closed my hand on the pack, I noticed that it was sitting on a plain manila folder.

Curious, I picked the folder up. Something fell out—a white business envelope and, to my amazement, a stack of bills secured with a rubber band.

I flipped quickly through the bills. My heart raced as I

realized they were all hundreds—there had to be thousands of dollars in my hand. I set the money on the dresser as though it was on fire, then picked up the white envelope and slid a piece of paper out. After scanning it I realized that it was a plane ticket. Dated two weeks from now, it was for a flight from STL to DUB. Saint Louis to . . . where?

Before I could examine the ticket more carefully, I heard Gram coughing my name from the living room. I jammed the ticket back in the envelope and slid it and the money into the manila folder.

In the living room I handed the cigarettes to Gram and tried to look like nothing was out of the ordinary. I smoothed an afghan over Chub and kissed his cheek. "I'm going for a walk. Be back in a bit."

Gram didn't respond. I didn't expect her to.

I didn't bother with the leash. Rascal didn't need it—he heeled and sat whenever I came to a stop. As we walked along the road, I tried to make sense of what I'd found. Neither of us had ever been on a plane, and I'd never seen that much money in my life. It had to have something to do with the men in the car, but what? Was she planning to make a run from the law? What had she done?

I was so intent on my thoughts that, as we rounded the curve a quarter mile from our house, I almost missed the familiar sound of the Hostess truck. It was a noisy thing with muffler problems that came along every Tuesday and Friday on its way to the Walmart in Casey. Rascal loved to chase it. Usually he wouldn't leave my side, but there was some-thing about the bright-colored truck that set him hurtling af-ter it, ears flying, tongue hanging out, taking pure joy in the chase.

I didn't worry about him—he was a smart dog, and fast, and he loved to give the truck a run for its money—but I hadn't counted on the curve. The driver couldn't have seen Rascal, who heard the truck's approach before I did and spun around in the gravel on the shoulder just as it rounded the bend.

I've replayed that moment a thousand times in my mind. I don't want to. I wish I could forget the sound Rascal's body made when the grill of the truck struck him, when he nar-rowly missed being dragged under the wheels, when he went flying through the air and slammed into the hard-packed dirt bank.

I ran, but it felt like my arms and legs could only move at half speed, and my scream was stuck in my throat. I know the driver pulled over and got out and called to me, but I don't remember what he said.

Somehow I made it to Rascal's side. It was bad. It was worse than bad. I won't say what I saw, the damage that can be done during a single instant of innocent joy. In the second that it took for me to kneel down beside Rascal and put my cheek to his head, I was covered with blood. Behind us the driver was yelling at me to put him in the truck and we'd drive to the vet, to move fast, there might be a chance—

But I knew there wasn't any chance. Not if we went in the truck. Not if I didn't do what needed to be done.

The rushing was already building in my body, the quickening in the blood, just like it had in the gym. But I couldn't do it here, not in front of the trucker. I stripped off my jacket and laid it flat on the ground and, as gently as I could, dragged Rascal's body onto the jacket. With tears welling up in my eyes and making it hard to see, I folded the fabric over Rascal's poor torn body and lifted him. He didn't protest. He was already slipping away.

I don't remember what I said to the driver. I don't know if I said anything at all. The driver was a kind man, and I think he knew that Rascal was nearly dead and he didn't want to intrude on my last moments with my dog. I know he drove away after placing a heavy hand on my shoulder and telling me he was sorry, but I was already turning back toward home.

I laid Rascal on the porch, still nestled in my jacket. I put my face close to his and waited for his breath against my cheek, but it didn't come. I put my hands to his torn flesh, the blood cooling and starting to crust under my fingers. I closed my eyes and let the feeling come, roiling rushing unstoppable, and the sounds of the afternoon fell away and the darkness turned to blindness and my fingers became electric as the thing inside me built and crashed and flowed from me to Rascal.

Tá mé mol seo draíocht
Na anam an corp cara ár comhoibrí

Did my lips move? Did I speak out loud? Did the words carry on the chilly spring breeze, across our ruined yard, out to the street, down to Trashtown, where frightened girls hid behind grimy windows, girls who knew more about me than I knew about myself, girls who cursed me? I don't know, but as the words mixed with the urgent need, I sensed that it was all connected, that what I was doing was not of my own making, that it came from a source that bound us all in some way. And as the rushing slowed and my senses returned with a prickly sharp sensation, I tried to push back the nagging feeling that I was in over my head, that I was invoking powers I couldn't control.

And then none of that mattered, because Rascal's body twitched. A small hitch, just a tiny jerk of his paws. I blinked sight back into my eyes and saw that his lips were curled away from his teeth, but under my fingertips I felt his heart beat faintly—a weak and irregular pulse—and I realized that he wasn't dead.

I hugged him, as gently as I could, and then I sewed him up. Thinking of it now, I can't believe I found the courage, but I fetched the sewing basket from the back closet, easing past Gram without waking her from her afternoon nap. I washed my hands and squirted Bactine from the bottle I kept in the bathroom. I got a carpet needle and strong waxed thread and I lined up the edges of the tear in Rascal's body as well as I could.

I apologized before I took the first stitch. "I'm sorry," I whispered. "I know this is going to hurt." But Rascal never twitched or showed the slightest sign of pain. He didn't look at me, his eyes still unfocused, and I made a neat row of overcast stitches, knotting them off at the place in the soft white fur on his chest where the wound began. I dribbled more Bactine onto the ragged stitches, and when I was finished, I carried him inside to the mound of blankets in the kitchen, where it was warm.

I talked to him some more, and even then I think I knew something was wrong. He didn't look at me, he just lay there, though his breathing was even and strong. I cleaned up the blood on the porch with rags and Windex, and then I carried the rags and my bloodied jacket to the burn barrel out back and stuffed them into the bottom, into the ashy remains of the last fire.

Back inside, Chub was waking up from his nap. He must have had a nightmare, because he blinked hard and started to wail and pulled at the blanket I'd covered him with. He was getting big, too big for this kind of thing, but I went to him and he wrapped his arms around me and hugged me hard. Slowly, his sobs diminished to whimpers, and he pressed his face into my neck, his tears mixing with Rascal's blood.

CHAPTER 8

RASCAL SPENT THAT NIGHT lying on the linoleum floor, close to the front door. In the morning I examined his stitches. The pink line of his scar was so faint that it was practically invisible, punctuated by the bits of thread I'd used to stitch him. Even more amazingly, fur was already growing over the area. How could flesh heal that fast—how could fur grow that fast?

Earlier, in the moments before my alarm went off, it had flashed through my mind that I had dreamed his injury. Now I was really starting to wonder. But the black threads were proof that it had happened.

I went to the front door and called his name. He got up obediently, without any stiffness or pain that I could see, and trotted outside and did his business, then came back in and returned to his blankets. I got Gram's embroidery snips with tiny pointed blades, and a pair of tweezers. I said, "Rascal, come," and he followed me to my room, where Chub was just beginning to stir under his mound of blankets, yawning and humming softly.

Rascal sat when I told him to, his pose show-dog perfect, erect and still. When I gently pressed on his shoulders he lay down, exposing his scar. He didn't complain as I cut the threads and tugged them out with the tweezers. It was almost as though he didn't feel it. I wondered if somehow the accident had damaged his nerves, had taken away his feeling without hurting the rest of him, and I prayed that he was healing on the inside as well as he was on the outside. I gathered up Gram's tools and threw the bits of thread in the trash, then shooed Rascal out of the room.

Behind me, Chub coughed and then mumbled sleepily. "Hayee. Mockingbird."

I turned around, Rascal forgotten in my amazement. Chub had said a word—one he'd never said before, three entire syllables as clear as a bell.

"What did you say, Chub?" I asked slowly, my mouth dry.

"Mockingbird," he repeated.

"You—you want me to sing? Sing you the mockingbird song?"

He rubbed at his eyes, nodding. Maybe it was a fluke. Maybe he hadn't said "mockingbird" at all but some other word.

But strange things were happening. Milla, Sawyer,

Rattler . . . nearly losing Rascal . . . the money and plane ticket in Gram's room . . . the things I had done without even understanding what I was doing. As I lifted Chub out of his crib and hugged him tight, the words from the pages played in my head, a whispered sound track that seemed almost like it had been running, the sound turned down, all my life.

But Chub wanted me to sing. So I lay down on my bed and held him and rested my chin on his downy hair and sang his favorite lullaby until he had enough and wiggled out of my grasp and ran out of the room to find Rascal. And then I lay there a few minutes longer, wondering what was happening to me, to us.

At school I skipped lunch to go to the library and use the Internet. I'd gotten pretty good at doing research online, trying to figure out what was wrong with Chub. Not that it helped much; there were so many things that could be wrong with him, I felt like the more I read, the less I knew.

I didn't have much more luck when I tried to research what was wrong with Rascal. I didn't know exactly what to search for: "fast healing" brought up natural remedies and health-food sites. Searching on Rascal's symptoms brought up "catatonia," which involved repetitive movements and ignoring external stimuli, but that didn't seem to be exactly what was wrong with him.

I gave up and unfolded the piece of paper on which I'd copied a few lines from the pages I found in the closet. I smoothed it out and entered the words in the search engine.

Soon it became obvious that the words were Irish, and after poking around in an online Irish-English dictionary for a while I had a pretty good idea of what the lines said:

I commend to this magic
The souls and bodies of our poor countrymen
Heal this withered flesh
These torn and cursed limbs
This tainted blood

I wished I had copied the whole page. I had no idea what kind of magic the author meant, but I felt a strange excitement building inside me. *Healing:* could it really be a coincidence that I'd found the words after the thing that happened to Milla in the gym . . . and right before Rascal had been hit by the truck?

Before I left the lab, I looked up the airport code from the ticket I'd found in Gram's room. DUB stood for Dublin . . . *Ireland.* How could the words from the pages in the closet be related to what was happening now, to the plans that Gram was making in secret?

I didn't know who had written those words or hidden the pages in the closet. I didn't know what Prairie Clover meant, but it still felt like those words held the key. I had to find out more, even if the one person who could help me hated me for reasons I didn't understand. There had to be a way to make her talk to me.

I waited until school was nearly over. When the last bell rang I bolted out of class and ran down the hall to the lab, because I knew Milla had science last period. When she shuffled out of the classroom, head down, at the end of the stream of kids, I stepped in front of her and blocked her path.

I opened my mouth to ask if we could go somewhere to talk, but her expression changed from wariness to recognition, her eyes widening and her lips parting in surprise.

"Where'd you git that?" she whispered.

"What?"

"The necklace."

My fingers went to the red stone pendant. I hadn't taken it off since I found it in the closet. I'd kept it under my shirt at home so Gram wouldn't see it, but at school I'd let it hang in front.

"I—I found it."

"Did your grandmother give it to you?"

I wasn't sure what to say. If I could have thought of a lie that would keep her talking to me, I wouldn't have hesitated. But I had no idea what she wanted, what would hold her interest. All I could think of was to ask her if she'd go somewhere to talk to me, somewhere private. "Look, could you, could we—"

Milla shook her head, already backing away. "I don't have anything to say to you."

"But I have to talk to you. To someone. I'm—I don't— I'll give you—I'll give you money if you want, I don't have a lot but I can get more." I could sense that in a second she would turn and run down the hall away from me. "The necklace! I'll give it to you."

"Don't take it off," she snapped. "I don't want that thing anywhere near me."

I wasn't sure what it was, what it could do, but it clearly had an effect on Milla. I held the stone delicately between my finger and thumb and twisted it in the light coming through the high windows. The sun bounced off the stone and danced across Milla's face in bloodred streaks. Her expression went from wariness to resignation.

"You won't let it drop, will you," she sighed. "So let's git this over with."

We went to one of the practice rooms by the band room, a musty space with old acoustic tiles lining the walls, and music stands and a scarred piano. There was only one chair, so we sat on the floor, our knees pulled up, the sound of someone practicing scales on a cello reaching us faintly.

I didn't tell her everything. I told her about the men in the car, about my fears that the authorities would separate me and Chub. I didn't tell her about Rascal—I didn't want her to think I was crazy. I told her about the men who came to the house, the deals Gram did out of the basement.

When I talked about Rattler, Milla dropped her gaze to the floor and went still.

"What is it?" I demanded, frustrated. "What is it with him?"

Milla didn't answer for a moment, but when she did, her

voice was so flat and quiet that I could barely hear it. "Seems like *you* might know."

"*Me?* Why? I've never done anything to him—"

She jerked her head up and there was anger in her eyes. "It ain't about what *you* done. Don't you git that? Ain't any of us Banished got any say in things. It's all laid out."

"Banished? I don't—"

"That necklace you're so proud of," Milla said, jabbing a finger at me. "Might interest you to know that it ain't the only one. There's three of them come over and they're all cursed. How do you think your grandmother got the way she is? Anyone who wears it's cursed too."

I touched the stone protectively. I couldn't say why, but it seemed to me the opposite was true, that the stone was a charm keeping even worse things from happening to me. "I don't believe you," I whispered.

"Really? Well, your mom had one of them, and look what happened to her. That one you got's probably hers. Your grandmother traded hers, is probably the only reason she's still alive. Only one missing is your aunt's, and who knows what happened to her?"

"My . . . what?"

"Your aunt, Hailey. Come on, don't act stupid."

"I don't have an aunt—"

"You *know* you do. And I don't have to sit here and listen to you sayin' whatever comes into your head like you think I'm an idiot, like you think I'll believe whatever you feel like sayin'—"

"I—I know you're not stupid," I said quickly, placing a hand on her arm, trying to calm her down, but she jerked away from my touch. "I don't mean to, you know, make you feel bad or whatever, but I really don't have an aunt. My mom died in childbirth and I—"

"Stop!" She wrapped her arms tight around herself as though she was cold. "Just stop. Your mom went crazy and killed herself and you know it. Bad enough your grandmother got the taint, and now ain't no one supposed to so much as say your name. Don't you get it? It would be better for everyone if you had never been born, Hailey." Her voice had gone cold and nasty. "You think you're a Healer, but who knows what you done to me? You probably cursed me."

"My mother didn't kill herself," I whispered. I could have said a dozen different things, but that was what came to my lips. "She . . . died. Having me."

Milla stood and pointed a shaking finger at me, her lips twisted in rage.

"I can't—" she started, and then she backed away from me. "If you really don't know, ask your grandmother. She'll *make* you believe it."

"Wait, wait! Ask her what?"

"Ask your grandmother," Milla said, and then she flung the door open and ran, and I was alone with only the mournful sounds of the cello for company.

CHAPTER 9

WHEN I GOT HOME, there was a car parked in the yard.

It wasn't the dark-windowed Lexus or Rattler Sikes's truck. It was a beat-up brown Volvo, and I knew from experience that was a whole other kind of bad news. A car like this—well maintained even if it was old, boring but socially responsible—screamed social worker.

The Department of Social Services, Family Support Division, sent people out to check on us from time to time. In theory they were supposed to visit every month. In truth I never knew when to expect them, so I could never prepare for their visits.

I bolted across the yard, ignoring Rascal, who was sitting on the porch. I let myself in the front door and hurried to the kitchen. It was worse than I feared: Gram hadn't bothered to do anything with Chub, and he was sitting on the floor wearing only a diaper that looked like it was about to burst, crusty bits of lunch on his cheeks. When he saw me he jumped to his feet and came running, throwing his strong little arms around my legs and pushing his face into my thigh, saying, "Hayee, Hayee," in his happy voice.

Gram hadn't bothered to ask the social worker if she'd like some tea or coffee. She had her cigarettes in front of her, and judging by the butts in the ashtray, she hadn't stopped smoking since our visitor arrived.

Last time one of the social workers came, she made a big deal out of Gram's smoking. I thought it would be a bigger issue that we still didn't have smoke detectors, and the porch stairs were still just a nail or two away from collapsing; that Chub was still barely speaking and wouldn't use a toilet, and Gram was still refusing to let him go to preschool.

It was time for damage control.

"Hello," I said loudly, pulling Chub's arms away from my legs. "I'm Hailey Tarbell."

The woman seemed to tense at the sound of my voice. She had shiny dark brown hair that came to little below her shoulders—no one I'd seen before, but that wasn't unusual. They came and went from this job all the time.

She pushed her chair back and stood up and turned toward me and started to speak. Then she stopped and we both just stared at each other.

The face looking back at me—it was my own.

I don't mean her face was a mirror image of mine. But she

looked like me if I was older and had money for nice clothes and makeup and a good haircut.

She had eyes like mine—more gold than brown, tilted up at the corners. Her eyebrows were high and arched like mine, though I'd bet she paid good money to get hers done in a salon.

She had my mouth, thin top lip and full bottom lip. She had the high, sharp cheekbones and the wide forehead I have.

My aunt—this had to be the aunt I never knew I had!

After staring at me for a few seconds, she did something that surprised me even more—she turned back around and smacked her hand down on the table so hard Gram's ashtray jumped, spilling ashes and butts. It had to hurt her hand, but she curled it up into a fist. For a moment I thought she was going to hit Gram, but instead she just squeezed her fist so hard her skin turned white. I realized I had stopped breathing the same instant that she put both her hands flat on the table and leaned down until her face was inches away from Gram's and said in a low and threatening voice:

"If you ever lie to me again, Alice, I'll kill you with my bare hands."

Then she turned back to me and all of the anger drained from her expression, leaving her looking sad and tired.

"My name's Elizabeth Blackwell."

Gram tipped her head back and laughed, an awful hacking laugh that showed her long yellow teeth. We both stared at Gram. Finally she ended on a skidding series of gasping coughs and wiped at her eyes with her hands.

"Now who's lyin'," Gram said.

The visitor blinked once, hard. Then she took a deep breath like she was trying to get her courage up to jump off the cliffs over Boone Lake.

"Okay," she said in a voice so soft I knew it was meant just for me. "I'm not—who I said. My name's Prairie, and I'm your aunt."

My throat went dry. *Prairie.*

Clover.

"What was my mom's name?" I said, my voice barely a whisper.

"What?"

"My *mother*. Your *sister*. What was her name?"

"Clover," my aunt said. "Didn't Alice ever tell you that?"

Suddenly my head felt both tight and dizzy. The words on the wall, the way they felt under my fingertips, the invisible pull they had on me . . . It was my mother's name there. I wondered if she had carved the letters herself. The dizziness escalated into something more, like my whole self had lost its moorings and gone drifting away. "I'm going to get some air."

I went out the back screen door. For some reason, when I heard her following me, I wasn't surprised.

She stayed a couple of steps behind me while I walked toward the woods, away from the road where Rascal and I had walked together just yesterday. A short path met up with the crisscrossed web of trails through the woods that connected the farms out past the creek to Trashtown in one direction and Gypsum in the other. I went straight and in a few minutes I was at the creek. It was nearly dry—we'd had little rain or snow over the winter—and there was a flat rock half submerged in the lazy flowing water. I'd come here to sit on the rock a hundred times, thinking and tossing pebbles into the water. I went there now, dangling my feet over the edge.

"Do you mind if I sit too?" Prairie asked.

I shrugged—*It's a free country.* She settled next to me and picked up a long, skinny twig that had blown into a crevice in the rock. Holding it loosely in her hand, she traced designs in the air. For a while neither of us said anything. Dozens of questions went through my mind. I kept thinking of the names carved into the wall.

"If you're my aunt, where have you been all this time?" I blurted out. It wasn't what I meant to say, and all of a sudden tears blurred my eyes and threatened to spill down my cheeks. I wiped my sleeve hard across my face.

"Oh, Hailey," Prairie said, and her voice wavered. "I . . . had reasons for leaving when I did. I didn't know about you. I meant to come back for your mom, but by the time I could, she . . . well, she died. I never even knew she was pregnant."

"But you . . . you left my mom here alone with Gram. And then she killed herself." I didn't bother to keep the accusation out of my voice, even though I wasn't sure I believed what Milla had said.

"I know." Prairie's voice got softer. "That's something I have to live with every day of my life."

I considered telling her that I'd never leave Chub with Gram. *Never.*

"Didn't anyone come looking for you?" I asked instead.

"Gram didn't report me missing," Prairie said. If she was bitter, she covered it well. "I was never officially a runaway. And the police had better things to do than search for me."

"But—why didn't you come back, you know, later? After I was born?"

I heard the crack in my voice and I hated it, hated that Prairie heard it too.

"I didn't know, Hailey. Alice said your mom—" She hesitated and I saw that she bit her lip the very same way I did, catching the right side of the bottom lip between her teeth. "She never let me know about you."

Why should I care? My mother was nothing to me. I had no memories of her. As far as I was concerned, I'd never had a mother at all.

"It doesn't matter, anyway," I muttered. "Chub's my family now. We're fine, we don't need anyone else."

Prairie nodded, more to herself than to me, I thought.

"I see you found your mom's hiding spot," Prairie said gently.

"Her . . . what?"

Prairie put her hands to the back of her neck and twisted the clasp of a thin silver chain. As she closed her fingers on the pendant, I knew what I would see.

"It's just like yours," she said. "When I saw it on you . . .

well, your mom never took it off. Neither of us did. Mary—our grandmother—she gave them to us. They're very old. She said they would protect us."

She handed the pendant to me, still warm from her skin. I had noticed that the stone in the necklace I wore absorbed my heat and held it, almost like it carried energy. The necklace in my hand was identical to the one around my neck, right down to the twisting, curling scrollwork that held the stone in place, the looping bale through which the chain ran.

I handed the necklace to Prairie. It would have been nice to believe there was magic in the necklaces, but I wasn't counting on it. "I guess we should go back," I said.

We didn't talk, but the silence felt all right. When we got to the house, Gram was still sitting in her kitchen chair. She gave us a calculating smile and blew smoke in our direction. "Look what the cat dragged in."

"I'm taking Hailey out to dinner," Prairie said. "We'll be a while."

This was news to me. Chub, who had been playing with his plastic magnet letters on the fridge, came over and pushed his face into my legs again. For just a second I was embarrassed for Prairie to see that Chub wasn't like other kids.

Gram stared at Prairie with her eyes narrowed down to slits. Prairie stared back. I found myself hoping Gram would blink first.

"Fine," Gram finally said. I could tell she was thinking hard. She had that look a lot. No matter what else you could say about her, she wasn't stupid. I couldn't tell you how many of her customers came to our house thinking they could put one over on her. She'd give them that look and sure enough they'd leave a lot more of their cash on the table than they had planned. If they didn't like it, she'd tell them to take their business somewhere else, which they hardly ever did. I thought of the money and the ticket again, and wondered what she was up to.

"Don't wait up" was all Prairie said as she took her keys out of her purse.

"We need to bring Chub," I said. I wanted to find out what Prairie was really doing here, but I felt bad about leaving Chub tonight. I could tell he was upset, the way he'd hugged me so hard.

"Chub's not going anywhere," Gram said. "I think he's catching something. I don't want him taking a chill outside."

I knew she was lying, but I also knew he'd be all right for an hour or two.

I followed Prairie out to her car. We didn't talk. She drove straight to Nolan's, taking the shortcut back behind the Napa Auto Parts, and I was surprised she'd picked the only fancy restaurant in town.

I was afraid the hostess wouldn't seat us, since I was wearing jeans. But Prairie gave her a smile and said, "We'll need some privacy, please. Would you find us a table that's a little bit out of the way?"

The hostess put us in a nice booth along the far wall, away from the waitress station and the kitchen. She kept sneaking looks at Prairie, and now that I had gotten over the surprise of how much our faces looked alike, I could see why Prairie drew attention.

I was tall and skinny, but Prairie was tall and elegant. Thin, but with nice hips and breasts, and her brown hair was shiny and hung exactly right, smooth and straight and curving under just a little where it went past her shoulders. Her jacket, plain and cut low enough in the front to show a little bit of her silky top underneath, fit her so perfectly it pretty much said money with a capital *M*. I guess the hostess was thinking the same thing. There were very few rich families in Gypsum; almost everyone was just trying to get by.

I was going to order the chicken sandwich. I read all the prices on the menu and added up in my head what dinner would cost. Part of me wanted to order the most expensive thing just to see what Prairie would do, to see if there was a limit to her concern for me, or maybe to see if I could get her to crack and show me who she really was. Like if under this nice exterior she was just waiting to tell me what she really wanted, and it would be something bad.

But when the waitress came around to take the order, Prairie said, "The filet mignon sounds really good, doesn't it, Hailey?" It was twenty-three dollars, but I hadn't had a steak in as long as I could remember and I just said yes, it did.

When the waitress walked away, neither of us said anything for a minute. Prairie fiddled with her knife, spinning it back and forth.

"Tell me about your dog," she finally said. "If you don't mind."

That caught me off guard. Rascal wasn't something I felt like talking about. "There's nothing to tell."

"It's just that I can tell he's . . . that something happened to him." Her face went soft, and her eyes were sad. "Where did you get him?"

"Um . . . Gram got him from a guy she knew."

"Alice traded him for drugs." Prairie's expression didn't change.

"Yeah." I shrugged like it was no big deal. "Probably."

"Hailey . . . I saw the scar. What's left of it, anyway. On his stomach."

I blinked. This morning the scar had almost disappeared. You had to push the fur to the side to see the faint pink line.

I wanted to ask Prairie how she knew, but I didn't want her to think I cared too much. Caring about things made you vulnerable. "He got hit by the Hostess truck a few days ago."

"Was he badly hurt?"

"He . . ." I swallowed, remembering the way Rascal looked. But I didn't want to tell her what I had done, didn't want to have to try to explain how he'd healed so well in one night. "No, just a little cut."

Prairie watched me carefully. "I bet you must have given him good care, Hailey. What did you do?"

Her voice was so kind that I had to look away. I swallowed hard and took a little sip of my ice water. "I, um, I just cleaned it with antiseptic and, you know, kept him inside."

"Did you talk to him?"

"Did I . . . what?"

"While you were cleaning up his injuries? I mean, maybe he was scared. I know how that can be. You must have wanted to make him comfortable."

She *knew.*

Somehow she knew that I'd healed Rascal, that something I'd done to him after the accident had fixed him, just like I'd fixed Milla during gym. I felt my face go hot. It was like she could read my mind.

"I don't think I said anything special," I answered her carefully, "while I was taking care of him."

Prairie nodded. "All right. Well, I'm glad he's . . . better."

"Yeah, it, um. I mean, he has that limp, you probably noticed. But that's all."

The waitress came along with our salads. We thanked her and just as I was about to pick up my fork, Prairie took a deep breath.

"I have some things to tell you, Hailey," she said. "I'm sorry to have to do it now, when we've only just met, but I think it's necessary."

Bad news, then; she was about to tell me what she *really* wanted from me. But, honestly, how much worse could my life get?

"Whatever," I said.

"Now I wish I'd ordered a drink," Prairie said, smiling a little. "A really strong one. Okay, where to start? How about this—Alice isn't as old as you think she is."

"What do you mean?"

"I think she's turning fifty this year," Prairie said. "Let's see, I'll be thirty-one, and she was nineteen when she had me, so, yes, she's still forty-nine, barely."

I thought of the old pages, the names and dates written there. *Alice Eugenie Tarbell, 1961.* But Gram was old—she had the wrinkled face, the thin gray hair, the bent fingers that elderly people have. And she was weak. She could barely get up and down the stairs to the basement. She couldn't do chores, which was why it was always me who mopped and swept and washed the windows and shoveled snow and carried the laundry and the groceries.

And she was sickly. She caught colds constantly, lying in her bed for days at a time, getting up only when her customers came calling. I found her hair in clumps in the shower drain, and her nails were yellowed and cracked. If she bumped into the furniture, she'd have purple and yellow bruises. Every time she lit up a cigarette, she hacked and coughed as though her lungs were about to fall out.

"That's impossible," I finally said.

Prairie sipped at her water. "I wish you could have known your great-grandmother. My grandmother Mary, Alice's mother."

I thought of the photo in the cheap frame, the woman's bright red lips and sparkling eyes. My great-grandmother—I could barely imagine it.

"She died when I was ten," Prairie continued, "but she was beautiful and strong and fun and smart . . . so smart. Most of the women in our family are."

"What happened to Gram, then?"

"Well, here's part of what I need to tell you, Hailey. Tarbell women—all your ancestors—are incredibly healthy and strong. It's—well, it's our birthright, I guess you might say. In our blood. Tell me, I bet you hardly ever get sick, right?"

"Uh . . . not much."

"And you're strong—stronger than the other kids. And more coordinated, right?"

I just shrugged.

"Well, like I said, it's in our genes. Except that every so often, maybe every five or six generations, there is an aberration."

"A what?"

"Someone born who doesn't fit the genetic pattern. Like Alice. Where the rest of the Tarbell women have phenomenal genes, Alice has been in poor health her entire life. She's aging much too quickly, her tissues are decaying. I don't imagine she'll live to see her fifty-fifth birthday."

I thought of Milla and what she'd said about the necklaces, about how they were cursed. *How do you think your grandmother got the way she is?*

I didn't say it, but if it was true, and Gram had been cursed, I wasn't sorry. Gram could die tomorrow for all I cared. I did the addition in my head—I'd be twenty. Twenty, and free of Gram—my heart lightened at the thought.

An idea came to me, a missing piece of the puzzle of my

life that maybe Prairie could supply. "Did you and my mom have the same dad? Do you know who he is?"

Prairie shook her head. I'd wondered, sometimes, looking at Gram with her withered skin and bent body, if she had ever been young, if a man had ever loved her. It didn't seem possible.

"Alice never talked about that part of her life."

"What about my dad?" I asked. "Like maybe my mom had a boyfriend or something?"

Prairie gave me a look that was so full of sadness I almost wished I hadn't asked. "Clover was my *younger* sister. When I left Gypsum, she was only fourteen. She was already pregnant with you. I never knew."

Fourteen. I couldn't believe it. I mean, I knew it was possible—they talked about it in Health enough.

"She would be . . . twenty-nine," I said. Barely old enough to be a mother of a *kid,* much less someone my age.

"Yes . . . Clover, your mom, she was very shy. She didn't really have many friends at school. And nothing like a boyfriend."

So she was like me, then. I knew what it was like not to have friends. "But maybe Gram knows something."

Prairie pressed her lips together for a moment as though trying to figure out what to say next. "*If* she knows, I'm afraid she'll never tell."

"Why not?"

"I know how hard it is to live with Alice," Prairie said

gently. "I . . . remember. She doesn't have the power that she wishes she had, and the way she is . . . it's left her angry and bitter. Maybe even unable to love anyone. I think it was hard on your mother, harder than it was on me. Clover was sensitive, and sometimes I think it bothered her more when Alice was mean to me than when she did something to her. I just . . . steeled myself, I guess. I decided a long time ago I wouldn't let her hurt me, and for the most part it worked."

I knew what she meant, though I didn't say it. You told yourself her words were nothing. When she refused to talk to you, you reminded yourself that you didn't care. You shut off the part of your heart that wanted a mother, a grandmother, and you made it through by remembering every day that she couldn't hurt you if you didn't let her, if you didn't make the mistake of caring too much.

My mother hadn't been able to do that.

"Whose child is Chub?" Prairie asked.

I felt my face get hot. "We got him from one of Gram's customers. He's Gram's foster child."

"For the state money," Prairie said thoughtfully. "Right?"

I nodded, surprised that she figured it out so quick. "Yes, but I think she also wanted him to be like . . . a project. Something she could fix. He has, um, problems? I mean, he's slow. He's really great and all, but he isn't really developing as fast as he should be."

I felt disloyal saying it. I waited for Prairie to say something mean about him, to make some careless criticism, and I was ready to hate her if she said the wrong thing. But she just nodded, her eyes sad. "He seems like a sweet boy. You take very good care of him. That must be hard."

"*No.*" The word came out harsher than I intended. "I mean, I don't mind. It's not hard, it's fun."

I didn't tell her how Gram had acted different for a while, after she applied with the state. I didn't want to admit that I'd been dumb enough to hope things had really changed during that brief time when Gram kept the house clean and cooked real meals and didn't do any business out of the cellar. That I had almost believed she could change Chub.

"Do you know his real name?" Prairie asked gently.

I stared at my plate. "No. Just Chub."

I'd thought about changing it. Charlie, I'd suggested to Gram, but she'd laughed and said she guessed he had a good enough name already. And the thing was, Chub *knew* his name, he answered to it. I figured he had enough confusion in his life that we didn't need to go adding any more.

"That's fine," Prairie said. "What about a last name?"

"Gram knows it, but she never let me see any of the papers," I said. "She just says he's a Tarbell now."

Prairie nodded. She had that look again, the one I was pretty sure meant a lot of thinking and figuring was going on.

The waitress came with our dinner, and I dug in. I couldn't believe how good the steak was. Tender and buttery and salty—the best thing I'd ever tasted.

Prairie barely touched hers. She sighed and sliced off a tiny corner and slipped it into her mouth. She chewed and swallowed, but it looked to me like she didn't even taste it. As hard as she was trying to seem calm, I could tell she was uneasy, almost frightened. I wanted to know why.

I set down my knife and fork. "Why are you here? What do you want from me?"

Prairie looked me right in the eye—something hardly anyone had ever done—and took a deep breath.

"I'm taking you with me," she said. "You can't stay here with Alice anymore."

My heart did a little flip at her words. *Leaving*—even if it wasn't the way I planned, even if it was with a stranger—the thought was almost irresistible. I wanted to say *Okay, fine, let's do it*. To hell with school, with the stupid Cleans who'd made fun of me forever. To hell with our falling-down house, the weedy yard, the long walk to the grocery. Anywhere would be better than here. I was tempted to say "Sure, let's go right now," before she changed her mind.

Instead, what I said was, "I can't leave Chub."

Prairie didn't look surprised. She dabbed at the corners of her mouth with her napkin and set down her fork.

"Look," she said, "I'll admit I hadn't planned on Chub. I was actually hoping to leave tonight. This complicates things a bit—but we're still leaving. We'll just go a little later than I planned, and we'll take him with us."

She said that last part kind of fast as I started to protest.

"But—but what about—"

She held up a hand to stop me. "Try not to worry. I want you to let me handle the details. At least for now. Okay?

Look, I know you probably aren't sure about me yet, and you may not completely trust me, and that's—that stands to reason. It does. I understand. But I just—I'm not doing this lightly, Hailey. After you get to know me a little more, you'll understand that I don't take *anything* lightly."

The way she said that, it sounded like a promise, but even more than a promise. Like something she'd worked hard to convince herself of and now she'd do anything to keep it true.

"I can't just—"

"You *can.*" Prairie reached across the table and patted my hand, but I pulled away from her. "I have . . . resources that I'll tell you more about later. I have some money. We can stay the night at the house and you can gather up a few things—not many, just one small suitcase. And we can't let Alice see you packing. She doesn't know. I told her that I was moving back to Gypsum so I could be closer to you. I told her I was going to look for a house here in town."

"You told her . . . ?" There was no way Gram would believe that. There was no way *anyone* would believe a person would come back here to live if they had a choice. "I don't have a suitcase."

"A box, then. Whatever you and Chub need, we can buy."

"And then what? Where would we go?" I knew it was crazy. But it was so tempting to believe in Prairie, in what she said she could do.

"I don't want to say just yet," she said. "I know I'm asking a lot from you, Hailey, but I promise you that soon I'll tell you everything. Right now I just need to focus on getting us all out of here. And you need to help me make Alice believe what I told her. Do you think you can do that?"

I didn't say yes—but I didn't say no, either.

Chapter 10

When we got home, I saw that Gram had made a few plans of her own. Dun Acey's truck was pulled up in the yard, the back fender hanging a little lower since the last time I'd seen it, the result of some accident that had probably been worse for the other guy.

Prairie pulled the Volvo into the yard about as far away from the truck as she could.

"Whose truck is that?" she asked, voice neutral, but I could hear the tension underneath her words.

"That's Dun Acey."

"What a surprise," she muttered, as if it was anything but.

"You *know* him?"

"I knew some Aceys." She said the name like it was poison.

She walked ahead of me. I let her, glad to have a buffer between me and whatever waited inside.

In the kitchen, Dun was tilted back in a chair across from Gram at the table. Rattler Sikes was standing at the sink, a lit cigarette in one hand. He was pouring a glass of water down his throat.

He gave me a tiny nod and then slowly lowered the glass to the sink. Leaning against the counter, he put the cigarette to his lips and drew in on it and smirked as the smoke streamed lazily out of his nostrils.

There were eight beer cans on the table, and I knew without having to be told that six were empty and Dun and Gram were working on the others.

"Hel-*lo,* Hailey," Dun drawled, letting the chair legs slam down on the floor with a thud. "You're lookin' hotter'n August. And who's this you got with you?"

Behind him Rattler laughed, an abrupt, rasping sound accompanied by a ghost of a smile.

Dun looked Prairie up and down the way he usually looked at me—lingering on her breasts and her legs. Dun and Rattler were both probably about Prairie's age, but Dun had always looked old to me, with a couple of missing teeth and greasy hair falling all around his face. After he'd stared her up and down, he gave a low whistle.

"Prair-ie Tar-bell," he said, drawing out the syllables. "I'd know you anywhere. You look even better than the day you left."

I could feel Prairie tense up next to me. "Hello, Dunston," she said, her voice steely. "Rattler."

"Damn—you recognize us after all, girl. Didn't think you would, now you gone all uptown on us. But I guess you just couldn't stay away from us local boys forever." Dun laughed as though that was the funniest thing he'd heard in a long time. Gram laughed with him, lighting up a fresh cigarette and ending on a hacking cough.

"I remember you." Prairie practically chewed off the words.

"Alice tells me you're moving back here. Ain't that nice. Course, if you come back to try an' git in my pants, you're a li'l late." Dun's words were slurred from the beer. "I got my eye on another girl."

Gram laughed again and they both looked at me.

"Lucky her," Prairie said icily. "Now, if you all will excuse us, Hailey and I are tired, and I'm meeting with a realtor first thing tomorrow to look at a house, so we're heading to bed."

"'Hailey and I are tired,'" Gram repeated in a high singsong voice. She did that sometimes when she was drinking, mimicking what I said.

Something told me it was a mistake to do it to Prairie, though.

I waited for her to snap back at Gram like she had earlier, but she said nothing. She put her hand on my arm and steered me toward the hall. "Come on," she whispered.

"Goin' to bed, are you, Prairie?" Rattler's voice came from behind us.

I could sense Prairie tense even more, but she didn't say

anything, just practically dragged me down to my room. Once we were inside, she shut the door firmly and leaned back against it.

I went to check on Chub. He was curled up in his crib, and I was grateful Gram at least had managed to get him put down. His little fist was pressed against his cheek. He always got hot when he slept, his face taking on a rosy color. I put my hand lightly on the back of his neck and felt his heartbeat—strong and regular.

Only then did I turn back to Prairie. "If Dun and Rattler knew about you, and probably a whole lot more people knew too, how come nobody ever said anything to me?"

"Keep your voice down, Hailey," Prairie said softly. "A lot of people are scared of Alice. Or else Alice makes it worth their while to keep their mouths shut. Besides, other than Alice's customers, not that many people in town would remember. Alice sent us to school in Tipton because she didn't want us mixing with the local kids. And it's not like we ever had friends over."

"What about Dun and Rattler? Seems like they knew you pretty well."

"There were a few families that Alice . . . socialized with. The Aceys and the Sikes, a few others."

"From Trashtown. Her customers."

"They weren't always customers, but—yes. Alice knew they had a taste for illegal substances. And she figured out how to capitalize on it. She had to find a way to make money, after all."

Prairie sighed and smoothed down the fabric of her jacket, the memories clearly taking a toll on her.

"But you got out," I said. "And . . ."

I almost didn't say it. I bit my lower lip and considered staying quiet, letting the past rest. It was probably the right thing to do. But in the space of a few hours I had learned that I had lost more than I ever knew I had. So when I spoke again, my voice was bitter.

"And you left my mom here to deal with Alice by herself."

Like me.

Prairie recoiled as if I had slapped her. "Hailey! I— It wasn't like that. You have to know that I loved your mother more than anything in the world. I would never have left, if—if—"

"If *what?*"

"The thing that happened. It would have been dangerous for both of us, if I stayed."

What could have been so bad that she had to leave town? "Did you kill someone or something?"

Sharp anguish flashed across Prairie's face, and for a second I regretted asking. If she was a murderer, maybe I didn't want to know.

"No," she said quietly. "Nothing like that, but what I did made it impossible for me to stay here. You just have to believe me. And I *was* going to come for your mom."

"It's easy to make promises," I said. "You told her you'd come back for her, and you didn't. Now you're trying to come in here and, what, *rescue* me? Because you feel guilty about what happened to my mom?"

I could feel my heart squeezing and hear my voice going high and thin. I knew I should stop. But it would be way too easy to give in to what Prairie promised—and way too dangerous. If I made the wrong decision, it wasn't just me that would be hurt. It was Chub, too.

Before Prairie could answer, I turned away from her. "Forget it. I don't want to know. I'm going to bed."

"Hailey—"

"If you're still here tomorrow, not that I expect you to be . . ."

I didn't finish the sentence, because I didn't know what to say. The truth was that I desperately wanted to believe in her. I wanted her to rescue me. But I was afraid that if I let myself trust her, she'd disappear like every other good thing I'd ever wished for.

Suddenly I was tired. Very tired.

"Hailey, we can go as soon as Rattler and Dun leave. Alice won't wake up once she's out. You know that." Prairie sounded desperate.

"What I know is that I don't want to talk about it anymore," I said, edging past her to the door. "I'm going to go brush my teeth."

When I came back, Prairie took a small toiletry kit from the bag she'd brought with her and went to the bathroom without saying a word. She looked exhausted. While she was gone, I fixed up a bed for her as well as I could. I put my sleeping bag down as a pad and added some old quilts and gave her my pillow. I made myself a pillow out of a sweatshirt.

When Prairie came back into the room, she looked at the makeshift bed and gave me a little smile.

There was one more thing I needed to do—I had to see what Gram and Dun and Rattler were up to before I could sleep. I slipped into the hall and peeked around the corner into the kitchen. The beer-can pile had grown, and Dun was slumped way down in his chair. Rattler was sitting at the table with an ashtray loaded high with butts, drinking another glass of water. Gram was saying something to him, low and serious, but his expression was stony. I wasn't sure Dun was even awake.

As I watched, something strange happened: Rattler suddenly raised his head and stared straight ahead, right toward where I was hiding. His eyes lost their focus and he squinted as though it hurt, and he held up a palm to Gram to make her stop talking.

"Who knows I'm here?" he demanded.

"Nobody," Gram said, chugging her beer. Some dribbled down her chin.

"No, there's—there's— You got that back door locked?"

"Yeah."

"Something's not right. A car . . ."

"Nah, that's just *her* car." Gram yawned, not bothering to cover her mouth. "That damn foreign thing."

Rattler shook his head. "Men. It's *men* in it."

Gram reached for a fresh beer, untangling it from the plastic rings that held the six-pack together. Even that effort was almost too much for her. I was always amazed that as frail as she was, she could drink so much.

"You're rusty," Gram said. "Ain't nothin' happened around here in so long, you're seeing things."

Rattler shook his head impatiently and scowled. I shrank back into the hall—I couldn't believe Gram wasn't scared of him.

"I ain't rusty, you damn woman."

"Okay, then you're just plum wrong. It happens."

"It happens to the *others,* Alice—not me."

Gram cackled, a sound I knew well. When she was drunk she thought plenty of things were funny.

I eased backward as quietly as I could, my heart pounding. In my room, Prairie was sitting on the floor, a quilt pulled up over her knees.

"Prairie, Rattler was talking to Gram. He says—"

But what had he said, exactly? Nothing specific, but I was thinking of the rumors, the women stumbling home barefoot in the chilly dawn.

"He's just so creepy," I whispered.

Prairie nodded. She didn't seem surprised. "I don't want you to worry about him. Let me worry about it. I'd lay odds that Dun's passed out by now—is he?"

I nodded, my heart thudding in my throat. "I think so."

"Okay, so one down, and Alice probably isn't far behind. Rattler's going to get bored sooner or later."

"I wish he'd just leave."

"I know," she said. "Me too. But let me worry about them. You need to rest, if you can."

I couldn't think of anything else to do. I lay down and Prairie turned the lights out, but there was enough moonlight coming in the window that I could still see her outline. She lay on her back and I could see her chest rise and fall steadily as she breathed.

"Good night, Hailey," she said. "I'm glad we're together."

I didn't answer at first. Her words had a strange effect on me—even though she'd brought even more chaos into my life, her voice was soothing, and there was a part of me that wanted very much to believe she'd come to help us. That I had some sort of family besides Gram—*real* family, the kind that cared about one another, like other people had.

"Good night," I finally mumbled.

A little later, before I drifted off to sleep, I peeked at Prairie. She wasn't lying on her back anymore. She was leaning on her side, up on her elbow, and staring at the doorknob. I closed my eyes again.

The next thing I knew, a scream tore through my dreams.

CHAPTER 11

It was coming from the other side of my bedroom door, and it sounded like Gram.

Prairie bolted to my side, clapping a hand over my mouth. Before I could protest, she leaned in close and whispered, "*Quiet.* Take Chub in the closet and close the door and stay there. Don't come out."

"But—"

"*Do* it, Hailey. Please."

Chub was a heavy sleeper—once he was out, he could sleep through anything. I picked him up, which took some effort because he'd gotten so big, and he snuggled in next to my neck, his skin hot and damp.

I glanced back, but Prairie was gone; the door to the room was open a few inches. My heart thudded as I went to the closet.

I yanked a bunch of clothes off their hangers, put them on the floor and laid Chub on them, covering him with a long sweater that I tucked in like a blanket. I kissed his cheek and then left the closet, closing the door almost all the way.

As I crossed my room, I heard a man yell, "Stop right there!" and a pair of sharp cracks and then Prairie's voice, speaking softly, something I couldn't make out. I had to find out what was happening. I wasn't worried about Gram, exactly—but I had to know what kind of trouble Prairie had brought with her.

I tiptoed down the hall, flattening my back against the wall, and peeked around the corner so I had a view into the kitchen and the living room.

What I saw made me suck in my breath.

A man stood a few feet from the door, pointing a gun at Gram and Prairie. It was one of the men from the car I'd seen at the drugstore—I recognized his gray jacket and his blond buzz cut. Gram was sitting in her chair and I could tell from the drool trail that still shone wet on her cheek that she'd passed out, like she sometimes did. She was blinking fast and patting at her hair nervously. Prairie stood behind her, hands held out at her sides.

Dun was exactly where I'd last seen him, slumped over the table, except there was a leaking pool of red coming from his mouth.

Prairie looked furious. I wanted to signal to her somehow, but I knew I couldn't do it without the guy with the gun seeing me.

"You," the man said in a clipped, calm voice. "Old lady. Get down on the floor. Lie on your stomach with your hands straight out to the sides."

"You ain't supposed to—" Gram protested. I suddenly smelled urine sharp in the air and I knew she had peed her pants.

A movement in the corner of the kitchen caught my eye. As it flashed past I realized that Rattler must have hidden behind the refrigerator—but why? Was he helping the man with the gun somehow? Before I could even finish the thought Rattler's arm came up and there was a flash of metal as he buried Gram's chef's knife deep below the man's shoulder.

I screamed. I tried to scream, anyway, but what came out was more of a choked gasp.

"Get back, Hailey!" Prairie screamed at me.

Rattler let go of the knife handle. He didn't wait for the man to fall but threw him onto the kitchen floor as he scrabbled at the knife sticking out of his shoulder. Then Rattler reached for Prairie.

"Get Chub," Prairie yelled. "*Now.* Run!"

I turned and sprinted for my room. I got Chub from the closet—he didn't even stir in his sleep. From the other room I heard a crash and glass breaking. I looked toward the window and considered jumping out with Chub—it was only a few feet to the ground, we'd be fine—but I realized that without Prairie, and the car, there was no chance we could get away. It was a long way across the yard to the woods, and we wouldn't have any cover.

And—I didn't want to leave Prairie.

As I ran down the hall there was another loud crack and then a man yelled, "Get *back!*" I skidded to a stop just before the corner and looked around it again, shielding Chub in my arms.

Dun had slid out of his chair and onto the floor, leaving a smear of blood on the table. The guy with the knife in his shoulder sat next to him, making gasping sounds, his blood-covered hands around the knife handle. A second man stood in the doorway, pointing his gun at Rattler. It was the other man from the car, slightly shorter than his partner, with black hair and eyes and wearing a black track jacket. He stepped neatly over the pile of splintered wood and glass that had been our storm door, and placed himself squarely between Prairie and Rattler. For a second I had the crazy idea that he was protecting Prairie, that they had come here to save us from Dun and Rattler and Gram, but then the man spoke, never taking his eyes off Rattler, who slowly sank to his knees and raised his hands in the air, looking not so much afraid as amused.

"On your stomach, arms straight out, or I *will* shoot you," the man barked, and Rattler complied. I saw Prairie's hands scrambling on the counter behind her, knocking against a glass, a dirty plate, a box of Cheez-Its. The toaster was just beyond her reach. I wanted to scream at her to grab it and throw it at the guy, nail him in the head, but I couldn't speak. I was clutching Chub so tightly that he was whimpering into my neck. I didn't know if I should run back down the hall and take our chances with the window after all, or try to help Prairie.

Before I could decide, Gram pushed her chair back and struggled to stand.

"Stop right there, lady," the man said. "Down on the floor like your friend here, arms out."

But Gram lurched toward him, her gray stringy hair plastered to her drool-damp chin, her hands paddling the air at her sides. "But I'm the one who—"

"Down!" he yelled as his arm swung toward her. I could see what was going to happen in the split second before the gunshot echoed through the room, as Gram kept lurching forward, straight for him.

Except it wasn't a single gunshot—it was two, one right after the other, and Gram flew back through the air, a misting red hole in her back. Then Rattler hurtled up off the floor, the first guy's gun in his hand.

The shooter took longer to fall than Gram did. Rattler had shot him in the side, but it didn't look that bad. He stumbled, putting his hands to the wound and sucking air. Rattler didn't have any more patience with him than with his partner, and he caught him under the chin with the butt of the gun. The man fell to the sound of his own jaw breaking.

There was a second of perfect silence. I took everything in: Gram on her back with her eyes wide and staring, Dun lying next to the two men Rattler had wounded. And in the center of it all, Rattler. If I'd thought his eyes were frightening in the past, they were ten times more frightening now. As I watched from the darkness of the hallway, he slowly lowered the gun to his side, dangling it loose in his hand.

"Ladies," he said, drawing out the word as though he was tasting it. "That was sloppy of me. What I git for doubtin' myself. Won't happen again. Prairie, guess we'll take your car."

"We're not going anywhere with you," Prairie spat.

Rattler shook his head. "Now, Prairie, don't you fret. I ain't gonna do nothin' besides take you somewhere's I can keep an eye on you."

Prairie's eyes widened and I saw fresh fear there. I couldn't believe there could be anything worse than this—four people lying in a sea of blood on the floor, Rattler threatening us with a gun—but Prairie looked terrified.

It was her fear that finally made me move. I remembered the kitchen scissors, in a mason jar with the spatulas and spoons next to the sink, and I ran for them. I waited for the slam of the bullet even as my fingers closed on the handles of the scissors and my hip hit the counter hard. There was an "oof" behind me and the gun went off and—Was I hit? Was Prairie hit?—I whirled around and Rattler had disappeared and Prairie was still standing and I was still standing—

"Now Hailey now!" Prairie screamed. I didn't have to be told twice. Chub wailed in my arms, struggling against me. I dropped the scissors and ran, holding him as tight as I could, and followed Prairie out the door, crunching glass under my feet, slipping on the blood, and then we were in the yard, sprinting for her car.

Rascal was sitting in the center of the yard. His eyes glowed golden in the moonlight. It looked eerie, and I couldn't figure out why he was so calm when strangers had been breaking in, shooting, trying to kill us. Why hadn't he come tearing after them, snarling and barking and snapping the way he did when he treed a squirrel or chased a rabbit?

I didn't have time to dwell on that now, though. "Prairie, I have to get Rascal!" I screamed. I thrust Chub at her and she took him, protesting as I ran and picked Rascal up.

I tightened all the muscles in my back, waiting for the impact of a bullet as I ran to the car, but none came. Rascal was warm and soft in my arms, and he didn't protest at being bounced around. I almost dropped him as I opened the car, and when he landed on the floor of the backseat, he nearly fell.

But there was no time to worry about him. Prairie had got the seat belt across Chub, and it looked like it would hold him in for now. She got in the driver's seat and started the engine, and I barely had time to jump in the backseat with Rascal and Chub before she started rolling across the lawn, accelerating as if she meant to plow straight through the speed of sound, the speed of light, as if she meant to put an eternity between us and the wreckage of my old life.

PART TWO: RUNNING

CHAPTER 12

WE HIT THE ROAD with a squeal of tires. Prairie yanked the steering wheel and the car fishtailed back and forth before straightening out.

Something was wrong with Chub. His cries turned to hiccups and I felt a widening pool of damp along his leg, his corduroy pants warm and wet. When I closed my fingers on his shin, he shrieked in pain.

"Oh my God, Chub's hit—"

Before I got the words out Prairie braked hard and headed for the shoulder. We had gone only a few hundred yards down the road, but she jerked the car into park and hit the dome light with the heel of her hand, twisting in her seat toward me.

"Give him to me," she commanded. I was terrified and didn't know what else to do. I lifted his heavy body feetfirst.

He was coughing and crying at the same time, and my muscles strained with his weight, but Prairie helped me slide him onto the front seat. She straightened his leg gently, the bloodstain black in the dim light, and then she did something that stopped my breath.

She skittered her fingers up and down Chub's leg and then stilled them. Ducking her head, she started chanting. I only had to hear a few words to know that she was saying the lines from the pages I'd found in my mother's hiding place.

It didn't take long—just ten or fifteen seconds—and as Prairie murmured softly, Chub snuffled and sighed and finally quieted. She took her hands off his leg and carefully rolled his pants up and ran her fingertips over his skin. Then she rolled the pants down again.

"He's all right now," she said. "He'll be fine."

She gently handed him back to me and I took him into my arms. His little hands went to my neck and he slumped against me. I could feel his long eyelashes brushing my cheek. I felt along his leg, the sticky hardening blood and the torn place in the fabric—and underneath, where his skin was smooth.

"See if you can buckle him in again," Prairie said, and eased the car off the shoulder and onto the road, picking up speed as the tires spun gravel. We were headed east, and as I fumbled with the seat belt, we blew past the Bargain Barn, the KFC, the old Peace Angel Baptist church that they'd tried to turn into a restaurant for a while and now was nothing at all.

"What just happened?" I asked when I had Chub more or less secured. "What did you do?"

But I already knew the answer, even as I fought back my hysteria. It was what I had done to Milla. What I had done to Rascal.

Prairie was silent for a moment, the outskirts of town blowing past in a blur of mailboxes and gravel drives and leaning shacks.

Finally she took a breath and slowly let it back out, and when she spoke, she was as calm as she had been when I first saw her sitting at our kitchen table that afternoon.

"I'm a Healer," she said. "And so are you. It's in your blood."

I knew it was true, yet her words still stunned me. I hadn't yet put a name to it. "I'm . . . it isn't—"

"I know you healed Rascal," Prairie said gently.

I felt my face go hot. I thought about denying it, but there didn't seem to be much point. Prairie already knew. And in a way, I wanted her to know. I needed someone else to understand.

"Was he your first?" Prairie asked.

"Um." I looked out the window at the farmland flying by, the barns and outbuildings dark shadows rising from the fields.

I almost didn't tell her.

And then I did. I told her about Rascal's accident, about the blood and the terrible damage to his body, about the way it had felt to carry him home, to put my face to his fur.

About the rushing, needful urgency of the energy inside me flowing through my fingers into his wrecked body.

I told her about Milla, about how I barely remembered running to her side, about the words in my head, about Ms. Turnbull shoving me to the floor, and the way my senses came back with a prickling abruptness. About watching Milla roll over and throw up—and how she was fine after.

"The gift is strong in you," Prairie said, a note of awe in her voice, when I finished. "I've never heard of anyone being able to do it without someone guiding them. Your mom and I practiced for hours with Mary in secret, so Alice wouldn't know, but it took us months before we could use the gift."

"But Milla says we're cursed," I said, hot shame flooding my face. "That we're freaks."

"No," Prairie corrected me sharply. "You have a *gift*, Hailey. You can do something that others can't."

That made me feel a little better. Just days ago I'd thought there was something wrong with me, one more difference between me and every other kid, but Prairie made it sound like something to be proud of.

But that didn't change the fact that we were running from killers, that the kitchen floor was soaked in blood, that Gram was dead. "Who were those men at the house? Were they there because I'm a Healer?"

Was it my fault?

"Those men were . . . professionals."

"What does that even *mean*? Like hit men?"

"More like trained . . . investigators, I guess you'd call them. They're killers when they need to be, but I don't think that was their main objective."

She was so calm. It made me panic even more. "What did they want?"

"I'm pretty sure they wanted *you*, Hailey."

"Me? Why would they want me?"

"Because you're a Healer."

"But how would they know that? I only just found out myself."

Prairie sighed. "That's a long story. I work for a man. Not a good man, though I didn't know that until very recently. His name is Bryce Safian. We were doing research, in a lab outside Chicago. Trying to find ways to use my healing gifts, to replicate them so they could be used to fight disease."

"What do you mean, like turn normal people into Healers?"

"Well, more or less. We analyzed my full genome and compared it with a control population to isolate the element that controls the gift. The next step would have been to figure out how to use a special process to change a person's DNA to match mine."

"I thought all that DNA stuff was, like . . ." I tried to remember what I'd learned in my science class earlier in the year, wishing I had paid more attention. "That it's still not understood all that well. That it's mostly a mystery."

"Yes, that's true to a great extent, but Bryce is very well funded. We had access to the latest research. We had a laboratory, equipment, a team of scientists. We were at the very forefront."

"But that all sounds like a *good* thing." Not like a reason to kill someone.

"Yes, but . . . Bryce had other plans. Other ideas about what to do with the research once we isolated the healing gene, to put it in simple terms."

"What do you mean?" I demanded.

"He . . . had figured out a way to use the healing gene in warfare. In a battle setting."

"What, like to heal wounded soldiers? To fix up their injuries so that they could keep fighting?"

"That's . . . well, something like that," Prairie said hesitantly. "The point is that he was willing to sell the research, our results, to the highest bidder. He didn't care who it was, as long as they paid."

Her words sank into my mind. "You mean like . . . other countries?"

"Possibly," Prairie said quietly. "Anyone who would pay."

"But I still don't understand why he needs *me* if he already discovered how to do it using all your research."

"It's not quite that simple. You can't really decode the DNA without a population, which means more than one person, and Bryce was desperate to find another subject. So he investigated me, and he found out things that even I didn't know." She gave me a small, sad smile. "Like, for instance, that I have a niece, someone who could be predicted to share the gift."

"So he had those guys spying on me, those men that were at Gram's," I said. "It had to be. They were following me around. I saw them outside the house one morning, and in town talking to people."

"Yes, I think that's what happened. Bryce must have hired someone in Chicago to find out everything they could about my background. Once they figured out I was using a fake identity, they tracked down who I used to be. Who I really am. And once they got to Gypsum, it was just a matter of talking to the right people. You know how it is in a small town, everyone knows everything about everyone else. And if they offered money . . ."

"Everyone's broke," I finished the thought. People in Gypsum tended to mistrust outsiders, but if money was involved, it probably wouldn't take a whole lot of convincing before they started telling everything they knew. "But nobody knew about the healing. I mean, I never did it before—I didn't even know about it myself."

"I'm afraid Bryce knew that it was hereditary because I told him," Prairie said, her voice heavy with regret. "I just never imagined that there was anyone left. I mean, besides Alice, and she can't heal."

"So if your boss knew that Gram was weak, that she didn't have the gift . . ."

"That's why his men didn't think twice about shooting her. She was useless to them. All they wanted was you."

"So they came here and . . . someone in Gypsum led them to us for a few bucks." I felt the bitterness build inside me, hot and sharp.

"I doubt anyone had any idea what it would lead to. These were professionals, Hailey. They would have had some story, some compelling lie that would make people trust them. And besides, the money Bryce would have offered—it would have been hard for anyone to resist."

"Your boss has that much money?"

"He has more than you can imagine, Hailey," Prairie said flatly.

"So if he's so rich and powerful and all, how did you get away from him? I mean, how did you get here without him stopping you?"

Prairie glanced at me, her expression troubled. Even in the glow of the dashboard, I could see the worry lines etched between her eyes. "A man can be . . . a genius in some ways, and completely dense in others. Bryce was my lover, Hailey. And even though he managed to keep me fooled for a very long time about who he really was, I guess there were ways that he didn't really understand me either."

"You were in *love* with him?" I demanded.

"I thought I was. But when I realized what he intended to do, well, let's just say I came to my senses fast. So fast that I was able to come up with a plan that would let me get to you first. I convinced him that I thought it was a great idea to find you, to involve you in our work. I pretended I didn't know about the worst of his plans. I told him I needed a day to buy a few things for you, for your . . . room . . . the room he had already prepared for you at the lab. And instead, this morning I drove like hell to get to Alice's, praying the whole way I would get there before he gave the order to pick you up."

"But I first saw those men three days ago. Why did they wait until tonight to try to take me?"

"My guess is they weren't allowed to do anything without the go-ahead from Bryce. And that they were trying to find a way to take you without drawing too much attention, ideally without getting the law involved. Bryce wouldn't have wanted that kind of trouble."

"So . . . how did he figure out you ran away?"

Prairie sighed, a long, sad breath that seemed to weaken her. "I don't think he did. Bryce is so . . . confident, I don't think it would have ever occurred to him that I'd go against his wishes. But his men must have recognized my car and tracked me to the house. I was sloppy; I didn't stop to think that Bryce would have given them details like that. And I bet as soon as they reported in, he gave them the go-ahead to come and get us."

"Oh." I thought about the two men breaking into our house. About the way a gun looked when it was pointed at you. About the way bodies looked when they were dead.

And I couldn't believe we'd escaped. That we had been attacked and gotten away.

Gram hadn't. Gram was dead. For all I knew, Dun was dead too. And the two attackers. I searched my mind to see if

125

there was some delayed grief, if I was upset about Gram and it just hadn't hit me yet.

But I came up empty. If I'd ever loved Gram, that love had died a long time ago. Now all I felt was relief. Relief, and horror at the blood that had flooded our kitchen floor, at the way her eyes stared out at nothing, at the knife sticking out of the blond man's shoulder, his fingers struggling to close around the handle.

To keep from focusing on those images I checked on Chub. He was sleeping contentedly, and I stroked his soft hair, smoothing it over his warm forehead.

It was only because I was turned around that the sudden headlights behind us cut directly into my line of vision. They came out of nowhere—one minute it was all black behind the Volvo, the next minute twin beams lit up the road, the distance between us closing fast. The other car—big, sleek, black—had to have been trailing close behind, but I hadn't noticed it, and I knew that Prairie hadn't either.

"Hold on," Prairie said. *"Now."*

I did. I couldn't see past the blinding light into the other car, but I grabbed the back of the front seat with my right hand, hard, to brace myself. Prairie jammed her foot down on the gas and we shot forward. I heard the whine of the Volvo's engine straining under the pressure, but the lights of the other car got steadily brighter.

Prairie swung the wheel to the left, into the passing lane, and then she hit the brakes so hard the tires squealed and I could feel the rubber screeching across the pavement, trying to keep hold of the road. There was a terrible jolt as the car behind us hit our back fender.

I was thrown against the passenger seat and my forehead slammed into the headrest, connecting with the hard plastic. Then I was thrown a second time, into the door, and my seat belt pulled up hard across my collarbone as Prairie hit the gas again and steered into the spin, flooring it and coming out of the turn in the direction we had come from.

How? was going through my mind, and I even moved my lips to say it, but nothing came out. My face hurt and I could feel warm blood trickling out of my nose, and realized I had smacked it against the headrest, but I was too scared to care.

"Hang on again," Prairie ordered, and I braced myself and checked on Chub. He was awake, and he looked surprised, his big eyes blinking slowly, one fist rubbing his mouth, but the seat belt held him in place, and he was unhurt. Behind us I could see more of the other car as it backed up into a turn, one wheel going off onto the shoulder. It lurched, then leapt forward and shot off the other side, onto the shoulder, before correcting and starting toward us.

My teeth clacked together hard as Prairie yanked the wheel again, and we headed off the road, into a field, the low-growing crop—alfalfa, maybe, or strawberries—thudding against the undercarriage. Prairie urged the car through the furrows, the wheels finding purchase between the planted rows and biting into the earth. The other car fought against the rows. I could tell the mistake they were making—trying to cut across at an angle, coming after us the shortest way.

But the foliage was too tall and it smacked against the car as it was mowed under.

We had a chance. Prairie increased the distance between us and the other car as they struggled for control, plants and clumps of dirt spinning up into the car's wheel wells and axles. I leaned forward to say something, I don't know what exactly, and the words died on my lips as I saw that Prairie was steering us straight toward a leaning structure silhouetted against the inky night, a big, old barn with a sloped roof.

"Prairie—" I managed to get out, terrified. I reached for her—to do what, I'm not sure, push the wheel away maybe, out of the path of the collision that would kill us—but Prairie spoke first, just as a cloud scudded in front of the weak moon and everything went even darker, leaving only our headlights cutting into the field ahead:

"Trust me, Hailey."

CHAPTER 13

I GUESS I DIDN'T TRUST HER. I squeezed my eyes shut and groped for Chub's hand. If we were going to die, I wanted to be holding on to him when it happened.

I pitched forward again as Prairie slammed on the brakes before we reached the barn.

And then we hit. The Volvo took the impact in its solid metal frame, and even though the jolt slammed me hard against the seat belt, I knew right away that the barn hadn't stopped the car. We'd hit it going about thirty, I guessed, and the big flat-sided wood doors splintered and went flying inward. Prairie pumped the brakes a couple more times, and I had the impression of a dark tunnel, the insides of the barn full of crazy angles and hanging rafters and spinning bits of hay in the headlights' beams. I could make out empty stalls on either side, and then we drove through the other side of the barn and it was like the first time, a thudding crash and wood flying everywhere—

I had time to scream "Prairie what are you—"

—before she yanked the steering wheel one last time, sharp to the left. The wheels bounced over ruts and rocks and spun, engine screaming, for a second, another, a third before they caught and the car jerked ahead. Suddenly everything went dark as Prairie cut the lights and ignition and the car shuddered to a stop next to the ruined barn.

"What are you—" I tried again, but Prairie clapped a hand over my mouth and twisted around in her seat to look out the back. As I did the same, I heard the roar of the black car and it came bursting through the hole we had made in the barn, faster than we had, hurtling past us, and then suddenly tilting up, its front wheels lifting off the ground. For a moment it looked as though it was going to go airborne, and then it made a sickening lurch and the back of the car rose up in the air.

It seemed to go in slow motion, the back end flipping over the front in a crazy somersault before it disappeared down, down and there was a horrible crash and a bright flash, sparks orange in the night, and then a series of smaller echoes.

"Where'd it go?" I asked, forgetting to keep my voice down. I think I might have screamed it. Chub started to wail.

But Prairie was already undoing her seat belt.

"Out of the car," she said. "*Now.* Get Chub."

I didn't have to be told twice. But when I turned to him,

I saw that he'd somehow been thrown clear of the seat belt onto the floor of the car next to Rascal. He was making short choked sounds, as though he was trying to cry but couldn't. I grabbed for him, but when I touched his arm, my fingers brushed against sharp bone poking from the skin and he screamed.

Terrified, I carried Chub from the car as carefully as I could. In the moonlight I could see that his arm was broken above the elbow. As my heart plummeted, his cries became even sharper with pain.

"He's hurt, he's hurt," I shrieked at Prairie. She ran to my side and stretched out her arms to take him, but I held him even tighter.

"I can fix him," Prairie said.

"No. I'll do it."

"But you're just starting, you're not ready yet—"

"I need to do it," I insisted. My fingers were already closing around the injury, carefully avoiding the protruding bone, gently finding their place on Chub's fevered skin.

For a moment Prairie said nothing, but our eyes met and there was almost a glow around us, an energy that bound the three of us. "All right," Prairie finally said.

I closed my eyes for a moment and willed my thoughts to slow down, my mind to empty, and soon I could feel the energy begin to flow from me to Chub.

"*Tá mé mol seo . . . ,*" Prairie murmured, and I joined in, my lips forming the words that seemed as familiar as if I'd been saying them forever. Our voices blended and twined together until they were almost one. I felt Chub's pulse go slow and steady, and then his whimpers eased and he was quiet.

The torn flesh met and closed beneath my touch, and I felt the shift of his arm bones as the broken place mended. I brushed my fingertips along his skin and found the ridge where it had split, but even that seemed to smooth out as the seconds passed.

"I healed him," I said in wonder.

"Yes." There was something like awe in Prairie's voice. "You are a true Healer, Hailey, a natural. Even your mother had to work hard at it, and she was twice the Healer I'll ever be. But you . . . you're something even more rare."

Through the haze of my focus on Chub, I heard the black car sparking and sputtering in what I could now see was a dry creek bed. The land behind the barn led to the creek bank and stopped abruptly. The banks had been carved by the rushing waters of years of spring floods, leaving behind craggy dirt walls that dropped several feet in places.

"We have to go," Prairie said, taking my arm and pulling me away from the Volvo and the barn and the wreck of the black car. "Tell Rascal to come."

Only then did I notice him sitting by the car. He didn't look frightened or even particularly interested in the commotion.

"Come on, boy," I said, and he got to his feet without hesitation and trotted to catch up with us. I looked past him at the wreck and wondered if the men inside had survived. "Shouldn't we see if—I mean, what if they need help?"

"They were trying to run us off the road, Hailey. Do you really want to give them a chance to catch up with us?"

"No." I quickened my pace to keep up with her, glancing back to see if our pursuers were clambering out of the car.

"Someone's bound to call this in soon," Prairie added. "The smoke's got to be visible for miles."

She was right; the smoke pouring from the wreck was an ugly cloud spreading across the pristine, starry sky. I forced myself to look at the ground in front of us; it wouldn't do to trip over something and drop Chub. He'd already been hurt and healed twice in one evening; I figured that was plenty.

"Where are we going?"

We were on a faint path, a trail of flattened weeds running parallel to the creek bed. Far off to the left, up a hill and past a neat vegetable patch surrounded by chicken wire, was a square farmhouse. The trail was narrow enough that we went single file, Prairie leading, then me and Chub, with Rascal taking up the rear.

"We're nearly to Tipton," Prairie said softly. "This is the Burnetts' place."

"Old Man Burnett?"

"Well, he wasn't that old, back when I knew him. I knew his youngest. Claude."

I recognized that name. Claude Burnett was a man in his late thirties, and people said he wasn't quite right. He came to Gypsum some Saturdays in a clean shirt tucked into pants pulled up too high, his father leaning on him and leading him at the same time.

With a flash of regret I remembered I'd once teased Claude. I'd offered him half of a Milky Way bar I'd been saving. He was waiting in the shade outside the drugstore while his dad picked up a prescription or something. I showed him the candy bar, and when he put out his thick hand for it, I whipped it around behind my back.

"You didn't say please," I'd said, relishing the feel of my heart pounding under my T-shirt. I was eight or so, and it was such a novelty to see someone who made people even more uncomfortable than I did.

"I know him," I said now.

"He was your mom's friend. She was always nice to him. She taught him to talk."

"What do you mean?"

Prairie shrugged. "He didn't talk much, only a couple of words. Clover got him saying whole sentences. Just another kind of healing, I guess. I played here too, when I was little. Mary used to bring us. There's a shortcut—just a little ways," Prairie said. "Or at least there used to be. Here, I think this is it."

She led the way off the path, down to a series of flat stones set into the creek bed, barely visible in the moonlight. We didn't need them to cross, since the creek was dry, but I stepped carefully so I wouldn't twist an ankle as we eased down the bank.

I was thinking about Claude . . . and about Chub, who was also not a talker. Could Chub be . . . healed? *That* way?

Prairie led us up the other bank. "This comes up on Ellis land. You know the Ellises?"

"I don't think so."

"Their kids went to school with me and your mom . . . but here . . . yes, I think this is it. . . ."

The path continued on the other side, a tramped-down, narrow trail that led up over the bank and toward a cluster of lights far ahead. As we drew nearer I saw it was another farmhouse with a barn and some sheds set back a few hundred yards.

"How did you know to do that?" I demanded. "How did you crash into the right part of the barn and all? How did you know the car would break through and not, like, hit a beam or something?"

"Luck," Prairie said, and I could almost hear a faint smile in her voice. "Don't you think we were due for some luck? Besides, barn doors, Hailey, they're just big pieces of wood."

"But how could you see the doors? I could hardly even see the *barn*. But you had to have hit it just exactly right, or—"

Or we'd be dead.

Prairie slowed, turned on the path in front of me.

"I just remembered," she said simply. "I thought about Clover . . . and how she and Claude liked to play cowboys here, and I shut my eyes and tried to picture it in my mind, where the doors were—"

"You *shut* your *eyes*?" I was dumbfounded.

She flashed me a grin, and it only lasted a fraction of a second in the weak moonlight. "It seemed like a good idea at the time."

The thought of Prairie flying across the field with her eyes closed was terrifying . . . and maybe just a little bit thrilling. At least, that was what I figured the zip of sensation was that snaked up my spine.

Prairie continued on the path, striding confidently, and for a crazy moment I wondered if she had her eyes shut now. If she was leading us away from trouble with nothing but a *feeling* to guide her.

I don't know why I didn't feel more frightened. Weirdly, the thought almost made me feel a little safer. Chub was so heavy in my arms that everything from my wrist down had gone numb, but at least he had quieted, his sweat-damp forehead radiating heat against my face.

I reached out and touched Prairie's pretty tailored jacket, and then I gripped it tightly and closed my eyes and willed my feet to walk in her footsteps, Rascal staying right behind me. If she noticed, she didn't say anything. She never stumbled, and neither did I, as we approached the cluster of buildings.

The Ellises' barn was in better shape than the Burnetts' barn, with hay stacked high in the loft and a couple of tractors parked neatly, gleaming in the moonlight, when Prairie and I opened the door.

"Stay here," she said. "I'll try not to be too long."

I didn't even ask her where she was going. I sat on the seat of the smaller tractor—really more like a big riding mower—and it felt good to relax my arms, aching from the effort of holding Chub. Rascal lay down next to the tractor, ignoring the scrabbling and scratching of creatures in the barn.

I used to be scared of things like that, mice and rats and bats. Now I was happy for the company.

I closed my eyes and tried to sort through the emotions swirling in my head. I felt as though my defenses were starting to fall apart at the edges. The past few days were like some sort of horror movie, and I couldn't quite believe that I was a part of it, that any of it had even happened.

But I had blood on my clothes to prove it. Gram was dead. A lot of people were wounded in our kitchen and in the wreck of a car less than a mile away. And the life I had led before—the one I had hated so much—was in the past.

I wondered how I'd stayed calm enough to get through the past few hours. Maybe I was in a state of shock, or maybe I had just gotten so used to dealing with the challenges of life with Gram that I'd built up more defenses than an ordinary person would have in a situation like this.

But I wasn't sure how long I could maintain my calm. What would happen if I started letting things bother me again, if I let myself start feeling things? The thought was terrifying. At least as terrifying, I realized as I sat shivering in the dark barn, as being shot.

I don't know how long I sat there, but when Prairie slipped back into the barn and said my name softly, I jumped.

"Let's go," she said, her voice full of urgency. I lifted

Chub and followed her to the front of the barn, where a gravel drive led to the road. A car idled there, exhaust billowing up white against the first pink streaks of dawn. I was surprised to see the car waiting, but Prairie *did* things. She got what we needed. I didn't know exactly how, but at the moment, it didn't matter.

"Is this the Ellises' car?" I asked.

She frowned, her eyebrows pinching together. "Yes . . . yes, it is. I'm sorry we have to take it, Hailey. We won't damage it, and they'll get it back. But . . ."

She didn't finish the sentence, but she didn't have to. We needed the car. We needed to get away. Even if I didn't understand exactly what we were escaping from, I understood *that*.

When I opened the door, Rascal jumped into the car and lay down on the floor, and I got Chub settled under the seat belt. I was getting good at strapping him in, but as Prairie drove slowly down the gravel drive toward the main road she shook her head and said, "We have got to get that boy a car seat."

I sank down low in the passenger seat and watched the farmhouse as we rolled by. The Ellises had a carport, so it would have been easy enough for Prairie to take the car—except she would have had to unlock it *and* start it, unless she knew how to hot-wire it.

And if that was what she did, I didn't want to know. Not quite yet, anyway. I wanted to think of her as someone who worried about Chub having a car seat. Because if she was thinking about Chub, he would be that much safer. As far as

I knew, I was the only person who had ever cared about him, and I knew he was a hard kid to fall for. He was behind in so many ways. But Prairie cared about him, and as we pulled out onto the main road and picked up speed, I was grateful.

I was so tired, riding in the Ellises' Buick. You wouldn't think a person who'd been chased and shot at, who had watched people die, would be able to lie down and sleep, but that was what I wanted more than anything. Just to sleep.

Prairie didn't look so good. Her mouth was pulled down in a thinking frown and her hands gripped the steering wheel tightly.

"We should make it in about seven hours," she said. "Six and a half if we really push it hard."

"Where are we going?"

Prairie was silent for so long I thought she wasn't going to answer me, but eventually she gave me a smile that looked like it took a lot of effort.

"Home."

CHAPTER 14

WHEN I WOKE UP, the sun was streaming through the Buick's windows, and I had to go to the bathroom.

"We're in Illinois, coming up on Springfield. There's a Walmart in twenty miles or so," Prairie said. "We need to pick up a few things. Can you wait that long?"

"Um . . . okay." I was hungry, too, but decided not to mention it. Somehow, it didn't seem like something I should admit to. After a night like we'd had, who thinks of food?

I did. Which made me wonder. On the one hand, I felt like I should feel worse. Like maybe in shock from the horror of it all, or something. I kept waiting for the guilt to sneak up on me, but it just didn't happen. I even felt a tiny sense of anticipation. Despite everything that had happened, we were going somewhere new.

I'd never left Missouri before. I'd only been out of

Gypsum a few times, on school field trips to Hannibal and St. Joseph, to see Mark Twain's childhood home and the Pony Express Museum. But I'd never been to a city.

My stomach growled again. To cover the sound, I asked Prairie something that had been bothering me.

"How could you not have known my mom was pregnant?"

Prairie's jaw tensed and she didn't look at me. She hadn't slept at all, and it showed in the faint lines under her eyes and around her mouth.

"When I left Gypsum, I moved to Chicago. I wrote to Clover almost every day," she finally said. "I knew there would be trouble if Alice ever found out that Clover knew where I was, so I told her to make up a story that we'd had a really bad fight and that we swore we'd never speak to each other again."

"Why would Gram care?"

"She had . . . plans for me. Just like I think she did for you."

Her words filled me with dread. "What do you mean?"

"You have to think about who Alice was, when she was younger. She tried to be a Healer for a long time before she gave up. Mary told me that Alice was devastated when she finally had to accept that she didn't have the gift. She never got over her failure, and to cope with it she turned all her misery into blame."

"Blame? But who could she blame for that?"

"Alice decided that the reason she was damaged was that the Tarbells had mixed their blood with outsiders. That they'd married and bore children outside the families, and that had corrupted the lineage."

"What do you mean, the families? What families?"

"Our ancestors all emigrated here together. The Morries, the Tarbells, we're all descended from the same village in Ireland."

"We're *Irish*?"

"Yes." Prairie smiled, but it didn't reach her troubled eyes. "Our ancestors lived in the same village for centuries. When they came here, they started over. New names, new skills, new homes, but the plan was always that they would stay together. They were known as the Banished, and they—"

"Wait." I cut her off. What had Milla said—*Ain't any of us Banished got any say in things.* "Why were they called that?"

"No one remembers anymore. I mean, there were all these stories. When your mom and I were little, Mary would tell us bedtime stories about faeries and blessings and curses."

"You don't believe in them."

"I . . ." Prairie hesitated, choosing her words carefully. "It's not that I don't believe. The blessings were real, even if I can't explain them, even if they don't fit neatly with what science tells us. The Banished are united by some . . . powerful things. Mary always told me that we Tarbells were meant to serve the Banished, to heal them when they needed us. But that wasn't the whole story. The rest of the women had a responsibility to keep the village, the people, together after they left Ireland. That's why we can sense each other, why we are drawn to each other."

At last, an explanation for the way I felt when I was around the Morries, even if it sounded crazy. A part of me was relieved that I hadn't imagined it. That it might be real, even if it was something out of a fable. "What else?"

"Well, when they left Ireland the men were all given the gift of visions. They could see into the future, or see things that were happening elsewhere. It was meant to protect them from enemies, disasters, even things like storms that could damage the crops."

"The Morries have *visions*?" I thought of the boys at school, their shadowed faces angry, stubborn, bleak. All but Sawyer's.

"Not much anymore. That gift, that power, is mostly gone."

"What happened to it?"

Prairie sighed. "A few generations ago, everything started to fall apart. I guess it came from marrying outside the Banished, it weakened the gift. Mary said she remembered the first broken Healer, when she was a little girl: a Tarbell daughter born like Alice, sick and weak and mean. But she didn't grow to adulthood. Mary said the strongest Healers were pure Banished. I think it broke her heart when one of her own daughters was . . . damaged. And Alice could never accept it. I think she always believed that if she could just go back to the source of the gift, she could somehow heal herself."

Go back to the source . . . to Ireland? My pulse quickened as I thought of the airplane ticket to Dublin. "There's something I haven't told you," I said, and explained about the folder I'd found in Gram's room.

Hailey frowned. "So Alice really meant to go. She used to talk about it, sometimes . . . only, I can't imagine it would have made a difference. I don't know how it could change anything just to go back to the village."

"If it did, then all the Morries—"

"—could be fixed?" Prairie said gently. "It doesn't work that way, Hailey. The changes in the Banished, they're deep in the foundations of who they are now. They are afraid of each other. Of what they've become. The men . . . they've lost their, their moral compass, I guess you'd say. A lot of them are addicts. They don't want to work, they don't take care of their families."

"But not all of them," I said, thinking of Sawyer.

"Oh, definitely not. There are still Banished men who are born with all the determination and idealism of the ones who first settled here. But in general . . . well, I guess that's how it got to be called Trashtown. You know, I saw a picture once, that Mary had. It was almost a hundred years old and you wouldn't even know it was Trashtown. Little houses all fixed up, flower beds, happy families, everyone dressed up and smiling."

I thought about the Morries at school, their patched and dirty clothes, the sickly, malnourished way they looked. I thought of Milla, the combination of fury and fear she wore on her face.

"I don't understand why they hate me so much now. The Morries."

"It's fear, Hailey. They think that after Alice was born . . . damaged . . . that the gift was turned into a curse. They don't believe you truly have the power to heal, just like they never believed Clover or I could. They're afraid that if you try to heal someone you'll end up cursing them instead."

"You never healed anyone when you lived here?"

"Alice wouldn't let us. She made us go to school in Tipton so we wouldn't be around the Morries. Mary taught us in secret. Alice always said she'd beat us if she ever caught us healing."

"Why?"

"I think because she never got over being damaged. She tried to heal, you know, when she was young. Mary told me. And she couldn't bear the thought that her daughters could do something she couldn't."

"And so you just . . . didn't?" I tried to imagine resisting the urge, now that I knew what I could do.

"I . . . took care of people sometimes, but usually I didn't even tell them. You know—a friend with a strawberry birthmark. Another one with bruises from when her stepfather beat her."

We rode in silence for a while, each lost in our own thoughts. "Did you ever know your dad?"

"No, and Alice never told me who he was. I never even knew if Clover had the same father."

I couldn't imagine Gram young. Couldn't imagine a man falling in love with her, wanting a child with her. "What about your grandfather?"

"No. He died young, not long after Alice was born, and Mary never talked about him. All Alice ever told me about him was that he was mixed blood."

"Was he?"

"Yes. There weren't very many purebloods left even a generation ago, and Mary's husband was part Cherokee and part German."

"How can you be sure about that?"

Prairie gave me a quick, sad smile before returning her attention to the road. "I studied genetics, when I finally went to college. And then I worked in a lab. By the time Bryce hired me, I'd traced my origins pretty thoroughly."

"You can tell all that? Just from blood?"

"You'd be surprised. The tests are a little complex, but you can track your heredity with considerable accuracy."

I thought for a moment. "Could you . . . test me? I mean, could you figure out what my dad was?"

"Not the way you're thinking, Hailey. Unless you were doing full-on DNA testing and looking for genetic paternity or something like that. And besides, if you're wondering about the healing, it doesn't matter. Alice was wrong. As long as a Healer's partner is part Banished, she will pass on the gift, nine times out of ten."

"You can tell that from your testing?" I demanded, surprised.

"No. That, I learned from Mary. It's not exactly scientific, but I have no reason to doubt it's true. Mary told me that some Healers are more powerful than others, depending on the blood of their fathers. And other factors too, some of which I doubt we'll ever understand. Like Alice. I don't know why the gift was corrupted in her. I . . . sometimes I can almost feel pity for her, for the way she was born, with the powers stunted along with her body. But then . . ."

She didn't finish the sentence, but she didn't have to. I guessed we both had our memories, of Gram's meanness, her cruelty. Yes, it was possible to feel compassion for her . . . until you remembered who she was.

"So Gram wanted to make sure you married one of the Banished," I guessed. "So your children didn't end up like her."

"That's right," Prairie said. "But it went further than that. Alice started to feel that she was responsible for ensuring that the Tarbell line continued. She used to say that when I graduated from high school, she'd choose one of the purebloods for me."

"And when you left—"

"There was only Clover. And I've always wondered . . ."

It took only a moment for me to figure it out. "You think Gram . . . *chose* someone for my mom. Once she realized you weren't coming back."

"Yes," Prairie said softly. "I think she didn't want to wait until Clover graduated. And I think she—Clover—didn't have any choice in the matter, that he—whoever he was—he must have . . ."

As Prairie struggled to find the right words, I realized why her pain showed through whenever she talked about Clover. About my mother. Gram had sacrificed her, had handed her off to one of the Morries—someone like the cruel-eyed, shadow-fleeting boys I knew from the halls of Gypsum High—so that she could be impregnated by a pureblood. So that her child would carry on the Tarbell legacy and be a true Healer.

Horror washed over me, closing my throat so it was difficult to breathe. I was the child of a violation of someone even younger than me. When I thought of my mother, alone, having lost the one person who cared about her, who could protect her, my heart fractured.

"Did she die in childbirth?" I asked. I had to know.

"Oh, Hailey." Prairie took a deep breath. "No. Clover killed herself."

"She . . ."

But I couldn't speak. I had always thought of my mother as a stranger, until I met Prairie. Gram had said she was mentally disabled and I had believed her, and somehow that made my mother less real to me. I felt like I had been born of nothing, in a way, like I had just appeared one day in the house I grew up in.

"You were a few weeks old when she died," Prairie continued quietly. "Bryce's investigators found the records at the county office, and he told me a few days ago. I was . . . devastated, thinking about how frightened Clover must have been."

"How did she . . . you know?"

"She hanged herself, Hailey. In the bedroom closet. Bryce found the police reports."

My closet. No wonder I had been drawn to that tiny space; no wonder I'd found the secret hiding place. It was her presence I'd felt there, her sadness. "But . . . why . . ."

"I think she felt like she was out of options. She was too ashamed to tell me she was pregnant. And I think she knew that if she had told me, I would have come back. I think she was *protecting* me, in her own way."

"But what about . . ." I swallowed the lump in my throat. *What about me?* I was thinking. Didn't she care about me? Didn't she want to make sure her baby was all right?

"You must *never* think that your mother didn't love you," Prairie said fiercely. "Clover loved you with all her heart. But she knew that Alice would have taken you from her, like she tried to take everything. Alice saw you as the future of the Tarbells, and that was all she cared about. A last chance for her to get it right. A last chance to purify the bloodline."

You are the future, Hailey.

"And she wouldn't have allowed anything to interfere with that. I am sure that she would have put Clover out on the street before she let her raise you."

I could barely absorb the full horror of what Prairie was saying. I thought of all the times Gram whispered and laughed with Dun Acey, the way he looked at me with his hungry eyes. I wondered if he was the one Gram had chosen for me, the man who would father my child, the pureblood Banished who would ensure that my baby was a Healer.

I thought I would throw up. I made a strangled sound in my throat and Prairie looked at me in alarm.

"Hailey, are you all right? The exit's coming up in a minute—can you make it?"

"I think so," I said, swallowing hard. "Just . . . tell me the rest. All of it. How did you find out my mom was dead? What did you do?"

"When she stopped answering my letters, I got worried. I had saved a little money by then, so I took a bus back to Gypsum to get her. But when I got to the house . . . she wasn't there, and Alice told me she had killed herself. I was just going to leave; all I could think to do was get out of there, out of the house, away from Alice. But she stopped me. She told me that she could make people think *I* did it. She said Clover had been talking about the huge fight we'd had. . . ."

"The one you told her to make up? When you wrote to her?"

"Yes. And she said I'd better not let any of the authorities find out I was in town, or they'd take me in for questioning or worse. Now I understand she was just trying to make sure that I never came back. Because if I ever found out about you, I might fight for you. And she was not about to lose you."

That was the final piece of the puzzle. Now I had the whole story of why I'd grown up without a mother. She hadn't abandoned me on purpose.

And if Prairie had come for me long ago, I wouldn't have Chub. I looked over the seat at him, rosy-cheeked in sleep, his mouth a sweet little O.

Until Chub, I had grown up with no love at all. But he had given me a reason to keep going, to keep trying.

Prairie had saved me last night, I thought as we reached the exit. But maybe Chub had saved me first.

We coasted off the highway, almost directly into an enormous parking lot. I was starving, and I knew Chub would be too the minute he woke up.

"We're going to eat here?"

"I'm afraid so. There's a McDonald's in the Walmart. I'll pick up what we need while you take Chub and get breakfast for the two of you."

"What about you?"

Prairie smiled, unexpectedly and genuinely. "If you would get me a sausage and egg biscuit, I would be very grateful. I haven't had one of those in ages. Oh, and some hash browns, maybe. And an orange juice. And a giant coffee, all right?"

She pressed some money into my hands and I closed my fingers over it. "How do you like your coffee?"

"Black's fine. Listen, Hailey, you've got some bruising. It might be better if you . . ." She reached out and pushed my hair across my forehead, arranging it so that it hung over the side of my face.

Prairie had taken off her jacket. At least there was no blood on her silk top. She'd combed her hair and put on lipstick, but she still looked like she'd been up all night.

"I need to walk Rascal," I said, leaning over to check on him. He was lying on the floor of the car, head resting on his paws.

"Okay, I'll get Chub ready."

By the time I had taken Rascal for a quick trip to a grassy median, Prairie had Chub out of the car. He was pointing to the giant store and making excited noises. I opened the car door and Rascal jumped obediently into the backseat.

As we walked through the huge parking lot, I decided two things: first, today was the day I was going to start drinking coffee. And second, I too would drink it black. Cream and sugar were things that could slow a person down.

By now, back in Gypsum, the Ellises would have realized their car was missing, wouldn't they? They would have gone out to get the paper, or let the cat in, and if they glanced over to the carport . . . although it *was* Saturday. Maybe they were sleeping in.

A quarter mile away, if the cops hadn't already been called to the scene, Old Man Burnett was waking up to discover a giant hole in his barn and a car crashed in his creek. Not to mention Prairie's car, that old brown Volvo, abandoned behind the barn.

I wondered how long it would take for someone to stumble on the carnage at our house. Gram was well known to a few people in Gypsum and the surrounding county, but they weren't the kind to call the authorities. It would probably be someone else—someone selling aluminum siding or checking the water meter—who would end up making that awful discovery.

Inside the store, an old man with a bright blue vest shoved a shopping cart toward us. "Welcome to Walmart," he said.

"Thanks, I . . . we're just going to, uh, have breakfast," I said, certain he would see how nervous I was and know something was wrong. But as Prairie slipped into the crowd of shoppers, he turned away from me and pushed the cart at the people who came through the door after us.

I saw a sign for the restrooms and dragged Chub toward them. Inside, there was one of those changing stations that pull down from the wall. I wondered if it would hold Chub, who weighed forty-two pounds now, according to Gram's old peeling scale.

"In here," I said, pulling him toward the largest stall. There were two other women at the sinks, one washing her hands, one putting on lipstick. I hoped they would just assume that Chub was using the toilet himself.

I realized I didn't have any diapers or wipes with me. How I was going to clean him? He was bound to be soaked. I grabbed a handful of paper towels and wet them at the sink before we went into the stall.

Chub said something I didn't understand and tugged impatiently at his elastic waistband. I helped him out of his damp diaper and then, to my amazement, he clambered up on the toilet.

A dozen times at home I had put him on the toilet, promising to read him stories or get him a cookie, anything I could think of to get him used to the idea of using it—and he always scrambled right back down and ran away.

But now he had done it on his own. He finished up, climbed back down and pulled up his pants.

I helped him wash his hands at the sink—he loved the foaming soap dispenser—and as we were drying our hands, a short woman with frizzy red hair turned to me and said, "Oh, he's sure a sweetheart. Is he your little brother?" and before I even really thought about it, I said, "Yes, ma'am."

She gave us a big smile and as we followed her out of the restroom I thought, Well, why not? There wasn't anyone who was going to argue. We could be related, both of us with pale freckled skin. And later, if he grew up looking totally different, if we were in the habit of thinking of each other that way—maybe it wouldn't matter.

Maybe we had a chance to be normal after all.

At McDonald's I ordered myself the same thing Prairie had asked for, and hotcakes and sausage for Chub. We ate quickly, and I tried not to look around at the other customers. I figured if I didn't look at them, they wouldn't look at me.

When Prairie wheeled up with her shopping cart full of bags, I was feeling better. We made our way back to the car, and she handed me a large box.

"Here's a car seat," she said. "See if you can get it figured out while I put the rest of this stuff in the trunk."

It ended up taking both of us to set the seat up, Prairie reading from the instruction book and me fiddling around with the straps and the seat belt. Rascal didn't seem at all interested in the process, barely looking up as we worked. Chub patted the plastic sides of the new seat with a thoughtful look on his face. I crawled back into the front seat. Prairie stuffed the instructions and the packaging back in the box and tossed it in the backseat. Then she pulled a plastic bag out of her purse.

"I thought . . . ," she said, and then hesitated. She reached in the bag and took out a small blue stuffed giraffe with glossy yarn forming a loopy mane down its long neck. The legs were loose and floppy, and it had a sweet face, with long eyelashes embroidered above little button eyes. She handed it to Chub, who held it close to his nose, turning it this way and that.

"Raff," he said. "Prairie. Raff . . . giraffe."

He really was talking. How was this happening? Was it because of me? Could I be healing him somehow, without even trying? I'd healed three times: Milla, Rascal and Chub, all in the past few days. Maybe it was now such a part of me that I couldn't turn it off.

It didn't seem possible . . . but so much of what had happened was unbelievable.

I handed Prairie the paper sack with her biscuit and hash browns. I fixed the coffee cup's lid so she could drink, folding back the little plastic tab, just like I'd learned to do twenty minutes earlier when I'd drunk my first cup of coffee.

Prairie nibbled at the food while she drove slowly out of the parking lot and back onto the interstate. She consulted her phone now and then, and I realized she was following downloaded directions.

"Where are we going?" I asked as she turned onto a multi-lane road lined with strip malls.

"Well, that's a little complicated," she said. "Keep your eyes out for a— Oh, there it is."

She turned into a parking lot in front of a row of low-slung buildings and passed a dry cleaner, a Thai restaurant, a bakery. She parked in front of a Hertz car rental agency, then turned to face me with a serious expression.

"This is going to sound a little strange," she said, "but we have to make it look like we're renting a car."

"Make it *look* like? But we're not really renting it?"

"Yes. How can I . . . Okay. Remember when I told you that Banished men used to have visions? That they could see the future?"

"Yes . . ." A prickly feeling had started at the base of my spine. I sensed that what was coming was more bad news, and I wasn't sure I was ready to hear more. But what choice did I have?

"Purebloods can still do it. Some of them, anyway. Well, a few." She bit her lip and stared at her hands, which were clasped tightly. "Rattler can."

"Rattler *Sikes*?" As if there was any other Rattler. Just saying his name dialed up the prickling to full-scale fear.

Prairie nodded. "Rattler and I have a . . . history. When

we were kids, he used to like to follow me around. Even then he had visions, and they just got stronger over time."

"But that means he knows exactly where we are!" The thought made me want to jump out of the car and run.

"It doesn't work quite like that. He can't see all of the future, or even choose what parts to see. He just . . . opens his mind, and he gets flashes. Pictures, pieces of the future. Sometimes he has visions of things happening at the same time but in a different place."

I remembered his unfocused gaze in the kitchen, the way he went very still, as though he was focusing in on something no one else could see. *Something's not right. A car . . . men. It's men in it.*

He'd had a vision of Safian's men.

"But what are we going to do?" I demanded, panicked.

Prairie laid a hand on my arm. "Stay calm, Hailey. That's why we're here. We're going to create a few scenarios, throw him off. We'll make it look like we're renting a car. We'll drive to the bus station. I'll take a few different routes, make it look like we could be going south or west. We just need to confuse him so he doesn't know which way to come after us."

"But eventually he's going to—"

"Stop," Prairie said gently but firmly. "Don't get ahead of yourself. Rattler can only see me when we're connected, when there's some energy between us. Right now we're scared and we're bound by what happened at Alice's, but we will get past that. We'll put it behind us and the connection will be broken and he won't be able to find us."

"I don't understand. What do you mean, you're connected?"

"The Banished . . . we're drawn to each other, like I told you before. And there's an energy around that. But if you were to leave, that energy would slowly fade. Your mind and your heart would focus on other things and the attraction would die down. The connection would be broken. Not forever, but you'd be functioning on your own, outside the influence of the other Banished. That's what I did, when I went to Chicago. The energy faded for me, and Rattler was a part of my past, and he couldn't see me anymore."

"But when you came back to Gypsum—"

"It opened it all up again. The connection, the energy. But we can fight it. I've fought it before. I've gotten away from Rattler before." There was strong conviction in her voice, but edged with something I didn't like at all, something dark and terrifying.

It almost sounded like she was trying to convince herself.

But it wasn't like we had any other options. "What can I do?"

"You and Chub take Rascal for a walk. There's bottled water in the trunk and a plastic bowl. Give me five or ten minutes."

I did as she directed, glancing in the plate-glass window as I took care of Rascal. She was having a conversation with the man behind the desk, who was consulting his computer monitor. Chub was happy to be out of the car, and he walked along beside me, picking up rocks and sticks that caught his eye.

In the bright light I could see that Rascal had blood along his neck and back, and I realized that Chub must have bled on him in the Volvo. I wiped him off with some of the bottled water and a handful of tissues from the box the Ellises kept in their car. He didn't mind, didn't even seem to notice. I put my hand in front of his face to lick, but he just stared at the lanes of traffic whizzing by. I wondered if he was thinking about chasing cars, but he didn't seem interested. He hadn't wagged his tail or perked up his ears at all, and I wondered again if he was having some sort of reaction to his accident, if something inside him was broken.

But when I said, "Rascal, come," he trotted along right away and jumped back in the car. If there *was* something wrong with him, it wasn't brain damage.

When Prairie came back out she seemed a little calmer. "One down," she said. After consulting her phone again, she pulled out of the parking lot. "Next stop, the bus station."

"Prairie," I asked after we'd driven for a few minutes, "what happened to Rattler? At the house?"

"Oh, that . . . ," Prairie said. A ghost of a smile flickered across her face. "I, uh, take kickboxing. That was a round-house kick. We're not supposed to use it in class. Well, anyway, I always wanted to try it."

"I guess it worked."

"Yeah—I guess so."

Rattler wasn't dead. He'd sold us out and nearly gotten me kidnapped, and as far as I knew, his only injury was from being kicked by Prairie. I wished he *was* dead—and then I wondered if he was "seeing" us even now. It made me shiver with fear and revulsion.

I barely paid attention as Prairie took smaller and less crowded streets, driving through a series of neighborhoods that grew shabbier and dirtier, before she turned into the parking lot of a bus station.

"This time we'll all go," she said.

We left Rascal in the car with an opened can of dog food that Prairie had bought at Walmart. We were gone for about a half hour, pretending to buy tickets. What really happened was Prairie asked a lot of questions about when buses were leaving for various places, and at the end she took a couple of folded paper timetables and tucked them into her purse. We sat in uncomfortable chairs for a while. I read an old magazine that someone had left behind, and Prairie got Chub a lemonade from a vending machine.

It didn't take long to get boring. That surprised me. I figured I'd never be able to relax, but when Prairie murmured that it was time to move on, I was relieved.

Next was the airport. That was a little more interesting, though Springfield's airport was tiny and didn't look anything like the ones in the movies. Still, there were people milling around, carrying bags, dragging suitcases—it made me wish I was flying somewhere. I'd never really thought I'd have a chance to, but now it seemed possible. Now that I was with Prairie. It wasn't just that she had money and experience, either; she made me feel like I could do things I'd never considered doing.

After the airport, Prairie took us into Springfield's downtown. There were enough tall buildings to make it seem like a real city. We circled for a while, sometimes barely moving in traffic, and by the time Prairie headed back out of town it was late in the afternoon.

The final place Prairie took us was a motel, an unremarkable place in a beaten-down neighborhood near the interstate.

"Okay," she said as we pulled into the lot. "I have got to get some rest before we go any further. I'm going to get us a room—stay here, okay?"

I didn't argue. I didn't want to admit to Prairie that I had never been in a motel before. Gypsum had two—a Super 8 and a motor court called the SkyView. I'd walked past them hundreds of times, wondering what it would be like to have a room to myself, everything clean and neat.

Chub was napping, so I left him in the car and walked Rascal nearby. I watched Prairie go through the glass doors and into the lobby, where I could see her talking to a man behind a counter. After a short while she returned.

"I got us a room near the back," she said as she drove the car around the corner of the motel to a space that was partly hidden behind a Dumpster. "I didn't tell them about Rascal. We'll have to sneak him in."

"You're worried about the cops looking for this car, aren't you. And . . . the guys Bryce hired."

She nodded. "I smeared mud on the plates this morning before we left, so the number's hard to make out."

I helped her get the bags out of the trunk. Chub held my hand and yawned as we followed Prairie to the last door on the first floor. Then I went back and carried Rascal in with my sweatshirt draped over him, not that anyone noticed us. Our room had a view of the end of the parking lot and a Denny's next door. Beyond, on the other side of the fence, was the back of another restaurant, with more Dumpsters and delivery doors and trash blowing along the pavement. A man sat on an upturned bucket, smoking a cigarette.

I knew what motel rooms looked like from TV. This one had a smell, not bad but both chemical and musty. I set my backpack down on one of the beds and watched Prairie unpack the Walmart bags.

"I hope you're up for a new look," she said, and I could tell she was trying to sound cheerful despite her exhaustion. She laid out a box of L'Oréal Couleur Experte on the nightstand between the beds. Next came a plastic comb and a pair of scissors. She upended the two largest bags and a pile of tangled clothing fell onto the bed. The last bag contained a handful of little plastic makeup cases, plus an enormous pair of sunglasses with white frames.

"Is that all like . . . a disguise?" I asked.

"Yes. We need to do what we can to make ourselves invisible. So we can get back to Chicago. And then find somewhere we can be safe."

Safe from things I never knew existed before today. From ancient magic and curses and dark secrets, things out of a twisted fairy tale. And at the other end of a spectrum, from a man who wanted to use me to experiment on.

A *scientist.*

I thought about the science class I'd never be attending again. Realized, to my surprise, that there were a few things I'd miss about my old life after all.

Chub was wandering around the room, touching things, exploring. He found the phone and pushed at the buttons. Prairie sank down on one of the beds, beside her purchases, and massaged her temples with her fingertips.

"Seriously, Hailey, we need to sleep, just for a couple of hours or so." She took her cell phone out of her purse and pressed the keys. "I'm setting an alarm. I'll get us up in plenty of time to do what we need to. Okay?"

"Okay," I said, sighing. It wasn't worth fighting her over. And I knew she was probably right anyway. Even though I felt wired now, I was bound to crash soon enough.

"Come here," I said to Chub. "Nap time."

"Nap time," he repeated, but instead of getting into the other bed he climbed up with Prairie. She must have been mostly asleep already, because she just made a sighing sound and looped an arm around Chub, who snuggled in close. Before even a minute passed I could tell by his breathing he was asleep.

I tried not to be jealous, to be glad that Chub was as comfortable around Prairie as I was. And mostly, I *was* glad. Except that now I was alone. And I didn't want to be. The fears, the anxiety, were simmering inside me, and I was afraid that if I was left alone with my thoughts they'd bubble up and take over.

I looked at Rascal, who was sitting motionless next to the door. "C'mere, boy," I said, and he got up and trotted over to me.

"Up," I said, and he jumped up onto the bed.

I wrapped my arm around him and pulled him a little bit closer. He didn't smell very good, a combination of wet dog and something else, something unfamiliar. But he was still better than nothing.

I was worried that he wasn't back to normal yet, but now wasn't the time to obsess over it. I switched off the lamp. With the heavy drapes pulled shut, the room was as dark as if it was midnight. There was a hum coming from the ceiling, a fan circulating the strange-smelling air. Prairie's cell phone glowed on the bedside table.

I was sure I'd never get to sleep with everything I had to think about, but the next sound I heard was Prairie's alarm.

CHAPTER 15

RASCAL WAS CURLED UP against me, oblivious to the cell phone's beeping. My mouth felt dry as a desert as I slid out from under the covers. In the other bed, Prairie sat up and turned off her phone. She rubbed her eyes and yawned.

I went to the bathroom, drank two glasses of water and splashed cold water on my face. When I came out, Prairie had gotten up and lined up her purchases on her bed.

"Well, hello, sunshine," she said cheerfully.

"What are you so happy about?"

"Nothing much . . . other than I think we managed to throw off Rattler. I mean, if he hasn't showed up yet, I guess we're doing okay."

"You think that worked? All that driving around?"

"He's not here, is he? So it seems to me he must have gotten sidetracked by one of our visits. For all we know he's on a bus to Texas." She gathered her supplies. "I know a shower would probably feel great right now, but how about if I color your hair first? You'll need to rinse out the color after it sets, so you might as well wait to get in the tub."

The sleep had done Prairie good; in the light of the lamps she'd switched on, I could see that the dark shadows had nearly disappeared from under her eyes.

I ran a hand through my hair. It was almost perfectly straight, rich brown with natural highlights. I knew people paid a lot of money for color like that.

"Uh, all right," I finally said. My hair was the one thing about me that I always knew was special. But if it meant our safety, I'd get over it. "What color?"

"I thought we'd try to match Chub's. Make it look like you're brother and sister."

I glanced at Chub, who was rolling over and sighing in a tangle of covers. His hair was so pale, it was almost white, with a wash of gold. I couldn't imagine that color on me.

"I need to cut it too," Prairie said, apologetically. "I wouldn't ask, if it wasn't so important."

While she mixed up the dye, filling the room with an acidy smell, I stripped down to the tank top I was wearing under my flannel shirt.

"Let me cut some first," Prairie said, after she spread a sheet from her bed on the floor in the center of the room, then put the desk chair on top of it. "Just get some of the length off. Then I'll shape it when the color's done, okay?"

I sat in the chair and she ran her hands through my hair. She gathered it into a ponytail and twisted it. I shut my eyes and tried to relax.

The first cut left my head feeling strangely light. I didn't want to think about my hair falling to the floor, so I asked Prairie something I'd been wondering.

"How could you not know that Bryce wasn't who you thought? I mean, you were . . . you know." *Sleeping with him,* I thought but didn't say.

Prairie paused. I could feel the heat from her skin, her hands inches from my face.

"I think deep down I knew something was wrong. But it's amazing what you can convince yourself of when you're in denial. Here, I'm going to start with the color, okay?"

She began to dab it onto my hair, starting at the roots and working out to the ends. It smelled terrible and stung my scalp.

"What did you like about him?" I asked. "I mean, at the beginning."

A little bit of the dye dribbled toward my eyebrow. "Well, for one thing, I thought he was *hot.*"

I brushed the dye away. "In what way?"

"Kind of a, I don't know, clean-cut look. He dresses well—really well. He likes expensive clothes. And he's always worked out a lot. He's a little compulsive about it, I guess you could say. He's average height, but he's got a naturally athletic build. Broad shoulders, strong arms . . ."

"Light hair or dark?"

"Brown . . . kind of a medium brown, I guess. And brown eyes."

He didn't sound bad, but he also didn't sound all that special. "What else?"

"Well, he's incredibly smart. I think that was the biggest thing, to tell you the truth. He has a doctorate, or at least he *says* he does, though now I don't know how much of what he told me was true and how much was lies."

I thought about that. The smartest guy at Gypsum High was Mac Blair, but it would be a pretty huge stretch to call him hot. He wasn't a geek, exactly—it was just that his mind was always on something else, usually some random fact he'd picked up online. "How did that make you like him?"

Prairie didn't answer for a moment. Her hands on my hair were confident and efficient, distributing the dye evenly over my head.

"Part of it was, I guess, that I hadn't known anyone like him before. Most of the guys I'd known—well, you know how it is in high school. It's not like anyone was even all that curious about the world outside Gypsum. And I went to this little junior college and night school, anything I could do to get enough credits to graduate, and it wasn't like I was around geniuses there, either. Even when I was working in the labs, a lot of the guys I met, they weren't really all that happy to be there, they weren't committed to the work. Not like Bryce.

"But it was also . . . I wanted so badly to do something

with my gift. I wanted to *matter*. And Bryce seemed like he could make that happen. I guess it was a little bit of a power thing, you know?"

"You thought that if you were with Bryce, he could open doors for you? Get you a better job, more money, stuff like that?"

"No, not exactly. More like, with his background and resources, he made me think the things I dreamed about were actually possible. That they could happen in my lifetime. I mean, now I know I was only seeing what I wanted to see and believing what I wanted to believe. But it was just so easy to put my faith in Bryce, this incredibly successful guy, and I was blinded by the fact that he wanted *me*."

"But what about other people? The people you worked with? Didn't any of them get suspicious about him? If they were closer to the data, didn't they wonder what he was researching?"

"Well, yes. About six months ago, Bryce started replacing a lot of the employees who'd been there a long time. He brought in people from all over the country, even a couple from other parts of the world. They were his inner circle, and when they weren't meeting with Bryce, they kept to themselves. I think they knew exactly what was going on . . . I think they're in on it. He can't do this on his own, not without getting caught."

"What about the people he fired? Weren't they angry? Or suspicious about what he was doing?"

"Bryce gave them a lot of money, made them sign all

kinds of nondisclosure documents. And most people knew about my relationship with Bryce and kept their distance, so I didn't stay in touch with the ones who left. I did have this one friend. . . ." She smiled at the memory. "He was hilarious. His name was Paul, and he was our tech guy, just this brilliant, geeky guy who could make you laugh. He only left a few weeks ago. I think Bryce had trouble finding someone who could do what Paul could; he was a genius at security and computers and all that."

"Weren't you mad when Bryce fired him?"

Prairie's smile faltered. "Yes . . . I guess I was. I mean, when I think about it now, I am, since he was the only person besides Bryce who'd have lunch with me or get coffee or whatever. And I don't think he really trusted Bryce. He made me a backup of some of the security systems without telling Bryce, said it was in case anything happened to him."

"Maybe he had a crush on you."

Prairie laughed. "Maybe. He was always blushing when we talked. His only hobbies were paintball and computer games, but you know, he probably would have been a better boyfriend than Bryce. Guess I need to work on that, my taste in men."

As she finished dabbing the dye around the crown of my head, I wondered if I'd ever have a boyfriend, and if so, whether I'd pick a good one. Maybe, being Banished, we didn't have the common sense other people did. We were attracted to people like us, and as far as I could tell, most of the men weren't great. Although Bryce wasn't Banished . . . and Prairie had still made a mistake.

"Did you ever think about dating Paul?"

"He never asked. I don't know . . . if he had, maybe things would have been different. I liked him a lot. He was shorter than me, not that it matters, and he had a ponytail, so if you like that . . . But it's a good thing we were friends, because he made me keep a spare prox card when they rekeyed the lab."

The familiar anxiety stirred in my gut. "Why is that a good thing?

Prairie didn't say anything for a minute as she wound the dye-coated strands of hair on top of my head. "It will let me get back into the lab. This won't be over until I destroy the data. I can't let Bryce move forward with . . . what he's doing."

"How are you going to do that?" I tried to keep the hysteria out of my voice, but all I could picture was the killers in our kitchen. "You think he'll let you just walk in there and—"

"Don't get ahead of yourself," Prairie said gently. "We need to focus on the moment, on—"

"Is that why we're going to Chicago? Can't we go somewhere else? Somewhere he can't find us?"

"We will. I promise. As soon as we do this last thing, we'll go far away and start over. But Hailey, neither one of us is going to be safe as long as Bryce is still active."

"But couldn't we wait a while? Let things die down? You

could get your friend Paul to help you, and when it was safe, you guys could, I don't know, sneak back in or something."

"I'm afraid it would be even more dangerous to wait," Prairie said. "I don't know how far Bryce has gotten. They were close to some key breakthroughs. But Hailey, you really need to try not to worry about that right now. Just relax while the color sets."

While Prairie cleaned up, I watched *SpongeBob* with Chub until it was time for me to rinse. On the sheet she had spread out, my hair lay in glossy piles, but I tried not to think about it.

I undressed in the bathroom and stepped into the shower, making the water as hot as I could stand it. I spent a long time lathering and even longer rinsing, standing under the shower with my head tipped back.

When I was finally done in the shower, I felt both worse and better. Worse because now I understood what was driving Bryce, and we were headed right back into it. Better because I was finally starting to believe that Prairie wouldn't abandon me. I dried off and wrapped the bath towel around my body. Then I took a washcloth and wiped away the steam on the mirror.

I was shocked. My hair was a pale, pale shade of gold. Nearly all the color was gone—and it hung in a heavy, straight line below my ears.

I felt my eyes fill with tears, and swallowed hard. It was ridiculous—my appearance was the least of my problems. But I still looked away from the mirror as I got dressed.

When I came out of the bathroom, Prairie pointed to the Walmart bags. "There's a new shirt in there. Go ahead and keep your shoes—I didn't know your size, and people won't be looking at those. Or your jeans. So really, it's just the top."

I unfolded the shirt. It was black with gray sleeves, and printed on the front was a silver skull with a leering grin, flames shooting out of its sides.

"I know, you hate it," Prairie said. "Sorry. I thought we'd do kind of a rocker look for you."

"It's . . . not so bad," I lied.

"I have these. . . ." She rooted around in the bag and came up with a pair of earrings that looked like pieces of bicycle chain. She also had a black leather cuff with snaps and rivets, and a silver ring with a skull on it. "If it's any comfort, I picked this because I thought it was the opposite of your look. I mean, you're so pretty, like your mom. . . ."

Her voice faltered and I turned away, partly to let her have her privacy and partly because I was kind of shy about changing in front of her. I found underwear and socks in another bag and slipped them on, then pulled my jeans back on and put on the new top. It smelled like the Walmart, clean and chemical-y, and it was tight enough that I had to tug on the sleeves to get them to sit right on my arms. I yanked off the tags and dropped them in the wastebasket.

"Very nice," Prairie said, with a smile that looked genuine.

"Hay-ee?" Chub, who had been tucking his giraffe into a pillowcase, seemed to have just noticed me. "Hair . . . What happen?"

I touched my newly short hair. "It's all right, Chub, it's just a different color. It's nice."

Chub liked his new clothes, the nubby sweatshirt and corduroy pants. As he went back to playing with his giraffe, Prairie got to work on me.

There was a lot of snipping, but it went fast, bits of hair flying to the floor as Prairie worked. Finally she stepped back and checked out the results. She snipped a little more and then got the motel hair dryer out of the bathroom.

"I wish I had a little product," she said. She ran the dryer for a few minutes, pushing my hair this way and that.

"Oh . . . ," she said when she was done. "I really like it, Hailey—I think it suits you. I mean, you can always grow it back but, well, I hope you like it too."

I went in the bathroom and stared in the mirror. Dry, my hair was a shiny platinum blond. It was cut so the front curved just a little past my chin, and then it got shorter in the back, with choppy layers I could feel with my fingers. A few chunky bangs were smoothed across my forehead.

It was amazing. It was better than anything you could get in Gypsum—I knew that instantly. For a second I wished I could go back to school just long enough for everyone to see. I looked like—I caught the thought and held it for a second— like someone in a band, like someone everyone else wanted to be.

"Happy with your new look?" Prairie asked, smiling, when I came out of the bathroom.

Before I could answer her, Chub jumped up from the floor where he'd been playing with his giraffe. "Bad mans," he mumbled, and pointed at the door. Then he pressed his face into my jeans and hugged my legs hard.

Prairie crouched down next to him. "Where are the bad men, Chub?" she whispered. "Are they close by?"

Chub nodded, his lower lip stuck out in a pout. "Outside."

She gave him a little hug and stood up, grabbing her purse off the bed and pulling out a little black canister.

"How, um, accurate is he?" she whispered. "With these predictions?"

"These *what*? I mean, he only just started talking. He never even went to the potty by himself until yesterday."

If Prairie was surprised, she didn't show it.

"Get that," Prairie whispered, pointing at the last of her purchases, a pale pink backpack with the tags still attached. "Pack up."

I jammed our things into it, our dirty clothes and the Walmart purchases. Prairie grabbed her plastic bags and stuffed them into her oversized purse.

"I'm really tired," she said in a loud voice. "I think I might lie down for a bit. Hailey, could you get my purse? I left it in the bathroom."

She was shaking her head as she talked, gesturing at the opposite side of the door. I grabbed Chub's hand and pulled him with me. When Prairie crouched down across from me, I did the same. Prairie felt around frantically on the wall until her hand found the outlet, never taking her eyes off the door. She yanked out the electric cords, plunging the room into semidarkness, and then grabbed the table lamp, holding it by the narrow top of the base. She held a finger to her lips. I could feel my heart pounding under my new shirt.

Chapter 16

When the door burst open, I jumped. Splinters of wood flew toward me and Chub. There was a crash and a man lurched into the room, landing on the floor.

"Go!" Prairie screamed.

She gave the desk a shove and it slammed down on the man's head. I didn't wait to see if he was hurt. I picked up Chub and hurled myself out the door, Prairie right behind. A skunky smell followed us. I could feel my throat seizing and I started to cough. When we were outside, I sucked down fresh air. The sun was so bright I was blinded for a moment, but Prairie pushed me, hard, toward the car.

"Rascal!" I screamed. "Come here, boy!"

He trotted out of the room, looking unconcerned. Prairie had the keys in her hand, and the locks clicked open as I reached for the handle. I didn't bother trying to get Chub settled, just pushed him and Rascal into the backseat and jumped in front as Prairie backed up.

The tires screeched as she twisted the wheel and aimed for the parking lot exit. A couple walking across the lot jumped out of the way, the man yelling and giving us the finger, but Prairie paid no attention. She pulled into traffic, wedging the Buick between a fast-moving compact car and a dawdling truck full of lawn mowers, and then shot across a couple of lanes, making a U-turn on a yellow light.

Then we were racing back toward the on-ramp and onto the highway.

I'd only inhaled a little of the pepper spray or whatever it was, and I managed to get my throat cleared and my breathing back to normal.

I leaned over the seat and helped Chub get buckled in.

"Car seat," he said. On top of everything else, he was adding new words faster than I could keep track of.

"That's right, this is your special seat," I said. "You did good, Chub. Good boy."

"They found us," Prairie repeated. She switched lanes again, pulling to the right and cutting off a slow-moving sedan. She veered onto an exit that led to an oasis of fast-food restaurants and gas stations.

"What are you doing?" *Keep moving!*—I felt the urgency in my gut to put as much distance as possible between us and the guy in our motel room.

"Bryce's men tracked us down," Prairie said, "and it

wasn't the car. It couldn't have been. Come on. Bring the backpack."

She pulled in to the first restaurant, a Wendy's, and parked crookedly in a spot near the entrance. I grabbed Chub and the pack, leaving Rascal in the car, and followed Prairie in. She went straight for the ladies' room and tried the door.

"Good," she said. "It's a one-person. Come on in."

I felt strange following her, and checked around, but no one was paying attention. There were a few customers in line, knots of two and three people at the tables, a hum of late-afternoon conversation.

Prairie locked the door behind us.

"My turn," Prairie said, digging into her purse for a Walmart bag. She stripped off her top, pulled a sweater from the bag and put it on. It was an ugly thing, brown, with leaves and pumpkins embroidered on it. It was too big, and it disguised her slim body.

"Here," she said, handing me a small plastic bag of jewelry and makeup. "Put this on, the earrings and all, and do your makeup. Lots of eyeliner, really thick."

I did as she said, starting with concealing the purplish bruise on my cheek, watching her out of the corner of my eye as I worked. She took a wide headband out of the bag and slid it into her hair so that all the layers were pulled away from her face. Then she added lipstick, exaggerating her mouth's natural shape.

I focused on my own makeup, doing my best to apply it

the way I'd practiced a few times at home for fun. Purple eye shadow, dark liner, several coats of mascara—I stepped back and looked at myself in the mirror.

"Wow," Prairie said. I hardly looked like myself at all. I guessed that was the point.

Prairie had swept on blush and some eye makeup. With the sweater and headband, she looked like a soccer mom.

"Wow yourself," I said back. "Um, not your best look."

Prairie arched an eyebrow at me and then we both burst out laughing.

We were in so much trouble, but laughing felt good. Chub looked at each of us in turn and then he surprised me by pounding his little fist against my leg.

He wasn't laughing.

Prairie knelt down in front of him. "Chub, honey, are they here? In the restaurant? The parking lot?"

Chub shook his head, rubbing his mouth with a little fist. "Not here."

"Okay. But back there—back at the motel?"

"Bad mans," he said again, looking like he was going to cry. Prairie put her arms around him and he went willingly, burying his face into her shoulder. She patted his back and murmured until he calmed down.

I felt awkward watching them. Chub had always had me—*only* me. I wasn't sure I was ready to share him.

But he turned from Prairie to me and hugged my legs hard. As I wet a paper towel to wipe his hot, tear-streaked face, I knew he was still mine. My little brother, if that was what it was going to be. The person who loved me for me.

As I finished patting his face clean, Prairie turned her purse upside down on the counter, the contents spilling out.

There wasn't that much: a set of keys on a simple silver key ring. Her cell phone and a couple of pens. A square black wallet. A small black leather case, which she unzipped, taking out a lipstick and comb and a compact.

"They're tracking us somehow," Prairie said softly. "At least they haven't followed us from the motel. Yet."

"You mean just because of what Chub said?"

"He's a *Seer*, Hailey." Prairie shut me down with her words. I tried to process what she had said. Sure, Chub had done an amazing amount of growing up in the past few days. Something important was going on with him, definitely—I was pretty sure no other kids on record had learned to talk and potty-trained themselves overnight. But Prairie wanted me to believe that, on top of all this, Chub could see into the future.

The men were all given the gift of visions, she'd said when she told me about the Banished. *They could see into the future . . . to protect them from enemies. . . .*

A thought was tickling around the edges of my brain. I shut my eyes and tried to focus. On days Gram's customers came calling, a lot of times Chub would stop what he was doing, set aside his book or toy and come to me, putting his face against my leg and holding on tight, which was what he had always done when he was scared or upset. And then a few minutes later I would hear the sound of a truck driving up onto the lawn, the slam of car doors, the shout of some half-wasted loser.

Maybe it was true. Maybe Chub *was* a Seer.

"Anyway," Prairie said, "I think we've got to assume the thing, whatever they're using to track us, is here with me. Or on me."

She unzipped the wallet, took out her credit cards and driver's license and cash, and stuffed them into a pocket of her jeans. She slipped a couple of keys off the ring and jammed them into her other pocket. She handed me her cell phone. Then she put the key ring, as well as the rest of the things on the counter, back into the purse and dropped it into the trash.

She took her phone back and gave me a gentle push.

"Let's move," she said.

In the parking lot she bent next to the front wheel while I got Chub settled into his seat and took Rascal for a quick walk.

"What did you just do?" I asked as we pulled out of the lot and back onto the highway, going at a normal pace now.

"Drove over my cell phone. Anyone trying to track us on that is going to find a pile of rubble in a Wendy's parking lot."

She was smart. She hadn't done anything yet that you couldn't learn from watching TV, but I was still impressed. There were moments when I felt the panic rising in my gut and I had to force it back with all my will. But I'd managed to do what needed to be done: to keep up with Prairie, to keep looking out for Chub. I was hanging on.

I wondered if it was a result of having grown up on constant alert. I was always watching out—whether for kids playing pranks on me when I was little, or for Gram taking a swipe at me as I walked past, or—worst of all—for the customers with their roving hands and hungry eyes. I was always thinking one step ahead.

"Prairie," I said. "Uh, thanks. You know, for the haircut and the clothes and everything."

She smiled, not taking her eyes off the road.

"Think I've got a future in it? You know, like I could be a stylist to the stars or something?"

"Um, not looking like *that,* I don't think so," I said, pointing to her sweater. "You look like you're going to a PTA meeting."

Prairie laughed and we rode along in companionable silence.

"So," I said after a while. "How do you know how to cut hair?"

"I worked in a salon."

"I thought you said you were a waitress."

"Yes, I did both. What happened was, when I'd been waitressing for a while, I went for a walk one day and found myself in a part of town I didn't know, in front of a salon. I felt a . . . compulsion to go inside. I couldn't resist, so I went in and met the woman who owned it. She was from Poland, and her name was Anna. We hit it off right away. She gave me a job. I worked there while I went to school, learned the trade. Then after I graduated I got a research job, and we . . . lost touch."

I could tell there was more to the story, from the way Prairie chose her words with great care.

"What aren't you telling me?"

Prairie bit her lip, and I waited.

"You remember how I told you that I got a fake identity?"

"Yeah."

"Anna was the one who helped me with that. She knew a guy who could get what I needed. Anna helped me become a new person."

"Why couldn't you just be yourself? Gram would never have come after you. You said it yourself."

"But I never stopped worrying. After I found out about Clover, I was done with Alice, I wanted no part of Gypsum—none of that. I saw what the people there had become. I thought I could take the Healing gift with me and leave the rest behind. The men, Gram's customers . . . their visions had clouded; most of them couldn't see the future anymore, and there was so much crime and violence. I saw how they treated the women, and I knew if I ever went back I'd get sucked into that life again."

"Why?" I demanded. "I mean, I hate Gypsum too, but you're acting like you didn't have free choice. Once you turned eighteen—"

"The Banished are bound together," Prairie interrupted.

"Haven't you seen that? Felt it? The Morries—the way you feel drawn to them?"

I felt my face redden: it was as though she could see inside me.

"It's not your fault," Prairie said, her voice softer. "It was ordained. But I knew I had to be away from all that. So I became someone new. Only . . ."

For a moment she said nothing, and then she laughed softly, but there was more hurt than humor in the sound.

"Anna was Banished too."

"*What?*"

"It's not just Gypsum, Hailey. There were others, from the village in Ireland. They lived there hundreds of years before the famine came and threatened to wipe them out. One group went to Poland. Anna came to the United States years ago, after her mother died."

"So there's . . . people like me, all over the world?"

"Not exactly. There were only a few original Healer families. I don't know exactly how many—maybe just us and the one that went to Poland, maybe a few more. But the Banished who went with them . . . yes, there are people like us out there."

"Are they all like the Morries?"

"Well, Anna isn't. Anna's . . . I loved her." She said it with a hitch in her voice and again I wondered why they'd lost touch.

"And she told you all of this?"

"Anna . . . filled in the gaps for me. I knew some of it

from my grandmother. Anna's pureblood. When she saw me, the day I went in the salon, she knew. She could sense it, that I was Banished. The ones who went to Poland, they kept the history alive better, they learned to recognize one another. Though now . . ." She shrugged. "Eventually the story gets lost."

"But how did she *know*? How could she tell?"

"It's not hard, Hailey," Prairie said. "You'll learn. I learned fast. You'll see it in people sometimes. Not often, and it's almost always weak in them. When the Banished left Ireland, they started to drift. Just like what happened in Gypsum, they married outside. The men lost the visions. Very little is left of the bloodline. But Anna showed me. Someone would come in, someone with Banished blood, and she helped me see it, or not see it exactly—it's a, a *sense,* I guess you'd say. Usually they don't even know it themselves. In a man, there might be some premonition, like sometimes things happen and they know in advance. Only, they talk themselves out of it, or chalk it up to coincidence. People can convince themselves very easily, you know, when they want to. It's human nature."

"Was Anna a Healer?"

"No. She says no one knows what happened to the Healer line in Poland, whether it died out or whether the Healers emigrated somewhere else."

For a while neither of us said anything. It was so much to absorb.

"So I guess Anna did her job, then," I finally said. For

some reason I felt bleak. "She found you. A gold star for her. Two pureblood Banished in a city the size of Chicago."

If Prairie minded my tone she didn't mention it.

"No, Hailey. Not two. Three."

"Three—what do you mean?"

"Anna has a son."

PART THREE: CHICAGO

CHAPTER 17

IT WAS TWILIGHT by the time we reached the outskirts of Chicago, the skyline a sparkling row of towers off in the distance, stretching out impossibly far in both directions. We left the highway on a looping cloverleaf crowded with speeding traffic.

Despite the brief nap in the motel, I couldn't keep my eyes open. I must have drifted off, because when Prairie gently shook my arm to wake me, we were parked behind another motel, this one huge and new and anonymous, backing up to a wide avenue across from a car dealership. I didn't even ask where we were. I went through the motions of getting Chub, who was fast asleep, as Prairie took care of Rascal. In the room, I collapsed with Chub and didn't wake up until late the next morning, when the sun was streaming in the windows.

I sat up, disoriented by the unfamiliar surroundings.

The room was almost a copy of the one from the day before, but reversed, the television on the opposite wall. Chub sat on the edge of the bed, swinging his legs, watching TV with the sound turned low. He was already dressed, and his hair was sticking straight up.

Prairie stood at the window, clutching the fabric of the drapes in her hand, staring out into the parking lot, Rascal sitting at her side, staring at nothing. When I said her name, she jumped.

"Good morning, Hailey," she said. "Are you feeling better today?"

To my surprise, I was. I felt rested and strong, and the events of the past few days had faded in my mind, like a movie I'd watched but would someday forget. Not that I would ever lose the images of the wrecked kitchen, of Gram on the floor, but as I washed up and packed, I felt like it was all in the past, like that phase of my life was over.

I felt the faint stirrings of hope.

It was almost one in the afternoon by the time we walked Rascal and put our things in the car. We went to a diner next to the motel for lunch. My appetite was back, and I ordered a burger and fries and a big glass of milk. Even Prairie ate most of her chicken salad, and the worry lines around her eyes had smoothed.

"So," I said as I finished the last of my fries, "I guess it worked, huh? The . . . thing you did. So he wouldn't be able to find us."

I didn't say his name, could barely stand to think it. *Rattler.* The image of him plunging the knife into the man in the gray jacket flashed through my mind and was gone, leaving only a shadowy outline of the terror of that night.

Prairie nodded thoughtfully and sipped at her coffee. "If he was going to be able to track us . . ."

She didn't finish the thought, but I knew what she was thinking. He would have found us by now, if his visions were able to lead him to us. I wondered if Prairie had slept, or if she'd stayed by the window worrying all night, waiting for his old truck to roll up in front of the motel, waiting for him to come crashing through the door the way Bryce's men had the day before.

I felt guilty because I'd collapsed and slept like a rock, leaving all the guarding and worrying to her. I almost apologized, but I couldn't quite find the words.

"So he probably stayed in Gypsum," I said hopefully.

Prairie nodded. "Mmm. With any luck I can finish . . . what I need to do tonight, and we can move on."

She was looking not at me, but out the window. I had so many questions. She said *we,* but did she mean all three of us? And I had no idea what she meant by "move on," or where we would go next, how we would live.

"What do you have to do tonight?" I asked.

She looked at me directly and chose her words carefully. "I need to destroy Bryce's research."

"How are you going to do that?"

"I have some ideas. First thing is to get into the lab. And for that I'll need my key. It's too dangerous to go back to my house, but I keep spare keys at my neighbor's."

"Don't you have a key with you?"

Prairie pushed her salad around on her plate without looking at me. "This is a special key, Hailey. It's a prox card for an electronic lock, and I'm pretty sure that by now Bryce has changed the code so I can't get in. But I have a master key at my friend's place."

"Does she know you're coming?"

"No . . ." Prairie hesitated and bit her lip. I could tell she was trying to figure out how much to tell me. "I thought it was best that I didn't call or do anything that might tip someone off. I do have a key to her house, so I can let myself in. The quicker I get in and out, the better."

I . . . She said *I*. Not *we*. Panic stirred in my gut—panic at being left alone, left to defend Chub against any threat that came along.

"I'm going with you," I said quickly, my tone harsher than I intended. "We're going together."

"I don't think that—"

"Please. We can wait in the car, it'll be better this way, we can watch for . . . for . . ."

I didn't finish my sentence, but I figured Prairie knew what I meant. I could watch for the men Bryce had sent or for Rattler or for any of the other threats I'd never thought to worry about, threats that until a few days ago hadn't existed for me, but that had changed the course of my life.

I'd argue with Prairie if I needed to. I wasn't going to let this drop. She had saved me from Bryce and Gram and Rattler, and I was grateful. But she couldn't leave us now. I wouldn't let her.

I didn't have any other choice.

"All right," she finally said, and I let out the breath I hadn't realized I was holding. "You can come with me to Penny's. But after that, when we get to the lab, I go in alone."

I wasn't going to argue that—yet. One step at a time.

She wanted to wait until dark to make the trip to her neighbor's house, so we spent the afternoon in a park. Chub played on the swings and the slides and dug holes and tunnels in a sandbox with a plastic shovel someone had left behind. I tried to interest Rascal in chasing a stick, but he just walked beside me and sat whenever I stood still. Late in the afternoon Prairie drove us north of the city to Evanston, the suburb where her apartment and the lab were. She parked near the lake and we walked out on a strip of land from which we could see Chicago to the south, the setting sun glancing off the windows of all the high-rise buildings, making it look like a city made from gold and mirrors. Chub was more interested in throwing rocks off the pier than at looking at the city, but I couldn't take my eyes off the skyline and the sun sinking toward the inky blue of the lake.

At last it was nearly dark. Prairie drove around for a while before choosing a parking spot on a quiet side street, near an alley. Cars were jammed in tight on both sides of the street, but a red Acura pulled out just as we were cruising past. It took several minutes of careful maneuvering to get the Ellises' big car into the spot, but when Prairie finally shut off the ignition, she seemed satisfied.

"I wish we had a leash for Rascal," Prairie said.

"He'll stay close. He won't run off."

"Yes, but there are leash laws here. Well, we'll just make do. When we get to Penny's house he can come inside. She loves dogs."

We started walking and entered a residential area. Prairie set a quick pace, cutting across a wide street and into an alley that ran behind a row of houses. We made our way down a few blocks, hurrying across when we came to an intersection. I tripped over a hose that had been left coiled behind a garage. We had to hush Chub several times; he was tired from skipping his nap and stumbled along half awake, rubbing his eyes and mumbling.

Prairie put her hand on my arm and pointed at a small, shingled coach house set back from a bigger house that fronted the street. I squeezed Chub's hand and he leaned against me, his face pressed into my legs. He was so exhausted that he started to cry silently, small sobs muffled by my jeans. We had stopped under the low-hanging branches of an elm that was leafing out for spring, and I hoped we were hidden from anyone who happened to look out their bedroom window.

"Is this Penny's place?" I whispered.

"Yes. I don't want to knock because she'll turn on the porch light, but she won't mind me letting myself in. We have an arrangement. We water each other's plants when we travel, that kind of thing."

Prairie didn't look as confident as she sounded. She dug for the keys she'd pocketed in the Wendy's bathroom.

I picked Chub up as she turned the key in the lock. He stiffened in my arms and I hushed him, holding his body tighter. I realized only after I heard the gentle click of the door opening that I had been holding my breath, waiting for—what? A gunshot?

Back in Gypsum, I was always on edge—I never knew what I'd come home to, who I'd find slumped at the kitchen table. But this was different. The things I worried about in Gypsum all seemed kind of stupid now—kids making fun of me, or Gram being in a bad mood, or Dun Acey trying to grab my butt when I walked past him.

"I guess she went to bed early," Prairie said as she stepped aside to let me into the dark foyer of the coach house, Rascal following.

She slid her hand along the wall. I could barely make out its outline in the moonlight coming through the door. There was another soft click as Prairie's fingertips found the light switch, and the room was illuminated by the soft light of a lamp on a low table.

A few feet in front of us, an elderly woman in a pink quilted housecoat sat in an overstuffed chair, her feet out in front of her at an odd angle, one of her satin slippers upside down on the wood floor.

For a second I thought she'd fallen asleep. Then I noticed a dark stain that ran down her neck and into the folds of her housecoat, and when I took half a step closer, the reason became clear.

Her skull had been bashed in.

CHAPTER 18

PRAIRIE MADE A SOUND next to me, a cut-off little cry. I pushed Chub's face hard against my shoulder, shielding him from the sight of the dead woman. When he'd been crying moments earlier—he'd *known* that something bad waited inside.

I saw that bits of shattered white skull showed through the woman's ruined scalp and blood-matted hair, and I took a step back. My foot hit something on the floor and I tripped, nearly dropping Chub. Instead, I staggered sideways and managed to stay on my feet. I looked down to see what I'd tripped over: a skillet, an old black one with a wooden handle.

"Welcome home," came a deep, rough voice. Another lamp switched on and I could see a man sprawled lazily on a floral-print couch, one arm slung along the plump cushions, the other hand dangling a handgun.

It was Rattler Sikes.

A purple bruise showed through the stubble on his jaw, but otherwise he looked none the worse for wear. My heart sank. All our efforts to throw him off—they hadn't worked. Had he seen every move we'd made?

As if reading my thoughts, he chuckled softly. "Bet you're surprised to see me. You really thought you could get me off your trail with that wild-goose chase? You must of forgot I ain't got any quit in me."

"Rattler," Prairie said, her voice choked with fury. "What have you *done*?"

"Before you go lookin' around for something you can throw at me, *Pray-ree*, you might ought to consider I got a gun and you got a little boy with you ain't done anything to anyone." The way Rattler said her name, it was like he was mocking her with it. "And I got a itchy finger, so's if you so much as make me nervous, why, I'm liable to go twitchin', and I know none of us wants that, right?"

"You'll have to shoot me first." I turned so my body was between Rattler and Chub.

"Hold up, there," Rattler said. "I ain't shootin' nobody just yet. Don't you want to know how I came to meet your friend here, Pray-ree? She weren't any too hospitable, though, I gotta say."

"How could you—"

"She saw me knockin' on your door, and come over wearin' garden gloves and waving her pruning shears and askin' me all kinda nosy questions. Liked to have pruned me to death, way she was lookin' at me. And I got to thinkin', maybe I'd just wait for you from her house here. Nice window I could look out of, make sure I saw when you got home. And now look, it must be my lucky day, 'cause you gone and come to *me*."

"She never hurt anyone—"

"Hey, all's I asked her to do was leave me be and set quietly in this here chair while we waited on you all. I wasn't fixin' to kill her or nothin'. Then I tell her to git me some tea and she come back with a skillet and she's ready to haul off and hit me on the head with it, only she didn't move quick enough. Guess that didn't work out too well for her, now, did it?"

I thought about how frightened the woman must have been when Rattler forced his way into her home. His grip on the gun looked sloppy, but I knew better. He could hit a can on top of the trash in the burn barrel in Gram's backyard while standing in the middle of the field next door. I'd watched out my bedroom window one summer twilight as he and a few of Gram's customers took turns shooting. The other guys hit the barrel or missed entirely, but Rattler nailed the can every time.

Now he was staring at Prairie with an intensity you could light fires with. And she stared back. There was something between them, all right, something crackling with tension and danger, something almost . . . alive.

"You slowed me down, girl," he said, so softly that I knew he was speaking only to her. I might as well have not even been there. "But you can't stop me. Not when I'm coming for you."

My fear curled and stretched into something new, a realization that Rattler didn't want to kill us—he wanted something worse. It was as if he wanted to *own* Prairie, and I realized that I was more frightened of Rattler Sikes and the other Banished men than I was of the professional killers who'd been chasing us.

More frightened of Rattler than *all* of those guys put together.

"You shouldn't have come here," Prairie said, but there was a tremor in her voice, and she shrank back from him. It was like the twisted energy around him diminished her.

Suddenly Rattler laughed, and the spell was broken.

"Now let's get back on a friendlier track," Rattler said, his voice oily. "Set on down, girl, I think you ought to be comfy enough in that chair. We got a little talkin' to do 'fore we all git on the road."

"We're not going anywhere with you," Prairie hissed.

But Rattler only shrugged. "I'm gonna take you girls home, where you belong. You can go easy, or you can go hard. Up to you. Hailey, go on, take the kid and git him settled in one of those bedrooms. And take that mangy hound with you."

I didn't need to be told twice. I edged through the room, avoiding looking at the dead woman, Rascal at my heels. I wished he was a better watchdog—it was like he didn't care at all that Rattler was threatening us. My heart was pounding so hard, it seemed like everyone ought to be able to hear it. In the hall a door stood open to a small room with a tidy bed made up with a quilt and a pile of embroidered pillows. As I put Chub on the bed and slid my backpack off my shoulders, I tried hard not to think about the woman with half her head leaking out in the other room.

"I like how you look all eased down in that chair," I heard Rattler say from the other room. "You're lookin' real good, Prairie."

I had to do something to stop Rattler. I unzipped the backpack and dumped everything out. I handed Chub his giraffe and sorted frantically through the rest of the contents.

"Bedtime?" Chub asked, yawning. "I want *my* bed." Even through my terror I noticed how well he was speaking, how clear his words were. Evidently he had forgotten his fear, or maybe he was simply too tired to care.

"You can just nap here for now," I said, pulling the quilts and covers back from the pillows. I could hear Prairie murmuring something.

"Okay. Good night." Chub got up on his knees to hug me and I kissed the top of his head.

Chub started to wiggle under the covers, but suddenly he sat up, frowning. "I don't want to watch."

"What, sweetie? What don't you want to watch?"

"Bad man's eye. I don't want to watch."

My nerves were so skittish, it took some effort for me to

smooth the hair off Chub's forehead and kiss him gently and get him to lie down again. "You don't have to. You just go to sleep."

"'Kay." He closed his eyes, his long lashes casting shadows on his soft cheeks.

In the other room Prairie and Rattler talked in low, intense voices. There was nothing I could use—just my old clothes and Prairie's purchases. I glanced around the room but saw only framed snapshots, a fancy silver comb and brush, china figurines, a basket of dried flowers. There was a chest of drawers pushed up against the wall and I ran my hand along the top of it.

"You can't tell me you don't remember how much fun we used to have," Rattler said, his voice rising. "You used to love skinny-dippin' with me and the rest of 'em."

"I *never* loved it," Prairie snapped. "I hated it."

"That ain't true. You know you an' me should of been together. *Everyone* knew it."

"No. *No.*"

I yanked open the top dresser drawer. Slips and camisoles, folded tissue. I tried the next drawer.

Scarves. A soft pile of scarves, lengths of silk in every color of the rainbow—beautiful, but nothing I could use. My heart plummeted.

"Only, you didn't do like you were supposed to," Rattler continued. "I waited, I followed your mom's rules, even if *you* didn't. You think I didn't know about you and that boy from Tipton?"

"He was—"

"You thought you were so smart, sneakin' around with him? Thought nobody'd figure it out, just cause you kept it from your mom? Well, I knew. I *knew*." I was shocked at the bitterness in Rattler's tone. Was he . . . jealous? Was that possible?

I stuck my hand in the drawer and seized the scarves and pushed them to the side. My fingers brushed against something hard and sharp. I picked it up. It was made of pale bone or ivory, with two delicate long, curved points at one end and a pearly fan-shaped decoration carved at the other. Some sort of hair ornament, I guessed.

I picked it up and held it in my right hand so that the long, curved points lay against my wrist, then stepped into the other room.

"Don't matter anyway," Rattler said. "'Specially since your sister beat you to the big prize."

I heard Prairie's sharp intake of breath. "What do you mean?"

Rattler laughed bitterly. "Only that once you took off, your mom said she guessed Clover was old enough to date after all. It took some convincin', like to hurt my feelings the way she kept turnin' me down, but I finally got her to see things my way. I guess I had a mighty fine time with—"

"Don't say her name!"

"I'll say what I want, Pray-ree," Rattler hissed. "You need me to spell it out?"

I stepped into the light.

Rattler glanced at me, and for a split second his face was open to me, his expression unguarded, and I saw something there I would have never imagined in a million years.

Pain.

Because of Prairie. It wasn't love—I refused to believe a man like Rattler could love—but a longing so strong he wore it like a second skin; and it was suddenly easy for me to believe that their connection went back not just generations but centuries. The thing binding Rattler to Prairie knotted tighter the more it was resisted.

But when Rattler saw me staring at him, the hurt vanished and was replaced with something else, something sharp-eyed and crafty. Amused, even.

"Little Hailey girl," he said. "Look at you, practically grown up."

"You never—you couldn't—she wouldn't—" Prairie gasped for words and looked like she was going to come out of her chair and attack him. But Rattler raised his gun hand without even looking and leveled it at her.

"Go easy, Prairie," he warned, his voice barely more than a raw whisper.

Then he looked at me full-on, his eyes glinting green sparks in the dim light. One corner of his cruel mouth quirked up.

"You know who I am, don't you, Hailey girl," he said softly, and suddenly I did—I knew, and my hand clutched hard at the handle of the hairpin as the knowledge thundered in my brain. "I'm your daddy."

I lunged at him and raised my hand, clenched that hair-pin tight, and the sound when those elegant curved points found their mark wasn't like much of anything at all, like sliding a knife into a melon—

But the sound that came out of Rattler made up for it, a sound that was neither human or animal but something in between, a wild something, a furious something, as he clawed at the thing that was sticking into his right eye.

"Prairie!" I yelled. I whirled around and saw her bolt out of her chair.

I ran to the bedroom and yanked back the quilts. Chub was propped on his elbows, his little face winding up for a scream of his own. He wasn't all the way awake, I could see that—it happened sometimes, when he was startled out of a deep sleep; it was like a sleep-waking nightmare.

"It's me, it's me, Chub," I said as I yanked him out of the bed, stuffing everything back in the backpack and shrugging it over my shoulders. He started to wail, squirming in my arms as I ran out of the bedroom. Rattler had got the hairpin out of his eye—blood covered the hand he had pressed against it—and he raised his gun hand and swung it from Prairie to me.

Then he shot at me.

I waited for a jolt of pain that didn't come, but there was a crash from the bookshelves behind me.

"Down," Prairie screamed, and pushed me away from her, but I stood my ground as she raced for the kitchen and jerked open a drawer and pawed frantically through the contents.

"Rascal!" I screamed, and he appeared in the hall, looking uninterested. "Sic him, boy!"

The change in Rascal was astonishing. In a flash he went from standing still to snarling and hurling himself at Rattler, teeth bared. He clamped down hard on Rattler's shin, and the sound coming from his throat was guttural and feral. Rattler yelled in pain. As he brought his gun hand down on Rascal's skull, the gun went off again and Prairie stumbled against me. She didn't say a word, just made a sound like "unh."

"Are you—"

"I'm fine," Prairie said, yanking on my hand and pulling me toward the door.

"Rascal, come on!" I yelled, and we ran as Rattler hopped back, clutching his leg where Rascal had attacked him.

When we reached the porch, Prairie stumbled and barely caught herself.

"You're *not* fine," I said, heart pounding. "Did he shoot you?"

I saw the spreading damp of her blood and the jagged tear in her sweater, the awkward angle at which she was holding her arm.

"Ahh," she said, breathing hard. "All right, I'm hit. But we have to get out of here. It's not just Rattler, Hailey. There were lights on in my house that weren't on before. Didn't you see? Bryce's men are over there, and they must have heard something going on."

"But—"

"They'll come here, Hailey. To see what happened."

And then they'd come after us.

Again.

"How— What can I—"

"Just help me run. We can get to a pay phone, there's one a couple of blocks back."

I remembered her cell phone, crushed under the Buick's tire.

If there was a moment for me to be strong, this was it. Prairie had taken the lead since the moment we'd met, and I'd followed. Not always willingly, and I hadn't always believed or trusted her, but I followed.

Now, though, she needed me. And I had to set aside my doubts, my questions, my fear. I set Chub down, yanked my old shirt out of the backpack and tied the sleeves tightly around her arm, above the bullet wound, to slow the blood flow. She stood still and pale, biting her lip but not making any sound.

I held Chub's hand and supported Prairie with my other arm, half dragging her, retracing our steps down the alley toward town. Rascal followed, docile again. Any traces of the vicious attack dog he'd been moments ago were gone. I listened for footsteps behind us, the sound of tires on gravel, but there was nothing.

We reached a shuttered drugstore and I could see the pay phone in a pool of light at the edge of the parking lot. I hesitated—we'd be a visible target for anyone who came along.

A taxi cruised slowly by.

I jumped into the street. I'd never hailed a cab in my life, but I held my hand high and waved it hard. For a moment I thought the cab was going to pass us by, but at the last minute it slowed.

"I can't—my arm," Prairie said.

"We can cover it—"

Prairie shook her head. "No. It's too dangerous. If he sees blood, he might insist on taking us somewhere. A police station, or a hospital."

"Would that be so bad? Come on, Prairie, you're *shot*. You need a doctor."

She shook her head hard. "No. You don't understand. Bryce is *connected*. In more ways than you can imagine. I'm sure he's got people covering the police scanners, the highway patrol—if we end up with the authorities, we're as good as dead. Besides, we can't take Rascal."

"But—"

The cabbie rolled down his window. "Excuse me, miss. You coming?" he asked in a thick accent.

Prairie shook her head again. I made a split-second decision. "I just need to use your cell phone, sir. Please. We'll pay."

The cabbie narrowed his eyes and frowned. "No ride?"

"No, I'm sorry, I just really need to use your phone."

He muttered something I couldn't understand and started to roll up his window.

"No! Please!" Frantically I gestured for Prairie to give me some money. She dug in her pocket and handed me a roll of bills. I peeled off three twenties. "Here. Just for a few minutes. I promise we'll give it right back."

The cabbie hesitated, then sighed and reached into the pocket of his coat. He handed me his phone and I passed him the money. "You stay right here," he said, stabbing a finger at me.

"Yes, okay."

I handed the phone to Prairie. She stepped back into the shadows while I waited next to the cab, Rascal sitting calmly at my side. Chub watched the transaction closely from my arms, his eyes wide and worried. "Phone," he said. "Prairie call."

"That's right, Chub. We borrowed the nice man's phone so Prairie could make a call." I glanced at the man, hoping his expression would soften when he saw how sweet Chub was, but he stared stonily ahead, arms crossed.

It didn't take long. Prairie shuffled back and handed me the phone. She was trembling. "Thank you," I said as I gave the phone back to the driver. He didn't respond but took off, wiping the phone on his shirt.

"I talked to Anna," Prairie said. She had started to shiver all over. "She's coming. We need to stay out of sight. I told her we'd be in that first yard."

She pointed back the way we'd come. A compact bungalow was separated from the street by a row of mature trees and a thick hedge. With luck, the trees would keep us hidden.

Before I could reply, Prairie started to sway. I grabbed her good arm and steadied her, then half dragged, half carried her. Chub walked behind us, hanging on to my jeans belt loop.

A low stone retaining wall ran along the side of the yard. There were no lights on in the house. I prayed that the people who lived there were heavy sleepers. Once I got Prairie settled on the stone ledge, I looked at her arm again. I couldn't tell in the dark whether it was still bleeding, but the makeshift tourniquet was wet with blood.

"Isn't there something I can do?" I asked. "You know . . . heal it?"

Prairie shook her head. "Healers can't help each other, Hailey."

"But why?"

"I don't know. It's just how it's always been. But we're strong. Stronger than most. I'm going to be fine."

Her shivering eased as we waited, but the stone was freezing beneath us and the night seemed to be getting colder with each passing moment. Chub burrowed against my knees. "Sleepy," he murmured, and I ran my fingers through his hair, over and over, the way he liked.

The minutes ticked by, the occasional car passing just a few yards away. Finally, a car pulled along the curb. It was small, and in the light of the streetlamps I could see that it was old and dented. The man who got out of the driver's seat was tall and broad-shouldered.

He stood silhouetted against the streetlight, fists clenched at his sides as he looked around. I couldn't see his face—he had a hood pulled up over his head—but something stirred inside me, the deep, intense feeling I sometimes got around the Morries, of longing and loss and connection and fear all run together. Could it be one of the other Banished men? How could he have gotten here so fast?

Prairie saw the man too, and I could hear her surprised murmur. Terror shot through my veins when I saw that he'd spotted us. I got ready to run, even though I'd never be able to move fast enough, not with Prairie and Chub.

But Prairie put her hand on my arm to stop me.

"It's all right," she whispered. "It's Kaz. Anna's son."

CHAPTER 19

HE CROSSED THE LAWN in a few long strides and barely looked at me before giving Prairie a careful hug.

"I can't believe it's you," she said, wrapping her good arm around his shoulders. "You're so tall! I think you were only twelve last time I saw you."

"Let's get to the car," he said urgently. "Mom'll kill me if I don't get you home fast, Aunt Eliz—"

He stopped and shook his head like he was embarrassed. "I mean, *Prairie.* Sorry. Mom told me."

"It's okay," Prairie said. "I was Elizabeth for a long time . . . don't worry about it."

"Yeah, it's just . . . I mean . . . Anyway, I'm Kaz," he said, finally turning to me and offering his hand. I couldn't make out his features in the darkness, but the faint light from the streetlamp glinted off his teeth as he smiled.

When I took his hand, I felt the electric connection I often experienced around the Morries. It wasn't as strong as when I touched Milla, but it was alive with energy. Kaz's skin was chilled by the night air, and his fingers were rough and callused, but his hand felt good in mine, and I held on for a second longer than I meant to.

And in one way he was different from any of the Morries I knew except Sawyer: he felt safe.

"I'm Hailey," I managed to say. "And this is Chub. And that's my dog, Rascal. Nice to meet you."

He nodded, then turned his attention back to Prairie. "We can talk more at home, but Mom's got everything ready and it looks like you're going to need it. How did you get here?"

"Drove," Prairie said, gritting her teeth. "But the car's fine where it is, no one will notice it for days."

"And . . . does the dog come?"

"If it's okay with you," I said quickly. "He's good." I couldn't leave Rascal after he'd come so far with us.

"Doesn't bother me. My car's seen worse. Okay, Prairie, how bad off are you?"

"It looks worse than it is."

"If you say so." He took her good hand and pulled her carefully to a standing position. "I'd offer to carry you, but—"

"Considering I used to read you Elmo books, that might take a little getting used to," she said with a weak laugh.

I followed, carrying Chub, who was nodding off. When we got to the idling car, Kaz helped Prairie into the passenger seat and fastened her seat belt while I got Chub settled next to me in the backseat, Rascal in his usual spot on the floor.

Kaz pulled away from the curb and accelerated fast. We didn't talk much on the drive, winding through tight-packed streets to the core of the city. Kaz took a road that curved along the lake, and suddenly there it was—all of Chicago laid out like a sparkling wonderland on the right, the black emptiness of Lake Michigan on the left. I couldn't take my eyes off the view, but soon we were back in a grid of city streets. Beautiful old buildings rose up all around us, but as we went farther, they gave way to plainer neighborhoods with run-down buildings.

"Almost home," Kaz murmured. "Hang in there."

He turned down an alley and into a tiny garage behind a little house tucked between others just like it. As soon as he turned off the engine, he got out and went around to help Prairie, easing her out of the car.

"I'd better get her inside," he said, almost apologetically.

Chub had fallen asleep again, and I tried to unbuckle him without waking him. I finally got him out, and found myself on a neat concrete walk in a tidy square of shrub-lined yard, tall fences separating it from the neighbors'. Rascal followed me and made an efficient tour of the yard. Three steps led to a brightly lit back stoop, where a woman waited, silhouetted in the door.

Yet another new thing to face. I took a deep breath and headed for the steps.

"Hailey," the woman said softly. She was about my

height, with softly rounded curves and pale hair curling around her shoulders. "I am Anna. Welcome. You come in. Dog too, is okay."

The door opened directly into a kitchen. It was warm and cozy and smelled like bread and spices. Prairie was seated at a round table, and Kaz was setting a steaming cup in front of her. He had pulled his sweatshirt hood down, so I could see his face. He had sandy brown hair that was just a little too long, and a strong jaw. When he smiled, his eyes glinted like blue ice.

"You're safe here," he said, and I *felt* his words as well as heard them, his low voice skimming along my skin, my nerves.

Anna went to the sink and began scrubbing her hands with a small plastic brush and a generous amount of soap. "Please do not think I am rude. I think I must fix Elizabeth now. I mean, Prairie. Yes? Then, we talk."

"We have tea," Kaz said. "Milk for Chub, if you think he'd want any?"

"Uh . . . I don't think he's going to wake up," I said. A clock on the wall read 1:40. I couldn't believe it had gotten so late, but a lot had happened already tonight. I was exhausted down to my bones, and Chub was unbearably heavy in my arms. I longed to sit, but the kitchen table was covered with first-aid supplies—gauze, scissors, plastic bottles—and I was afraid I'd be in the way.

Anna turned from the sink and shook her hands, droplets sprinkling the air. "Kaz, show Hailey their room. This handsome boy—"

"Chub," I said. "His name is Chub." I'd carried him for hours, and my spine felt like it might never be straight again. I could smell the stink of my sweat and fear. Even worse, I felt the hot pooling of tears that threatened to spill onto my cheeks.

"Chub," Anna repeated. "Let's get boy to bed, okay? You and Chub have Kaz's room tonight. Prairie will stay with me, I have big bed. I will take good care of her—I am studying to be nurse, so no need for worry."

"I can't take your room," I protested, but the hitch in my voice was obvious even to me.

"Oh. Oh, *ukochana*. You poor child, go with Kaz now." Anna pursed her lips as she settled in the chair next to Prairie. Then she took Prairie's arm gently and began to cut away the shirt I had knotted in place. Prairie stayed silent, but her skin was pale and shiny with sweat, and she had purple circles under her eyes. Her hair hung in greasy clumps and her mouth was set in a bunched line.

"Come on," Kaz said. "Do you want me to take him?"

Before I could protest, he lifted Chub out of my arms and laid him over his shoulder, Chub's face tucked into his neck. I slid my backpack off and dangled it in my hand, my muscles numb from carrying Chub. Anna was dabbing at Prairie's wound with cotton, and there was a strong smell of antiseptic in the air. The skin around the wound was black with blood, but the cotton came away bright red. I shivered and turned away.

I hoped Anna knew what she was doing.

The hall was narrow. At the end I could see a tidy living room. On one side were a bathroom and another room, with its door slightly ajar and a lamp glowing softly inside. Kaz opened a door on the opposite side.

"I'm, uh, sorry about the mess," he said. "I didn't have a lot of time to clean before you got here."

It wasn't cluttered or even messy, like kids' rooms on TV shows or in the movies. I had been a neat freak my whole life, but I knew it was due to the rest of my life being so out of control, and Kaz's room wasn't like that either. It was comfortably disordered, with an iPod and books lying open on the desk and an empty soda can on the floor near a big bean-bag chair.

On the shelves, books were lined up neatly along with lacrosse trophies and a compact set of speakers. Posters of lacrosse players lined the walls, as well as pennants from Johns Hopkins and Syracuse and a few other teams. Crates on the floor held gear—gloves twice the size of an average person's hand, rolls of tape and elbow pads and other things I could only guess at. A blue and white helmet sat in a place of honor on top of the dresser along with more books and a Mac laptop. The bed was made—barely, a quilt pulled crookedly over a lumpy comforter and pillow.

"If you pull back the covers, I can set Chub down and maybe he won't wake up," Kaz said.

"You're good with him," I said as we got Chub settled.

"I babysit for a family down the street," he said with a shrug. "They have four kids. I like this age. They're so . . . determined, you know?"

I did know. It described Chub perfectly. And suddenly I wanted to tell Kaz all about him, about our life with Gram, about the way it had all ended. I felt like I could talk to him for hours, without the staggering shyness I usually felt around kids my age.

Maybe there would be a chance, later. But right now I had other things to focus on. "I need to go see how Prairie's doing."

In the kitchen, Anna had finished cleaning the wound and stopped the blood flow, but I had to look away—the sight of Prairie's torn flesh was more than I could handle.

I knelt in front of her, grabbing her free hand and squeezing. I wanted to do something more—but I didn't know what. I knew that if all the bad things hadn't happened, she would never have let me see her weak or scared, the way she looked now.

But what was I supposed to do? Prairie and I had saved each other—well, mostly she had saved me—over and over again. She had proved herself to me.

"I'll be good as new soon," she said, trying hard to sound cheerful. Anna clucked under her breath and poked black thread through the eye of a curved needle. The smell of antiseptic was almost overpowering. "Anna took the bullet right out. It was just a little thing."

Bullet—that word did it. I laid my face on Prairie's knee, my shoulders shaking. Prairie patted my hair, my neck, whispering that it was going to be all right. That made me cry harder, but I was afraid that I would jostle her when Anna was taking a stitch. And besides, my nose was running all over her pants, and even though they were grimy from the past two days, I still couldn't stand the idea of messing them up. So I got to my feet, shaky and stumbling, wiping my nose on my sleeve and swallowing my tears down hard.

"Hailey, there are tissues on counter," Anna said, her voice calm but kind. "Please help yourself."

I did. I blew my nose and splashed water on my face from the sink, and washed my hands and dried them on a pretty yellow dish towel. And then, even though I was afraid to look, I sat down and watched Anna close up the wound with tiny, careful stitches, the line of black *x*'s the only proof that Prairie had been shot just a few hours before.

Kaz had wandered in without me noticing. "Chub went right to sleep. I left your backpack in there. You can, uh, use the bathroom or go to bed or whatever when you're ready. You can use my mom's stuff."

"Yes, of course," Anna said. "Thank you, Kaz. Hailey, please make yourself home. There are towels in closet in hall, okay?"

"Thank you." I knew I was filthy and that I probably smelled, and I was embarrassed for Anna and Kaz to see me like this. But I wasn't ready to leave Prairie. I stood behind her chair and watched as Anna finished up.

"So, Hailey, you are sophomore in high school?" Anna asked, glancing up from her work and giving me a smile.

"Um, yeah." Though it seemed unlikely I'd ever be setting foot in Gypsum High again.

"Kazimierz is junior at Saint Michael's. That is Polish name, we call him Kaz. Saint Michael's is nice high school, lot of good teachers. You do good in school?"

"Me? I— No—"

"Hailey's smart, like her mom," Prairie said, her voice soft. She had closed her eyes and rested her head against the chair back.

"Is she going to be all right?" I asked, worried.

"Oh yes, there is nothing to worry about. I think she is just very tired. This little wound, mostly I just make sure no germs, no bone chip. Bullet comes very close to bone here, see."

I looked where she was pointing, at the neat stitches in Prairie's arm.

"But all good. I have to poke around a little, that does not feel very good for Prairie. But I give her something strong to drink, make her relax, make her feel little bit sleepy."

I watched Anna finish the stitches and carefully bandage Prairie's arm. I wished I could just put my hands on her and heal her like I had with Milla and Chub, but the rushing urgency wasn't there, and I knew it was true—I couldn't help her. Anna, Banished like us, was using thread and a needle and medicine, traditional tools, and in comparison they seemed so . . . inadequate. And I understood how Prairie could have been tempted to try to use her gifts to heal as many people as she could, how she could have gotten dragged into Bryce's crazy scheme if she believed that she was going to find a way to share the powers.

I had Prairie's hand in mine, and I could feel her pulse slow and steady in her wrist. I thought she might have gone to sleep, but when Anna started to pack her supplies back into the case, Prairie sat up and blinked a few times.

"Anna, I don't know how to begin to thank you."

"No need to thank—we are family."

I figured that whatever had caused their rift, it couldn't have been that bad if Anna still considered Prairie family.

Anna turned to me and patted my knee. "Your aunt has told me all about your grandmother Alice. I am so sorry you had to live with her. In Poland, there were stories among the *Blogoslawiony*—"

"That's what they call the Banished in Poland," Prairie said.

"Yes, the people who came from old country. Anyway, after they left Ireland, sometimes a Healer woman is born who is not right. The gift is too much for them, they are not strong enough to use it right way. They turn mean, families have to lock them up. Usually very sick, die young."

"Gram was . . ." I couldn't think of what to say. She was so many things, all of them bad.

"Anyway, now you are with aunt, with our Eliza—our Prairie—much better."

Prairie sighed and reached out to touch Anna's hand. "I owe you so much. You were right. You told me to leave that job, and you were right. I don't know what else to say . . . except that I'm sorry."

That must be it, the reason they'd grown apart. Anna shook her head, eyes cast down. After a moment she squared her shoulders and met Prairie's gaze. "There is no need to speak of it again."

"But . . . all those years. I thought I'd lost you. And Kaz . . . he's a man now."

Kaz looked from one of them to the other. "That's what you argued about? Prairie's *job*?"

"Don't be angry at your mother," Prairie said. "It's my fault. Your mother asked me what we were doing at the lab, and I lied. I felt terrible about it, but Bryce made me sign a confidentiality agreement. He said we were getting funding from the university. I didn't find out it was coming from the government until a few days ago. And he told me what to say . . . told me to tell people we were working on a vaccine, for livestock."

"I can tell when you lie," Anna said sadly. "Kaz, too. You are not good liars."

"But Mom, how could you send Prairie away like that?" Kaz was angry now.

"I had to," Anna said. "She was trying to do science with Healing gift. There is no good in that. *Bajeczny* powers were meant for one village only, *czarownik* cursed those who left.

Banished maybe should die out. Since the people left Ireland, the men lose the visions, there is fighting and crime. The women are weak, they forget history."

"What about me? What about Dad? And Prairie? And Hailey?" He looked at me as he said my name. "Do you wish we hadn't been born?"

"Of course not."

"Well, do you want us to do something good with our lives? Something important? Or do you want me to be an accountant or a shoe salesman or something?"

"There is nothing wrong with honest trade," Anna shot back. I could see how they escalated each other's tempers. "Be shoe salesman—be *good* shoe salesman, I don't care."

"*You* didn't marry a shoe salesman," Kaz muttered angrily.

"Your father was warrior. You know that. He was hero in Iraq."

"And Prairie is a *leader*. An innovator," Kaz said. "She can't help it if her boss is crazy."

"Thank you, Kaz." Prairie cut in. "But I made mistakes and I have to make up for them. Terrible things are happening because I was stubborn, because I refused to see what your mother tried to tell me. Now I have to fix them."

"This is conversation for tomorrow," Anna said. "Now is time for everyone rest. Tomorrow is Sunday, salon is closed, everyone get some sleep."

"What about . . . ?" I asked. As welcome and safe as I felt in Anna's house, as relieved as I was that Prairie was going to be all right, I couldn't stop thinking about Rattler, seeing him holding his hand to his face, blood streaming through his fingers. "What if Rattler comes after us?"

There was a brief silence. Anna and Prairie glanced at each other. I could tell they were troubled, that they weren't saying what they were thinking.

"Please," I whispered hoarsely. "Don't keep things from me, I have to know."

"I think . . . we are safe for now," Prairie said carefully. "The injury . . . I wouldn't be surprised if Rattler loses that eye. The blood loss alone will be enormous. He won't be able to do much of anything until he gets some help. Even if he tries to just rest and wait until he's well enough to travel, it's not going to be tonight."

"Your aunt, she describe . . . what you do." Anna made a stabbing motion with her hand and I flinched, the memory of the hairpin going into his flesh more than I could bear. "She say it went in far, to eye? Is possible there is damage to brain. Possible he gets much worse after you are gone. You are very brave girl," she added quickly.

I knew what she was worried about: that I would fall apart if I thought I'd killed Rattler or even disabled him. But that wasn't going to happen. I wouldn't grieve over him. I hoped he was lying on the floor even now, his blood leaking out until he was too weak to say his own name.

And I also felt, deep inside where instinct worked against reason, that he *wasn't* dying. That whatever damage I'd managed to do to him, it wasn't enough. That after he healed he would be as strong as ever, and as determined, and that when that happened he would come after us again.

But I had bought us some time. For now that would have to be enough.

Prairie allowed me to help her stand up. Kaz rushed to her other side and together we helped her down the hall, Anna in the lead. Anna opened the door to her bedroom, where a pretty comforter was turned down on the wide bed.

"I will help Prairie freshen up," she said. "I have night-gown and robe. Now you two, go to bed."

Kaz offered to take Rascal out for me while I brushed my teeth and washed my face. They weren't gone long, and Kaz gave Rascal an odd look as he said goodnight. I closed the door, glad for the solitude. All the tension from the day welled up in my heart and I knew I was close to breaking down.

Instead, I climbed into Kaz's bed and patted the mattress next to me. "Come, Rascal," I said, and he jumped up and lay down.

It felt good to put my arms around his warm body, to feel his heartbeat strong and regular under his fur. It almost didn't matter that he'd lost his personality, that he didn't ever play anymore. I closed my eyes and remembered the way he used to be, and as I stroked the soft ruff of fur around his neck, I felt a little better.

Until my fingers touched something that shouldn't have been there.

I worked my fingertips through the dense fur and found

a small, hard object embedded in the skin. Anxiety raced along my nerves as I rose up on one elbow and switched on the bedside lamp. I parted Rascal's fur and looked closer. A little bit of black metal protruded from a swelling where the skin was growing over the object. I felt its outlines with my fingers. Small. Knobby.

A bullet.

I jerked my hand away and sucked in my breath, scrambling away from him. My legs were tangled in the sheets and I half fell, half crawled out of Kaz's bed. Shock mixed with disgust as I wiped my hand against the carpet, hard, making my skin burn. "No, no, no," I heard myself whispering, and when I closed my mouth and tried to stop, the words became a desperate moan.

I remembered Rascal waiting in the yard at Gram's, with blood on his back—he must have been shot when Bryce's men first came to the house. They must have tried to kill him to keep him quiet.

Maybe it had been a superficial wound, just a minor injury that Rascal was healing from on his own. I clung desperately to that thought, even though I knew it was unlikely, as I forced myself to look at him. He hadn't moved; he was lying still and indifferent on the mattress. I had to know. Nausea roiled through me as I approached the bed on my knees, staring at the place in his fur where the bullet had entered, trying not to look at his expressionless eyes. I gritted my teeth and reached with a shaking hand and touched him, and when he didn't respond, I felt like I was touching evil itself and my entire body resisted, my heartbeat pounding a crazy tempo.

I almost couldn't do it. I squeezed my eyes shut and felt hot tears leaking down my face, and still I couldn't stop making sounds, quiet little sobs of desperation and horror. But I made myself trace my fingers through the fur around his torso, finding two more dented places where bullets had gone into him. One I could barely feel, lodged deep in the muscle, but one had entered his body far enough that I couldn't feel it at all, right over his heart.

Rascal had been shot three times. He should be dead. But he wasn't.

Bullets couldn't kill him. Because he was already dead.

Because I had made him into a zombie.

I *was* cursed. I was no Healer—I was a zombie-maker.

I'd known it all along, deep inside. The accident came rushing back and images freeze-framed through my head in rapid succession: all the blood, his organs spilling from his body, the way his eyes rolled up a final time.

Their emptiness when I brought him back.

I brought him back. From the dead.

And now he couldn't die. He'd been shot and the bullets were in his body as proof; they'd ripped through skin and bone and his very heart, and yet he soldiered on, a robot of a dog.

A *zombie* of a dog.

I screamed and pushed him from the bed, as hard as I

could. His body fell to the floor with a thud, and he got up slowly and stood there unblinking, staring at nothing.

I scrambled to my feet and started backing toward the door, and when the wailing didn't stop I realized I was still screaming.

The door pushed open and strong arms circled me from behind, practically lifting me off the floor. I fought and kicked and tried to break away as Kaz dragged me down the hall to the living room.

"Stop, Hailey," he commanded, but he didn't try to protect himself. Slowly, I ran out of energy and stopped fighting him, and my screams turned to sobs and he held me tight against him.

I heard a door open and Prairie's and Anna's voices.

"What happened?"

"Is Hailey all right?"

"He's not healed," I cried, letting go of Kaz and running to Prairie. I wanted to throw myself into her arms but I knew how fragile she was, so I just hugged myself, shaking all over. "I turned Rascal into a zombie."

CHAPTER 20

"You have to tell me the truth," I said as Anna tucked an afghan around me and Prairie. We were sitting together on the living room couch. "*All* of it."

Kaz had taken Rascal out to the yard after I insisted I couldn't stay in the house with him for another second. He put water on for more tea, and the four of us huddled in the living room. Chub, thankfully, slept through the whole thing.

"We never . . . I don't know if *zombie* is really the right word," Prairie began hesitantly.

"That's what Rascal is!" I burst out. "He can't be killed. He came back from the dead." I was struggling to control my breathing, and my hands were shaking so badly that I jammed them together. "Just, please, tell me how it happened. Tell me what I did."

Tell me Milla won't end up like this
Tell me I'll never do this to Chub

"This won't happen again," Prairie said carefully. She exchanged glances with Anna, who'd said little since I woke everyone up.

They both looked so worried that my anxiety threatened to bubble up again. I felt the scream building inside me, so I squeezed my hands even more tightly together, the knuckles going white. "How can I be sure?"

"It's only . . . you must never heal someone who has died. That's the one rule. Mary taught us that from the start, me and your mom, before we ever healed anything, even a lizard. She wouldn't even let us heal a dead squirrel or mouse—she made us promise." Prairie reached for my hands and tugged at them gently until, like a chunk of ice thawing, I relaxed my grip and let her lace her fingers through mine. "I am so sorry you didn't have anyone to teach you, to explain it all to you."

You know you're the future, Hailey

Gram's words, the dozens of times she'd given me that strange, hungry look—they chased each other around my head, trying to take hold, to grow into full-blown terror. I fought back, focusing on the feeling of Prairie's warm hands on mine. After a moment, I realized something—the bandages were off her arm, and the wound that Anna had stitched closed already looked better.

Healers can't help each other, but we're strong. That was what she'd told me.

I was strong. I grabbed that thought and held it tight.

"So explain it all to me now."

"There's not much more to tell. Just the one rule: you must never heal someone who has died. Their body will come back, for a while anyway, but their soul is gone. They don't feel love, or pain, or any emotion at all. They respond to basic stimuli and will eat and even sleep, though they don't dream. They can't make decisions for themselves, though they can hear and process instructions and will do whatever they are told."

"Rascal does what I say. If I tell him to come, or stay, or— You *knew*, didn't you?"

"I . . . yes, I was pretty sure from the moment I saw him. That's why I went looking for scars on him."

"How could you not tell me? How could you know what I had done to him and, and let me keep him in the car with us, let me keep *touching* him—"

"Hailey, I'm so sorry, but I didn't know how to tell you without upsetting you—"

"Without *upsetting* me? I'm so far past upset, I can't believe—"

"I had to keep you calm," Prairie cut me off. "I truly am so, so sorry, Hailey, but you weren't ready to know."

We were silent for a moment, and I realized it was true. I had been so close to falling apart these past few days. One more thing might have tipped me over the edge.

"How long have you known about . . . what happens? If you heal, after?"

"Mary used to tell us stories," Prairie said. "Horror stories, I guess, meant to scare us so we wouldn't be tempted. When she was a little girl, one of the other Healers couldn't help herself and she brought back a cat, a pet she loved, and it was just like Rascal. It frightened all the children, the way it just sat on the porch, not moving. People wouldn't walk by the house."

"What happened to it?"

Prairie bit her lip. "Mary said it started to . . . well, its body began to decompose. The bodies of the healed dead can't sustain life forever."

"Oh my God," I cried, fresh horror surging through my brain. Would Rascal start to decompose? Was his body rotting already?

"One day someone—they never found out who—broke the cat's neck. It was a blessing, Mary said."

"But I thought they couldn't be killed."

"There are a couple of ways—the brain stem has to be destroyed. A . . . decapitation would work. Crushing of . . . that area of the brain . . . A sharp break of the vertebrae could accomplish that, if . . . Well, you get the idea."

"It was good person, compassionate person," Anna cut in.

I noticed Kaz in the doorway and realized he'd been listening, a pair of steaming cups in his hands. He came forward and set the cups down. His eyes met mine and there was sadness in them.

"I'm sorry about Rascal," he said quietly, "but it's not your fault."

"It *is*. I did it. No one else." I didn't add that at some level I had known that what I was doing was wrong, when I felt the energy rushing from me to Rascal's lifeless body. Even before I knew I was a Healer.

"How . . . long?" I asked when nobody spoke.

"The decomposition takes longer than it would in a normal death," Prairie said carefully. "Depending on the health of the person—or animal—it can take up to two or three times as long for the tissues to fail. And other conditions affect it too, of course."

Heat, I thought, and humidity and insects, all the things we'd learned about in science. I felt like I was going to throw up. I hadn't noticed anything yet, except the bad smell, and Rascal had been a young, healthy dog, but how long until his fur began to fall out and his body filled with gases and his skin began to break down?

I pulled my hands away from Prairie's and covered my face, trying to keep the tears at bay. "I can't stand to see him," I whispered. "Don't make me look at him."

"He's outside," Kaz said. "You're *here*, with us. It's all right."

I wanted to believe him. He knelt in front of me and Anna leaned in and we all huddled together. Their hands comforted me, patting my shoulders and squeezing my fingers, and it helped. I felt closer to Anna and Kaz than to people I had known my entire life. And as for Prairie—I couldn't imagine life without her now.

But I knew I was still alone in one important way. I'd

done the thing that must never be done, the thing Prairie and my mother had been warned about since childhood. I'd done the unforgivable. And I couldn't help wondering how many ways I would suffer for it.

I thought of Prairie when her face clouded over with private grief. I recognized the solitary pain at her core. She carried a secret with her too, and I wondered if I would be like her someday, marked with a kind of suffering that other humans couldn't understand.

"What did you do?" I asked her. I had to know if it was connected to the things that had happened, to the thing I had done. "Why did you leave Gypsum?"

Her face went pale, but it wasn't surprise I saw on her face. Almost the opposite—a kind of resignation. "Not tonight," she said, exhaustion making her voice husky. "There's been enough to deal with tonight for all of us."

"Stop putting me off," I protested. "You owe me the truth."

"I'll tell you in the morning. I promise. After we've all had a chance to rest. The sun will be up in a few hours, and we won't be able to do what needs to be done unless we get some sleep."

I wanted to fight her, but fatigue was winning. Despite the shock of learning about Rascal, despite having a whole new nightmare to worry about, I was desperate to close my eyes and let sleep steal in and erase everything, if only for a few hours.

"Promise," I begged in a whisper.

"I promise." She looked directly in my eyes when she spoke, and in the pale green depths I saw reflected a shadow of myself.

She stayed in Kaz's room with me for the rest of the night. I insisted that she take the bed, and when she protested, I curled up in the nest of blankets with Chub. I was asleep before she finished telling me not to worry.

CHAPTER 21

IN THE MORNING she was gone, the bed neatly made and sun streaming through the window when Chub and I woke up. I found her in the kitchen, after I'd taken Chub to the bathroom and washed my face and brushed my teeth.

Before I could demand that she keep her promise and tell me the story, she handed me a travel cup of coffee.

"There's someone I want you to meet," she said. "Grab a bagel and you can eat on the way. Anna will watch Chub."

Anna came into the room just then, her face pale and tired, but she gave me a smile that looked like it took some work. There was no sign of Kaz in the house, and it seemed smaller without his presence.

"Go, go, you two," she said, giving my arm a little squeeze. "I'm making *gulasz,* we'll have big lunch when you get back."

I wasn't hungry, but I took a bagel from the platter Anna had set on the table. It had been split and spread with cream cheese studded with dried apricots. Anna pushed a paper napkin into my hands.

"I don't want to go out there," I said, hating the way my voice went high and thin, but the horror of last night was stirring and threatening to return. I was desperate to keep the panic under control, but I knew if I had to walk past the creature that used to be Rascal, I'd lose it all over again. "I can't see him, I just can't."

"It's all right," Prairie said gently. "He's gone. He's . . . at rest."

"What do you mean?" I demanded. "What did you do to him?"

"*I* did it," Anna said. She stepped forward and placed a hand on my shoulder and gave me a look that was kind but firm. "It was humane, Hailey. I am nurse, I know what to do. Kaz is burying body in park, a place where there are trees, nice place, forest. When you come back, it will all be over."

I started to shake, and tears dotted the corners of my eyes. I put my hand up to Anna's, covering it, trying to find a way to say thank you, but I was afraid my voice would betray me. "All right," I managed to get out.

"Anna is letting me borrow her car," Prairie said. "Let's go, and we can talk on the way."

We didn't talk much, though. Anna's car was only slightly newer than Kaz's, and it sputtered at every intersection as though it was about to die. Prairie fed it gas, revving the engine, as we made our way through the neighborhoods, away from the lake, back to the cloverleaf and onto the highway.

"Where are we going?" I finally asked as she headed north, away from the distant skyline.

"Not far now."

A few minutes later, she exited into a neighborhood of tidy brick bungalows and the occasional church or tavern. There were no signs on the brick building she pulled up to. It had neat white shutters at the windows and tulips pushing their way up from planters out front. Long sloping ramps were the only clue to what kind of place it was.

"Is this a nursing home?" I asked as we made our way to the front doors, which glided open at our arrival.

"A convalescent home," Prairie said. "A very good one, with some of the top doctors in the country on call."

"Ms. Gordon," a woman at a desk called out cheerfully. "Vincent's having a good day. He'll be so glad you're here."

Prairie exchanged a few words with the receptionist as she signed in. Looking over her shoulder, I read *Susan Gordon* in a neat script.

"And who have you brought with you today?" The woman smiled at me with open curiosity.

"This is Hailey. Her family just moved to the area and joined the church. She's interested in doing outreach ministry too."

"Oh, that's wonderful! Hailey, we love our volunteers

here. And so do our patients. Especially the ones who don't have family. Visits just do them a world of good."

"What was that all about?" I demanded after Prairie thanked the receptionist and guided me across the lobby. We were buzzed through a set of doors and walked down a hallway with a shiny waxed floor and rooms opening up on either side that held hospital beds, many with patients in them. Some sat, others appeared to be asleep. None looked our way.

"I visit every week. I use a fake identity, as you saw. They don't ask a lot of questions when it's church people visiting. And I've been coming to see Vincent for years, so they're used to me."

"Who's Vincent?"

She slowed as we reached the end of the hallway and took a deep breath. Then she gestured for me to enter the last room on the right.

"Vincent was my boyfriend," she said as she followed me into the room.

A man sat in the bed, a thin blanket covering his body, his hands folded neatly on its surface. There was something wrong with him. His skin was puffy, with an oily sheen, and his color was off. He had a network of fine scars on his face and also on what I could see of his arms, below the cuffs of his shirt. His dark hair was thin and it hung lank in his face.

But the worst part was his eyes. They stared straight ahead at nothing, blinking slowly every few seconds. They were the emptiest things I'd ever seen. There was no emotion, no evidence of dreams or hopes or plans or disappointments in their depths. As we entered, they flicked over and looked at us without a trace of interest or curiosity, and I had to fight an urge to run from the room and get as far away from him as I could.

"I never told you why I left Gypsum," Prairie said softly. "I never told anyone but Anna. And I lied to you earlier, when I said I never healed someone who died. The truth is that I did. I healed Vincent. I was sixteen and we were in love. We were going to run away together—Alice never knew. We were just waiting until we had enough money to get someplace far enough away that Alice could never find us, and we were going to take Clover with us."

She walked to Vincent and put a hand to his face. I couldn't imagine how she could stand to touch him. He didn't seem to notice.

"We had an accident on prom night," Prairie said, adjusting the collar of Vincent's shirt before she stepped away from the bed. "He was thrown from the car, and he died. And unlike you, Hailey, I should have known better. I had been warned about what would happen if I ever tried to bring someone back."

"How could you . . ."

"I loved him. I thought I would die without him. I wished it, I actually wished I was dead too, but I didn't have the courage to make that happen. So I brought him back instead. I think there was a part of me that believed if I prayed hard enough, if I wanted it badly enough, that just this one time it would work, that God would take pity on me and let him live. A *real* life, not . . . this. But of course that didn't happen. And once I realized what I had done . . . I left. That part was all true. The only thing I didn't tell you was that I took Vincent with me."

"How did you get him in here?" I asked, horrified.

"We came to Chicago by bus, on the night of the accident. I had a little money, enough to get a change of clothes and the bus tickets. It was the next day when we finally got there. All night long, all he did was stare ahead, sitting in that bus seat. . . ."

"But what about his parents? When he didn't come home, didn't they freak?"

"I'm sure they were upset, Hailey, but unlike Alice, they knew about me and Vincent. They knew he loved me, and he'd told them if they didn't give their blessing he was leaving with me anyway, as soon as we graduated. They'd argued about it; they wanted him to go to college, not to spend all his time with me, but he wouldn't listen. I think they—everyone who knew us—just assumed we'd run away together. And I'm sure they looked for us, for a while. But Vincent was eighteen. Legally, there wasn't anything they could do."

"They must have been heartbroken," I said, imagining how his parents must have worried—after all this time, if they were even still alive, they had no idea what had happened to their son. From the misery in Prairie's eyes I knew it was a thought that haunted her as well. "Where did you go when you got to Chicago?"

"I took him to a hospital, the best in the city. I made sure of that. I spent almost the last of the money for a cab and took him to the emergency room. There was no one there, so I sat him in a chair. I pretended to be there for myself, which wasn't hard, since I'd been in the accident too, and unlike Vincent, my cuts and bruises weren't healed. I told them my parents were undocumented and they treated me as an indigent. I stayed around long enough to eavesdrop on what they were doing with Vincent."

"Wait, so they didn't know you were together?"

"No, and he couldn't tell them. He didn't even look at me once. After that, I kept track of him, which wasn't easy, since I was trying to find a room and a job, but I found ways. I . . . learned to be creative. And convincing. One of the doctors on ER rotation was a young resident who studied immune disorders. That's what they think he has, by the way . . . after all this time they still think Vincent has some rare immune problem, and they've got him on all these clinical trials."

"They can do that? Just experiment on him like that?"

"Technically, it's not allowed, since no one ever claimed him, and they never made contact with his family. He's a John Doe, but he had an ID bracelet with his name engraved on it, so they've always called him Vincent. I used to find that . . . a comfort. Anyway, as you'll learn yourself someday, when money's involved, lots of things are possible. The doctor I mentioned—the one who studied immune diseases—

had plenty of funding, and arrangements were made." She shrugged. "They've found ways to keep his skin and organs functioning all this time."

"But how . . . ?"

"The miracles of modern science." Prairie's voice was heavy with regret. "It's ironic. I've often wondered what would happen if the doctors here got together with Bryce, what they might be able to accomplish. But I could never tell them about each other. They work at cross-purposes, I guess you could say."

"What do the doctors here do to him?" I asked, my throat dry.

"They're doing research into cell regeneration," she said. "His systems have responded well. I guess I should thank them."

She didn't look all that thankful. I didn't blame her. What must it be like to see someone she loved here, kept alive artificially? I tried to imagine him at Kaz's age, full of life, laughing, but all I saw was an empty shell made of skin.

"What does he . . . do?" I asked.

"He's very good at simple tasks, like sorting beads and solving shape puzzles. But he's completely nonverbal. They keep hoping. I . . . don't know if that's worse. Here, watch this."

She stood in front of the bed, in Vincent's line of vision. "Vincent, clap three times."

Without any change to his blank expression, the man raised his hands and slowly slapped them together. Once, twice, three times. Then he let his hands fall back on the covers. His eyes never focused.

Watching him sent a chill through me, but I didn't want Prairie to know how horrified I was. "You can't blame yourself. You couldn't have known."

Prairie shook her head miserably. "I *did* understand. And I did it anyway. I have to make sure this doesn't happen again, and that means I have to stop Bryce, no matter what."

I couldn't stand to see her this upset. "Don't worry. If people know what happens when you heal a dead person, they would never do it, not on purpose. Even if Bryce manages to make more Healers, he wouldn't make—"

"Hailey," Prairie cut in sharply. "You don't understand. This is *exactly* what Bryce wants to make . . . *things* like this. He wants to sell them, to the highest bidder. The Healers are just a tool, like an assembly line."

I looked at Vincent, who was staring at nothing, a faint, shiny bit of drool pooling at the corner of his mouth. I didn't understand. "What could he possibly want with . . ."

Prairie's face darkened. She grabbed my wrist and pulled me to the bedside, until I was standing only a few inches away from Vincent.

"Vincent, hit yourself," she whispered, and he immediately started to smack himself on one side of his face and then the other, his palms flat and hard, the sounds of flesh on flesh sharp.

Prairie turned to make sure I was watching, and the pain

in her eyes was staggering. "Harder," she whispered, and the thing that used to be Vincent curled his fingers into fists and now each blow caused his head to jerk and roll, but still he kept at it—

"Stop!" I cried. "Please, Vincent, stop, don't, don't hurt yourself." And just like that, the Vincent creature, the zombie that lived in the ruins of his body, put his hands back in his lap. His face bore fresh bruising and a few cuts; his lip was beginning to swell. But there was no sign at all that he noticed, much less cared.

Prairie backed away from him, her eyes shining with unshed tears.

"Why?"

"Because you can send them into battle, Hailey," she said, her voice cracking with emotion. "You can load them up with explosives and tell them to blow themselves up, tell them to walk into shopping malls or schools, and they'll never think twice, never blink an eye."

"No," I whispered, horrified. "No one would—"

"*Yes.* A dozen of them, deployed the right way, could bring a major city to its knees."

"But Bryce couldn't . . . he wouldn't . . ."

"I saw it. I saw the *list.* On Bryce's desk. Unstable governments overseas . . . there were half a dozen or more. And he doesn't care who he sells to, as long as they show him the money first."

"But where would he get the . . ." I stopped, unable to

come up with the right word. Raw material? Bryce would need the newly dead, and a lot of them, if he was going to manufacture enough zombies to sell.

Prairie laughed bitterly. "He's smart, Hailey. He'll find people that won't be missed. There are so many more of those than you'd ever imagine . . . the homeless, and mental patients, people abandoned by their families. And that doesn't even scratch the surface. If he's getting help from inside our government, and I have strong reasons to believe he is, he could go to veterans' hospitals. Soldiers killed overseas—the remains shipped home could be faked, while the real corpses were taken."

"You can't think our own government would be involved in something like this!"

"No, of course not, not officially. But there's corruption at every level. Hailey, Bryce used to get visits from men who looked official. I never paid much attention, since I assumed it had to do with our funding. But thinking about it now, you could totally tell they had once been in the military. They had that air about them. There was someone he just called the General, and we used to joke about that in private—but now I'm thinking that was his principal contact."

"But why would they let him sell to enemies of the United States?"

"The governments on the list, their battles are on their own soil. They're extremists, terrorists, at war with each other—or with their own people. I've wondered if that wasn't part of the plan, that some rogue branch of the military might *want* them to exterminate each other."

Zombies.

Terrorists.

Shadowy operators, working outside the control of our own government, funding this study in horror.

It was too much. Especially when I thought about the fact that, without even knowing it, I was one of the keys to its success.

A day ago I would never have believed that there could be something worse than being hunted by killers.

But now I knew different. There was something much worse, and it was in *me*.

Chapter 22

When we got home, Kaz was in the backyard with Chub, teaching him to throw a lacrosse ball.

"Hailey, watch me, watch me!" Chub shouted, waving the stick around, his voice clear and distinct, the improvements in his speech growing every day. Kaz waved, grinning. But I raced past them with nothing more than a mumbled hello.

Anna had been cooking, as promised, and the house smelled wonderful, but I couldn't bear to talk to her. I went straight to Kaz's room, closed the door and lay down on the bed and pulled the pillow over my face, trying to block out the images in my mind.

Vincent in the hospital bed, staring without seeing.

Rascal, after I found the bullet wounds and pushed him to the floor, unhurt and uncaring.

Zombies walking straight into battle, unfazed by the sights and sounds of war.

Public squares full of people, erupting into explosions and flames.

I didn't know how long I lay there trying not to think. There was a gentle tap at the door. I pulled the pillow off my face but didn't answer.

"May I come in?"

I couldn't very well keep Kaz out of his own room, so I sat up and pushed my fingers through my hair, hoping I didn't look too messed up. "Come on in."

He opened the door hesitantly and gestured at the bean-bag on the floor. "Mind if I . . ."

"It's your room," I said, blushing. "I mean, I should be asking if *you* mind."

He sat, strong forearms draped loosely over his knees, and looked at me. I mean, *really* looked at me, in a way I wasn't used to.

"Prairie told me about Vincent and everything. Wow, that's a lot, you know, to find out. I'm sorry."

I shrugged. "Yeah, I guess. At least the healing . . . well, I was kind of getting used to that part."

"But the rest?"

"It. Um. I can't . . ." I tried to think of a way to describe how I felt—almost like I was guilty of something, because if Bryce did manage to find me, I was pretty sure he could force me to go along with his plan. "The zombie thing. Just, I don't get how anyone could do that on purpose."

"Yeah . . ."

"Did you know? About Rascal?"

"No. I mean, I thought there was something wrong with him, and I was kind of surprised. I knew Prairie could heal animals, because she fixed our cat's leg once when it fell out of a window, a long time ago. And when I met you I could tell you were a Healer too. So I thought it was strange that you weren't able to fix your dog. But I never knew about the . . . reanimated dead thing until Prairie told me just now."

"Reanimated dead?" I grimaced.

"Well . . . that's what Prairie said. I think she has a hard time saying 'zombie.'"

"But Kaz, if you'd seen him—"

"Hey, it's okay with me, you can call them whatever you want. I mean . . . decomposing flesh walking around, that's kind of the definition of a zombie." He flashed me a tentative smile and I felt a little bit better. "Besides, other than that little issue, I think it's cool, what you can do. Your gift."

That surprised me, but then I remembered that he'd grown up knowing he was Banished. "What about you?" I asked. "Do you . . . you know, have visions?"

"Sometimes. Usually only when something really bad's going to happen. Like when I was a kid I had this vision of our garage burning down. I made Mom go look, and some paint rags had caught fire in the corner. Or when our downstairs neighbor had a heart attack, I saw it a few days earlier, how she was lying on the floor of her apartment, dead. Stuff like that."

"Can you make yourself have a vision of something you want to see?" Like whether a crazed one-eyed redneck is coming after you.

Kaz shook his head. "No, it doesn't work that way. You can't, you know, summon it or whatever. It just happens sometimes . . . I get a dizzy feeling and then there's a sort of extra layer on top of my vision that fades in and out. If I close my eyes, I just see the vision. Otherwise it makes me feel like I'm going to hurl, like motion sickness."

"So you don't want to have it while driving or something."

"Yeah. That would be bad." Kaz grinned at me and I realized he'd done the nearly impossible: he'd lifted my spirits.

"Thanks," I said. "For taking care of . . . burying Rascal."

"Oh, that was no big deal. No problem." For a minute I thought he was going to say something else about it, but then he just stood, offered me his hand and pulled me up off the bed. "You missed lunch. I saved you some."

After all that, unbelievably, it was a good afternoon.

Prairie and Anna were having a serious conversation when we came out of the room, and Chub had managed to corner Anna's cat and was trying to pick it up and hug it, an experiment that ended with him getting a couple of scratches on his forearms, which made him cry. I thought about healing them, but then I decided that healing should be reserved for when it was really necessary. Chub still needed to experience the little hurts and challenges of childhood so he would grow up strong and self-sufficient.

After Kaz microwaved me some lunch, we all walked to the park, Kaz carrying a couple of lacrosse sticks and a duffel bag. He tried to teach me how to throw and catch, and we lost a few balls in the hedges circling the park. We pushed Chub on the swings and fed stale bread to some ducks, and by the time night was starting to fall, I'd managed to forget for a while, which was what I suspected Anna and Prairie had intended.

On our way to a pizza place that Anna and Kaz raved about, Prairie caught up with me.

"I'm going up to the lab tomorrow, early. There's only one guard on duty on Sundays. I'm thinking I can wait until he goes to the bathroom or something and get past him. Then I have the prox card to get in the lab."

She didn't look all that confident. I figured there was more to the plan, but that she didn't want me to worry. "Do you want me to come along?"

"No . . . I think it's best if I do it alone."

I didn't argue. Maybe I should have, but it had been so nice to not think about it for a few hours, and I wasn't ready to give that up. Instead, I tried to put it out of my mind, telling myself there would be plenty of time to worry later, but when we returned home and got Chub bathed and put to bed, I was exhausted. I hadn't had more than a few hours of sleep in days, and it hit me hard. I crawled into Kaz's bed,

Chub on his nest of blankets on the floor, and fell into a dreamless sleep.

I woke to someone shaking my arm.

"Hailey, wake up." It was Kaz, whispering, his face hard to see in the moonlight. "There's a problem. I'll get Prairie. Meet me in the kitchen."

I got up quietly so as not to wake Chub. I splashed water on my face and went to the kitchen. When Prairie and Kaz came in a minute later, she looked completely awake, as though she'd never gone to sleep.

"You've been through so much already," she said when she saw me. "Kaz, I wish you'd let her sleep."

"She has a right to hear this."

"What?" I demanded as a door opened down the hall and Anna came into the kitchen.

"What are you all—"

"I had a vision, Mom," Kaz said. "They need to know."

Anna tensed up, and I remembered that Kaz said his visions always signaled something bad. "What is it?" she whispered, her face going pale.

"Bryce . . . he's medium height? Brown hair, going gray here?" Kaz gestured along his hairline.

"Yes."

"I saw him, in a room . . . looked like a motel room? Or a dorm room? There were people in the beds . . . hurt people. Hurt bad, Prairie, they weren't even conscious."

"What was he doing?"

"It wasn't what *he* was doing. He was just sitting there, taking notes or something on his laptop—"

"What was it?" Prairie demanded, her voice going high and thin. "What did you see?"

"I'm sorry, Prairie . . . he's got another Healer."

CHAPTER 23

"WHAT DO YOU MEAN, another Healer?"

"I couldn't see her all that clearly. She had long hair, and she was leaning over them, chanting or talking. I couldn't hear. I don't hear anything with the visions."

"What made you think she was healing them?"

"Well, first of all, it was so obvious they were . . . dying." Kaz hesitated. "I mean, they were unconscious, and one of them had his head shaved and what looked like a recent scar. And the other one had a breathing tube and a body cast. Young guys."

"Military," Prairie said. "Had to be. Only question is whose."

"And the Healer, this woman, she put her hands on them, on their faces." Kaz demonstrated, cupping the sides of his face with his hands. "And after . . . it was hard to tell because the visions jump around, but, after, they, ah, woke up."

"Woke up?" Prairie repeated sharply.

"Yes, they moved, you know, opened their eyes, sat up. That was about it, all I saw."

Prairie was silent, but I could tell she was thinking hard.

"Who could it be?" Anna asked after a moment. "There was no one else in your village? You are sure?"

"No one." Prairie was vehement. "Clover's dead. Hailey's here. Alice is broken. Mary's dead. There's no one else. I don't see where he could have found one."

"One of ours, then," Anna said. "The Healers must have made it out of Poland after all."

"We have to go *now*." It was me speaking, to my amazement. "Prairie, we have to stop him. You have to destroy the research. We can't let him find her, we can't let her make zombies."

"But we can't—"

"There isn't much time," I insisted. "Isn't that right, Kaz? How much time between your visions and what happens?"

Kaz looked from me to Prairie. "I don't know. Maybe a day or two. Maybe . . . less."

"There still might be time," I pleaded.

"I'll help," Kaz said, pushing his chair back from the table. "The three of us will go. Mom can take care of Chub. You will, won't you, Mom?"

"What do you mean to do?"

"Whatever needs to be done to stop that bastard."

"Kaz," Anna snapped. "There is no need for that."

"No need for what, Mom? No need to call Prairie's boss what he is? She's right—he has to be stopped. We have to destroy everything."

"What is this *we*?" Anna demanded sharply. "There is no *we*—"

"I'm going with her," Kaz said. "She can't do it alone."

"Do not talk crazy." Anna was shaking with fear or anger or some combination of the two emotions.

"I'm not crazy," Kaz said. "Prairie is right. We have to destroy the research and stop this guy."

"This man is *dangerous*, Kazimierz. He hired people to kidnap Hailey. They kill all those others."

"Papa went to war," Kaz said. "There was killing there, but you didn't stop him."

I saw that he wouldn't back down, and I had a feeling no one was going to be able to tell him what to do. I could relate: no one was ever going to tell *me* what to do again either.

"Anna," Prairie said softly. "I understand. I'll go alone."

"You can't!" I protested. "You can't go alone. Bryce will kill you."

"Not if I plan," Prairie said, but I could tell she was grasping at straws. "Not if I come up with a strategy—"

"Strategy is not enough," Kaz interrupted, his voice hard

as steel. "You need help. I can see things. Especially if I'm there, if I'm close. It might make a difference."

"I can't ask you that," Prairie said. She raised her shoulders and let them fall. Her arm, I saw, moved easily, bandage or no bandage. "It's my fault all this happened, and—"

"I'm not letting you go alone," I said.

"We're going with you," Kaz said. He turned to Anna. "Mom, you didn't raise me to be afraid. My father was brave, you tell me that every single day of my life. You can't deny that."

"Your father is *gone*, Kaz. I can't lose you, too . . . I can't."

Anna's face reflected a mother's agony. Prairie, too, looked uncertain.

But *I* knew. I knew that Kaz would not be stopped.

"If something happens, if Kaz gets hurt, we'll be there too," I said urgently to Prairie, praying she would understand. We could *heal* him—he'd be safe with us there.

Anna looked at me carefully, her eyes narrowed. Then she looked at Prairie again. "What do you think?" she asked softly.

"I cannot ask anything more of you," Prairie said. "Even this, even taking me and Hailey in, this is so dangerous."

She was right. Bryce didn't care about the innocent people who got in the way.

He wouldn't stop. He didn't care how many people died for his research, for the chance to study Prairie and me and learn how to use our gifts to turn people into killing machines. Everything this man touched seemed to be about killing.

He wanted to use me as a tool, a way to make him stronger and richer and more powerful while other people died.

There was silence in the room. Kaz went to the picture window and stared out into the dark streets with his arms folded across his chest, tense and ready.

After a long moment, Anna nodded slowly. I could tell the decision had been made.

We'd won this round, Kaz and me.

We were going with Prairie.

"I'll guard him like my own," Prairie said softly. "Hailey too. I will do everything I can to bring us back from this unharmed."

Anna nodded. And then we were gone.

Kaz drove. Prairie sat up front with him, not saying much. She had slicked her hair back into a ponytail and was dressed in jeans and a sweatshirt, with an old pair of Anna's sneakers. Dressed that way, she looked more like a college student than the elegant woman who had first appeared in Gram's kitchen.

Kaz drove smoothly along Lake Shore Drive, the way we'd come only last night. Tonight the moon—nearly full—hung over the water near the horizon, its reflection shimmering beneath it. When we got to Evanston, I suddenly wished the drive had been longer. I didn't feel ready.

Prairie murmured instructions. She took us through a neighborhood of stately old homes that got smaller as we drove farther from the lake, until they were mostly squat little bungalows. We crossed the commuter train tracks and I could see Evanston's downtown ahead.

On the next block there was a cluster of low-slung modern office buildings. "Pull in," Prairie said. "Park over here, by the Dumpsters."

Kaz did as she directed.

We were shielded by a row of trees, the Civic nosed in under low-hanging branches. There were plenty of cars in the lot, customers of the Thai restaurant and the Laundromat across the street.

"Here's what I'm thinking," Prairie said. "The data is on computers in the secure lab. The prox card will get us in the main part of the lab—"

"Do you think Bryce could be in there?" I asked.

"Possibly . . . but what's more likely is he's got extra security guarding the place, with instructions to bring me in if I come poking around. By force, if necessary. Although I doubt there would be anyone here in the middle of the night."

"Let me go," Kaz said. "Alone. They won't be expecting a man."

Prairie shook her head. "No. I have to go with you."

"What about me?" I demanded.

Prairie closed her eyes for a moment. When she opened them, they were clouded with doubt. "There will be a guard in the lobby," she said. "A night guard. Unless they've hired someone new, it will be an older man who likes to nap on the job. Still, he's a danger. He can trip an alarm that will shut the whole place down and bring security running from off-site. And Bryce may have paid the guard to contact him first."

"You want me to distract him?" I asked.

Prairie looked uncomfortable. "I don't see any other way. I thought maybe you could pretend to have some emergency, I don't know, like maybe you're hurt or something. As soon as we're in, you get out. Figure out any excuse, tell the guard you were mistaken, whatever you need to do. And then you come back and wait where you can see the car."

She dug into her pocket and handed me a cell phone. "This is Anna's. Kaz's number is on it. Press and hold the three key and it will dial him direct. Call if you see anyone coming in the building after us—anyone at all. Or if there's any kind of trouble."

I didn't like being left behind, but I didn't see an alternative. "What are you going to do to the computers?"

"I have full administrative access to all the servers. Paul gave it to me, along with the master keys. We've got to hope that Bryce never found out. I'm sure he locked me out, but he might not have changed the admin log-in. I just need to get in and start the wipe-disk program."

"How much data is there, anyway?" Kaz demanded. "Because it takes hours to wipe a big disk."

"I—I'm not sure."

"It doesn't matter," Kaz said, his voice edgy and low. "It's going to be fire."

We both looked at him.

"What do you mean?"

"I saw it. A vision . . . Tonight will end in fire."

Chapter 24

"You had a vision?" I demanded, but Prairie interrupted.

"Fire? Oh my God . . . I should have thought of that."

"What?"

"The walls . . . all around the inner offices. They'll burn."

"I brought some stuff from the garage," Kaz said. "To use as an accelerant. I didn't want to say anything in front of Mom—she would have lost it if she knew—but it should help spread the fire—"

"No, what I mean is, the walls are flammable. Bryce had us working with volunteer subjects who claimed to have predictive powers. We had a few who kept hitting it off the charts. Seers, you know? I was sure of it. And Bryce was researching ways to block their visions."

"For the military application," Kaz broke in.

"For the what?" I was lost, but the two of them were practically running over each other's words.

"Like if the other side had Seers? You'd want to block them, right? You wouldn't want them to be able to sense your next move."

"Only, it's very hard to do," Prairie said. "The only thing we found that seemed to impair the subjects was iron. But it wasn't like Bryce could put up iron walls in the lab, so he found this guy who came up with a way to embed iron filings in polyurethane foam. The kind you spray? You know, that expands? Only, it's like a hundred times more flammable than wood, so he hired these guys off the books to spray it in all the drywall one weekend last fall."

"That's perfect," Kaz said.

Perfect for destroying the building, I thought—but not for getting out alive.

"What sort of accelerant did you bring?" Prairie asked.

"I got a couple of cans of lighter fluid and some paint thinner. And matches."

"Okay, good." Prairie sighed. "You've got this all figured out, haven't you?"

"Uh . . . yeah. But don't tell Mom. She'd ground me for the rest of my life."

We got out of the car, Kaz carrying his backpack filled with supplies. I stayed back, leaning against the car while they slipped off toward the building. They kept to the edge of the parking lot, as though they were strolling along the street toward downtown. When they got to the building, they cut over and edged along the front wall, barely visible in the shadows.

It was time. I took a deep breath and touched my fingers to my necklace. The red stone felt warm to my touch. I closed my eyes for a second and tried to empty my mind of everything other than what I had to do.

Then I sprinted across the parking lot and slammed into the glass doors at a flat-out run, smacking my palms against them and shoving. I didn't take a chance on looking for Prairie and Kaz in the shadows. The doors swung open and I was into the building's lobby. To the left was a bank of elevators, and to the right was a curved desk where an older man with a brown uniform sat reading a folded newspaper.

He looked up, his eyes wide with surprise, as I ran through the lobby to his desk. I leaned on it, panting.

"I need help!" I yelled. "A car—it was driving by—it hit someone. It ran up on the sidewalk by the parking lot. I think they're hurt bad."

The man lowered the newspaper more slowly than I figured the situation called for. "You're saying there's some kinda accident out there?"

"Yes, please, can you come out? I need—"

"They got procedures," the man said gruffly. I read the name on the gold rectangle that was pinned to his shirt. *Maynard.* "I got to call—"

"There's no time!" I was shouting now, fear making me

loud and careless. If he called for help, it would ruin everything; the police would come and Prairie and Kaz would never be able to get into the lab. "Please!"

"Just as soon as I—"

But that was as far as he got. Because when my hand shot out over the desk and came down gently on the side of his neck, his eyes went very wide for a second and his body tensed up as though he'd touched a power line.

Then he slumped over on his desk.

I'd had no idea that I was about to do what I did.

And at the same time, I had somehow known exactly how to do it.

Powerful. The word thrummed in my mind as I backed away from the desk. The gift that I had doubted, that I had resisted, that I had finally used and claimed for my own—it was more powerful than I'd allowed myself to realize.

I knew the guard wasn't dead or even hurt. What I'd done was like a surge of calming energy that overrode the circuits of his brain and shut him down temporarily. Like sleep—really deep sleep. I knew it in my blood, in the understanding that flowed somewhere inside me where it had lived since I was born. Since I was conceived, even, in the violent union of my mother and father, the source of my gifts descended from the first families.

Behind me I heard the whoosh of the doors being pushed open.

"I saw that," Prairie said.

I just nodded. Then I remembered.

"We can't leave him here, not if there's going to be fire—"

Kaz jogged around behind the desk, picked up the guard and slung him over his shoulders as though he weighed nothing. Prairie hesitated only a moment before pointing down the corridor.

"We'll put him out the back door. He'll be hidden there—and safe."

Then she turned to me.

"You're done for now, Hailey. Go back out. Wait for us."

I watched them head down the corridor, the guard's head bumping gently against Kaz's back.

Prairie had only just come into my life, and I didn't want to lose her. I didn't want anything to happen to her.

But we would always be in danger unless we finished this. Bryce would keep chasing us as long as he thought we were useful to his work.

I followed.

Around a couple of corners in the hallway was a reinforced door with no identifying sign. Prairie held up the little plastic prox card, and when the lock clicked, she pushed the door open. I ran to catch up. When Kaz saw me he hesitated only for a second before holding the door for me.

"Hailey, no!" Prairie hissed.

"She deserves to be here," Kaz said as I pushed past him.

I grabbed Prairie's hand and squeezed hard. "I'm not going back."

She stared into my eyes for a moment and then nodded once. "All right. All right. You two start dousing the edges of the room, along the walls. I'm going to start the wipe-disk program. I doubt I can get in the server room—that requires a retinal scan and I'm sure I've been blocked—but I can do it from my workstation. And take this, just in case." She pressed the prox card into my hand and I pocketed it.

Prairie snapped on a bank of lights and I saw that we were in a huge lab, with workstations and sleek monitors and equipment I couldn't begin to name. There were robotic-looking devices in various states of assembly on platforms, and banks of blinking boxes with cables running in and out in loops. More cables snaked along the floor.

The one thing that was missing was a human presence. Other than stacks of papers and coffee cups and a sweater or two left over a chair, it was as if the people who worked here brought nothing of themselves with them. There were no photos, no kids' drawings tacked to cubicle walls, no plants or paperweights or figurines.

Prairie disappeared down a corridor at the other end of the room, and Kaz dug in his backpack, then handed me a can of lighter fluid.

"Shouldn't take much," he said. "Just concentrate it along the drywall."

We set to work, stepping around the equipment. At first I was cautious, but then I followed Kaz's example and shoved things out of the way, pushing desks aside to reach the walls. The acrid smell of chemicals filled the air, stinging my eyes and making me cough, and adrenaline pumped through my veins.

I thought I heard something—a slam, a muffled cry—from the corridor Prairie had entered. Kaz heard it too, and we both went still, looking at each other and trying to listen over the hum of the equipment. Then we were both running toward the source of the sounds.

We were barely into the hallway when there was a crashing of metal on wood and a heavy door rebounded off the walls a few feet in front of us.

Prairie stumbled into the hallway, followed by someone else.

Bryce Safian—it had to be. A well-built man with close-cut brown hair and a starched button-down shirt was holding a gun jammed against Prairie's back. Kaz reacted before I could absorb the scene—he rushed forward and slammed between Bryce and Prairie, knocking her to the floor. He grabbed for the gun and it went off, and a split second later he grabbed one hand with the other, wincing, blood dripping between his fingers. He'd been shot in the hand, and now Bryce had the gun aimed straight at his heart. Kaz backed up slowly as Prairie crawled out of the way and got to her feet.

The man's eyes met mine, narrowed, and then relaxed. He smiled, a cruel and calculating expression that wasn't all that different from the way Gram used to look when she thought Dun or one of her other customers had said something funny.

"You must be Hailey. I'm Bryce Safian. Please call me Bryce." His smile grew wider. "It's a good thing I decided to come check on things in the lab when I heard that my employees had managed to let you slip away yet again. You should be congratulated on your ingenuity. Remarkable, really."

"Your hand . . . ," I choked out, watching Kaz bleed onto the floor.

"Don't worry about him," Bryce said dismissively. "He's not worth your time. You know, Hailey, if things had gone differently, I might have been your *Uncle* Bryce."

I looked from him to Prairie. I had never seen her look so angry.

Bryce followed the direction of my gaze. "Yes, that's right. I had been thinking of proposing to your aunt. That is, until she made it clear that we had profound, ah, you might say, fundamental character differences."

"You *have* no character," Prairie spat. "You have no shame. You're—you're inhuman."

Bryce laughed, a rich and cultured sound. "That's pretty funny, coming from you, darling. Seems like it might be *you* that deserves that title. Did you know," he said conversationally, tipping his head to me, "that your aunt has chromosomal abnormalities so severe that technically she shouldn't even be alive in any condition known to science?

"Oh dear," he added, creasing his forehead and pretending to be sorry. "I shouldn't have said that, seeing as you—and your young friend here too, I take it—have the same . . . deficiencies."

Kaz raised his bloody hands as though he was going to go after Bryce again, but Bryce swung the gun between me and Prairie and back at Kaz. His gun hand was steady.

"Don't get any bright ideas," he said to me. "You all bleed regular blood—and I should know, considering all the testing we've done here. Presumably, losing enough of it will kill you just like it would any normal human. And I know you can't heal this one without touching him."

I could feel the rushing that signaled the need to heal. I couldn't take my eyes off Kaz's shredded hand. My fingertips pulsed with the compulsion to touch him, to find the wound and let my energy flow to it. But I couldn't reach him. Bryce would never let me get to him. And without touching, I couldn't heal. Milla, Rascal, Chub . . . I'd had to lay my hands on them to feel the energy from my fingers go into their bodies.

"Kind of funny, really," Bryce went on. "If you could get to big boy here, you could probably fix him up, but I've got lots of extra clips, so I'd just keep shooting holes in him. No doubt who'd win that race, huh, sunshine?"

"You have no idea what you're doing," Prairie muttered.

"Oh, but I do! Who's been running those tests for all these months? Hmm? I'd say I'm intimately familiar with just how your special little powers work, wouldn't you? In fact, I think I'd be able to hurt your young friend here just badly enough that you'd have a very difficult choice to make. Isn't that so, Prairie?"

She looked stricken, a choked sob dying in her throat. I remembered her promise to Anna. *I'll guard him like my own.*

"It doesn't matter anyway," Bryce went on, smiling lazily. "I don't need you anymore. I found someone new. She's not as pretty as you, and I doubt she'll prove as . . . amusing. But she's cooperative—very cooperative, considering she's become, let's say, a permanent guest of the laboratory. And now that I have Hailey, the two of them are all I need to get the last of our work done. It's a shame, really, that you won't be around to share in the glory."

So Kaz's vision had been real. Bryce had found another Healer, and locked her up here just as he intended to lock me up. My heart sank as I realized that all our work might have been for nothing. Bryce planned on keeping me alive, but he clearly didn't intend to keep Prairie or Kaz around. I felt despair overtaking the determination I'd started the night with.

"You won't live that long," Prairie said, surprising me with her fury. She stepped toward Bryce, unafraid. "Shoot me if you want. Go ahead, I dare you. Your new girlfriend's never going to make zombies for you. That's not what was ordained, and you can't fight it."

Bryce chuckled, genuine mirth crinkling his eyes at the corners. "Oh, Prairie, such idealism, it's so refreshing. I've always loved that about you. If you only knew."

"Knew what?"

"Where do you think I found out about your little niece here?"

Prairie hesitated, and I saw uncertainty flicker in her eyes.

"The guys you hired," I said, trying to edge closer to Kaz. "Your men. Your *dead* men."

Bryce laughed harder. "That is so amusing to me, you see, because once they traced Prairie's true identity, we found an unexpected ally. Someone who was willing to tell us every-thing we ever wanted to know about you, little Hailey, for a price. Someone willing to set up the perfect opportunity for my men to come and get you, someone who not only wouldn't miss you, but would make sure no one else did, either."

A murmur started inside my ears and built quickly into a roar. I shook my head and whispered "No," but I knew exactly who he was talking about.

"Your grandmother, Hailey," Bryce said, barely able to conceal the smug satisfaction in his voice. "Alice Tarbell. Gave you up for five thousand dollars and a ticket to Ireland. Oh . . . and the promise that, not to be indelicate, when it was time for you to procreate, we would furnish you with one of your own kind."

Kaz shot forward, launching himself low against Bryce's torso, trying to knock him down. But I could see that Kaz's injury had weakened him, made him miscalculate. Bryce stepped neatly out of the way and his finger tightened on the trigger, almost in slow motion. I heard the shot and saw Kaz's injured hand fly out at an odd angle and bang against the wall in a spray of blood.

CHAPTER 25

THE HOLE IN Kaz's bicep stayed neat and round for a second before blood began to leak from it. I could see now that his hand was badly damaged, the fingers bloody and bent at odd angles, his index finger hanging by a thin strip of skin. A wave of nausea rolled through my stomach, followed by shame. I was supposed to be a *Healer*—how could I be so weak?

Prairie reached for Kaz, but Bryce jammed his gun under her chin and drove her back against the wall. Kaz sank to the floor, his face going white as he tried to squeeze his uninjured hand around his arm, above the bullet wound, and stop the flow of blood.

Bryce sighed. "I told you we could do this the hard way or the easy way, Eliz—I mean, Prairie."

I stepped toward her, but Bryce swung his arm around and aimed at me. "That's far enough, Hailey. It might be wise for you to remember that your aunt won't be a bit of good to you if you get hurt. Kind of an interesting arrangement, wouldn't you say? It's going to be fascinating to study that, Healers' natural resistance to each other's gifts. I'm certainly looking forward to that research."

Prairie was inches away from Bryce, backed up against the wall, and the second he turned away from her, she tensed. I could tell she was going to attack him. I shook my head and tried to form the word *no,* because I knew Bryce would kill her, but I also knew that she was past caring. As she lunged at him, I waited for the sound of the gun, a silent scream building inside.

But Bryce surprised me.

He brought the gun crashing down against Prairie's skull, above the temple, and she crumpled to the ground like a puppet with cut strings.

But he didn't kill her.

When he looked up, there was something in his expression I recognized. It was part longing and part defiance. It had something in common with the way Rattler had looked at her. The ancient blood connection was missing, but in that second I realized that Bryce too had loved her, in his way. Enough that he couldn't shoot her.

And I realized that love could be dangerous. "Don't think I won't enjoy killing her slowly," Bryce said, but now we knew he had a weakness, and for the first time I saw uncertainty in his eyes. He kept his gun trained on me, but he knelt beside Prairie and felt for her pulse.

If only there was a way to use his weakness against him. I glanced at Kaz. His eyes were squeezed shut with pain. I could tell that he was starting to lose his balance. A shocking amount of blood was leaking from his arm. The bullet must have hit something important.

The need to heal surged hot and demanding inside me, pulsing its way along my nerves to the tips of my fingers, and my desire to put my hands on Kaz, on his wound, was irresistible.

I willed him to open his eyes and look at me—and he did. The second his eyes found mine, I felt it again, the connection I'd noticed when he first took my hand.

Only, now his life depended on it. All of our lives.

I stared deep into his eyes and tried to shut out everything except the gift that was a part of my lifeblood. Kaz's eyes flickered, his lips parted slightly. I could feel my heartbeat slowing and then I sensed my breathing diminish to almost nothing. Something happened to my vision, too; the edges fell away, replaced with a haze of shimmering shadow, and there was nothing but me and Kaz. My vision began to fade and my lungs screamed for air, but it was beautiful, too, exquisite and so sharp that it felt like it might tear my heart in pieces, this link between us that was more powerful than either of us could ever be alone.

I fell.

I didn't realize it was going to happen until I collapsed onto the floor at Prairie's feet. Bryce yelled something and turned his gun from Prairie to me, and I braced for the impact of the bullet, wondering where he'd shoot me, wondering whether it would be better if he merely disabled me and kept me alive in his laboratory—or if he killed me.

And then Bryce slammed into me hard. It took me a second to figure out that Kaz had shoved him, that he had found the energy, a last reserve of strength, to attack.

"Get away, get away from him!" Kaz yelled. I tried, but Bryce was so heavy and he was scrambling on top of me, heavy knees and elbows—God, it hurt—and what about the gun? He still had the gun, and then he was pulled off me and slammed into the drywall and that was Kaz. Kaz, whose good arm was plenty good; Kaz, whose bad arm was good enough, because I'd healed it, not very well because it was damn hard to heal without putting your hands on someone, but enough. Enough.

Kaz kicked Bryce and the gun went skittering out of his hand and down the hall. I pushed against Bryce as hard as I could and managed to roll out from under him. I tried to reach Prairie, but I knew I couldn't do anything for her now. I couldn't heal her, couldn't wake her up.

Kaz was fumbling in the backpack that lay open on the floor, pulling out the last can of lighter fluid, holding it in the crook of his wounded arm while he twisted the cap off. The smell hit me hard as Kaz shook the can over Bryce, the clear liquid splashing his clothes and his face, and he clutched his eyes and started screaming, a scream of rage that turned to terror when Kaz lit a match.

So much screaming. I had finally found my voice and it joined Bryce's. I backed away from the fireball that Bryce had become, dragging Prairie with me, watching the trail light up like a sparkler in the dark.

Bryce's scream turned into a horrible yowl of pain as he rolled toward the door he'd come through. Kaz grabbed my arm and pulled me upright.

"You don't have much time," he said urgently. "Check the server room, make sure she got the program started. Just in case it doesn't all burn. I'll take care of Prairie until you get back."

"Don't wait for me," I said, already backing down the hall. "Just go, take her with you."

But our eyes met and held and dark energy passed between us, and I knew he wouldn't leave.

I wouldn't have either.

I bolted down the hall. Smoke rolled down in hot, gritty clouds after me, and I knew the fire must be raging in the main room. The last thing I saw before entering the server room was Kaz bending low next to Prairie, pulling his shirt over his mouth, and I prayed there would be enough air for them.

The door was open to the smaller, inside server room. It was still cool and dark in there, where the fire hadn't yet reached, and glowing numbers scrolled at lightning speed along the single monitor on the desk. So Prairie had succeeded—the data on the disk was being scrubbed out of existence.

It was about time for some good news.

I emptied the lighter fluid around the equipment and had turned to go, to run back to Prairie and Kaz so we could try to race the fire out of the building, when I noticed a door along the other wall of the server room. It was a heavily reinforced door, like the one to the main lab, with a scan pad set into the wall next to it.

I hesitated. The fire was burning, and the data was being erased. It ought to be enough.

But the door was locked. Something in there was important enough that Bryce had secured it separately. More data? Specialized equipment?

And then I remembered what he had said: *She's become a permanent guest of the laboratory.* His new Healer—she was imprisoned somewhere nearby, and this was the last place we hadn't looked.

Fear shot through me. I had to find her and get her out of the burning building, to save her if I could.

I didn't have a gun, didn't even have any more lighter fluid, but I pulled the prox card from my pocket and jammed it against the pad. I heard the click of the lock releasing; without thinking I grabbed the door handle and yanked it.

What I saw struck me with such blinding horror that I nearly fell back into the raging flames. A scream started in my throat and burst from me with the ragged, howling desperation of a trapped animal. I tried to run, but my legs weren't working—my terrified brain couldn't control my movements as electric panic shot along my nerve endings and adrenaline threatened to drown my conscious mind.

Inside, sitting motionless on a dozen folding chairs, were a dozen men dressed in plain T-shirts and khaki pants. As I blinked away smoke and gulped the poisonous air deep into my lungs, I saw that these were no ordinary men. They were decomposing. Their skin ranged from pasty white to gray and purple, and in a few cases it had started to separate from the bone. The smell hit me next, worse than anything I had ever smelled, and bile rose in my throat. Some of the men weren't wearing shoes, the flesh swollen and splitting from the bones of their feet. The one closest to me had stains on his shirt. With a wave of nausea I realized that his torso was leaking bodily fluids.

Worst of all were their eyes. Empty, as though the souls of these men had been sucked out through the sockets.

Their heads slowly turned to me. One by one, they rose from their chairs and started toward me, arms outstretched.

They were zombies. And they were coming for me.

CHAPTER 26

FOR A MOMENT I couldn't move, my legs still frozen in place from the shock. Then the closest zombie stumbled in front of me and its fingers scrabbled at my arm. They were crusted with black filth, and the skin covering its hands had started to separate from the bone. I screamed and backed away, but not before I saw that its eye sockets drooped with rotting flesh, that its gums had shriveled back from broken teeth, that its hair was coming out of its head in clumps. The smell was so strong that I gagged on my own vomit.

I turned and bolted for the door, but the zombie managed to grab the back of my shirt. I was yanked backward, and I realized the zombie wasn't weakened at all by decomposition. A second gruesome hand reached for my neck and spun me around, and I saw that they were all converging on me, their hands out, their mouths slack and open.

I screamed and shoved at the reaching hands. I screamed harder when my own hands touched flesh that was wet and slick and loose. A hand snaked around my face and pressed against my nose and mouth, cutting off my air. I breathed in the stench of rot. My screams turned to fury as I fought to pull away from the bodies pressing in on me, but there were too many.

I bit down. Hard.

My teeth closed on a finger. As I threw all my strength into fighting, I heard a soggy crack and the finger separated from the hand. I spat it out and kept screaming, my voice going hoarse. I stomped on the shuffling feet around me, but there were too many. Another hand replaced the first, and then another, tugging at my hair, thumbs poking at my eyeballs.

I was going to die. The zombies had been ordered to destroy me—to destroy anyone but Bryce, I guessed. How long had he been building this ragtag army? Judging by the state of their bodies, it must have been days. Weeks, even, given what Prairie had told me about decomposition slowing. Even longer, if Bryce had been working on ways to retard it.

I was going to die, but my rage kept me fighting. My fingers found flesh, and they shoved and poked and fought, undaunted even when they sank into rotting tissue. I knew I couldn't kill the zombies. Their pathetic bodies would keep going until all the flesh had fallen away and they were nothing but skeletons, and only when the last of the tissue had rotted would they be truly dead. I, on the other hand, would die as a human dies; they would squeeze the breath from my throat and twist and crack my limbs and take me to the floor to kick and pummel the life from me.

"Hailey!" Kaz burst through the door. He hesitated only a second, taking in the scene, and then he picked up one of the folding chairs. Wielding it in front of him, he charged the zombies. They were clustered in front of me, for some reason lacking the instinct to circle behind and surround me, and Kaz slammed into them, knocking several down right away, and then, with stunning force, going after the ones that remained. He jabbed and slammed the chair the way I'd seen him use his lacrosse stick in the park, with deadly accuracy and the force of all that hard-built muscle.

Their hands fell away from me one by one. They were slow to adapt to the change of circumstances, and they bumped into one another and hesitated, their hands closing on air, their expressions unchanged. The ones that had been knocked down were getting off the floor and coming at Kaz, and I knew I had only seconds until they adapted to the new threat.

I put all my energy into kicking and clawing. I managed to tear my arms free as I delivered a kick to the legs of the last one holding me, and its feet slipped and it went down.

"Now!" I screamed, and grabbed Kaz's arm and pulled him toward the door. He threw the chair at the advancing zombies, and we both fell through the door as I pulled it shut hard.

"They're locked inside," I said, as much a prayer as a

statement. Kaz grabbed my hand and we ran back into the smoky hall.

There were flames licking along the floor, and I realized that the fire would reach the server lab in seconds.

"Prairie?" I asked, choking on the smoke.

"Got her to the lobby," Kaz said. "Try not to breathe until we're clear."

I took a last lungful of breath and held it. We ran until we couldn't see through the smoke, and then we put our free hands to the walls and guided ourselves that way, following the corridors until we were running through fire. The flames licked against us, and I knew that if our clothes caught fire, we were doomed. Then, suddenly, we burst into the lobby, where the smoke was thinner, and I saw Prairie laid out along the floor near the guard desk.

She looked dead, her head lolling against her outstretched arm, and my heart plummeted.

"She's going to be all right. I'll get her," Kaz managed to wheeze, and he slung her over his shoulder, much as he'd carried the guard earlier. I coughed hard, trying to clear the smoke from my lungs, and when I followed him through the doors, out into the chilly night, I breathed the sharp, cold air greedily. Before I could catch my breath, Kaz grabbed my arm and pulled me away from the building, into the shadows of the trees lining the street.

"We need to hurry," he said.

"What about the Healer?" I said, my voice hoarse and raw. "She's still trapped in there somewhere!"

That was when I heard the sirens.

Kaz heard them too. He looked back at the building, where flames were now pouring from every window. Then he looked at me with such pain in his eyes that I knew there was no hope. The Healer would die, alone and in agony, alongside the horrible creatures she had been forced to create.

Prairie moaned softly and stirred.

"We need to hurry," he repeated, and I knew we wouldn't speak of the Healer again.

By the time we got Prairie settled into the backseat, police and fire vehicles were hurtling down the block toward the lab.

I turned away from the burning building and stared out the windshield into the night as Kaz drove us away.

CHAPTER 27

PRAIRIE WOKE UP right before we reached the house. She had a wicked bruise on her scalp, but otherwise she seemed all right.

Kaz filled her in on the terrible discovery I'd made in the room behind the lab, and described how we'd escaped. I couldn't bring myself to talk about it yet. I kept feeling those cold hands grasping at me, and I knew I would never be able to forget the sensation of my fingers sinking into the ruined flesh of my attackers.

Anna got a much-condensed version. By unspoken agreement we spared her the worst of the details. Kaz's wounds looked like little more than scrapes now—full function had been restored to his hand, and the hole in his arm closed over—so we didn't tell her the extent of his injuries. We skipped the zombies entirely.

She had the news on, though, and she nearly cried with relief that we'd escaped the fire, which had turned into an inferno that was expected to consume the entire building. Crews had come from up and down the North Shore, and they were trying to save the adjoining buildings. There had been two survivors. One was the security guard, who had been found wandering around the back of the building, dazed and disoriented, but otherwise unharmed. He was unable to supply any details about the start of the fire, because his memory of the night's events ended at the sandwich he'd had on his dinner break.

The other survivor was taken from the building on a stretcher. We saw the same footage played several times. None of us could look away. "It's him," Prairie said the first time, as the paramedics carried the stretcher past the news crews to the waiting ambulance. "Those are his shoes."

There was only one shoe, though. It was an expensive leather loafer that had blistered and peeled in the heat, but stayed attached to Bryce's foot. His other foot was bare, and it was clear his pants had burned away. The blackened flesh of Bryce's leg was visible in the instant before the camera cut away.

"Burns over eighty percent of his body," the reporter confided in tones that barely concealed an undercurrent of excitement. It was a story that would lead for days, that much was clear, especially as "breaking details" about the lab revealed it had been carrying on important scientific efforts endorsed by the university, though reporters were having trouble getting confirmation.

We drank strong coffee while we watched. Anna set out a plate of sandwiches as the first hint of morning colored the edge of the sky, but no one touched them. I wondered if I'd ever sleep through another night, if dawn would become a familiar sight for me.

As I was beginning to doze off, leaning against Prairie, an announcer cut into the broadcast. "There it goes, folks," he said, barely containing his excitement. "As predicted, it looks like the building's a total— Oh my God, would you look at that."

We all leaned forward as the building fell in on itself in slow motion, the upper floors collapsing like papier-mâché.

I reached for Prairie's hand. "They have to be dead," I whispered. We both knew it was a question.

She nodded. "They said the temperatures got well over a thousand degrees. And now this . . . they won't find anything by the time it's finished burning. Maybe some bone fragments."

I nodded and snuggled a little closer, praying she was right, praying zombies burned like everyone else. And trying not to think about the Healer trapped inside.

A moment later, though, she stiffened.

"We forgot," she said, tugging at the blanket that covered us both. "We forgot his apartment. We've got to get over there and destroy his papers and his backup."

I sat up straight. Kaz was already getting to his feet.

Anna tried to pull him back down. "This is not the time," she said. "You're exhausted. Everything is destroyed there. Bryce is in hospital, probably going to die."

But she hadn't seen the zombies. We had.

The argument was cut short when Kaz hugged Anna hard. "I love you, Mom," he said, every syllable a promise. "And we'll be back safe."

The trip back to Evanston was harder than the one before, even though there was nothing left that could hurt us. It had all been destroyed in the fire. But we were no longer fueled by the energy of our quest. This was a sad trip, the culmination of a journey that had as many losses as gains, and we barely spoke at all except for Prairie's occasional directions.

We found a spot on a crowded street. Kaz eased the little car into a tiny space. The apartment building was only a few years old, a ritzy, gleaming brick and steel and glass tower.

"What's in the documents, anyway?" Kaz asked as we got out of the car. He'd brought his backpack, but this time it was to take things with us. Prairie said there was less than a single filing cabinet drawer of documents, plus Bryce's laptop. We planned to shred the documents back at Anna's, and destroy the laptop there too.

"From what I could tell, it was mostly his notes to himself. He may have transferred them to electronic files later, but these were handwritten lists, like the one I told you about with his contacts in foreign militaries. I don't really know what's there, but I figure we need to be safe."

In the gleaming lobby, the guard nodded and smiled at Prairie. Clearly, he recognized her from past visits. Bryce must not have told the guard that she was no longer welcome. As we got to the elevators, Prairie leaned in close to me, close enough that I could see the fine network of lines around her eyes, the deep purple smudges beneath them. She looked so tired.

"It's almost over," she said quietly, and I wondered if she was trying to reassure herself as much as me.

The elevator glided smoothly to the top floor. We walked down a softly lit, carpeted hallway. There were only two apartments, the penthouses. Prairie slid her key in the lock and the last possible obstacle was removed—not that Bryce would have had time to change the locks, but I had learned to take nothing for granted.

The door opened on a beautiful if sparsely furnished apartment. The midday sun sparkled off tabletops, wood floors, a vase of tulips. Sleek furniture was arranged around a richly patterned rug.

Everything looked normal. Inviting, even. My shoulders practically sagged with relief. At last it felt like we had reached the end of our journey.

"I'll just be a minute," Prairie said, going to the desk in the den off the main room and starting to gather up papers.

Kaz put out his arm and I leaned into him, letting him support me, breathing in the comforting scent of clean laundry and soap. As my eyes fluttered shut, I wondered if it would be possible for me to fall asleep standing up, because I felt like I could sleep forever.

That was when the voice called out.

"Mr. Safian?"

It was a woman's voice, heavily accented, like Anna's but

far closer to its speaker's Polish roots. I froze as Kaz stiffened at my side. Prairie dropped the papers in her hands.

The voice came from behind a closed door in the apartment's long hallway. I looked at Prairie questioningly.

"Guest room," she whispered.

I started toward it, but she stopped me, a warning hand on my arm.

"She's Banished," I said. I sensed it, even through the closed door, even across the distance. The stirring of the blood, the heightening of my senses, it was all there.

"Mr. Safian!" the voice said again, now wailing. "You leave me all night. Mr. Safian!"

"It's her," Kaz said. "The one I saw in the vision. It has to be."

"We don't know," Prairie said. "We can't be sure—"

"You not come back, you promise come back, you not come back, I am so scared." The voice broke down in sobs as Prairie's hand tightened on my arm. "Please don't be angry, Mr. Safian. We will do your work. No more fight, no more resist. We do what you ask. Now you bring my sisters, yes? Now you bring my sisters back to me?"

ABOUT THE AUTHOR

Sophie Littlefield is the author of several thrillers for adults, including *A Bad Day for Sorry*. She lives with her family in Northern California. Visit her online at www.sophielittle field.com.